AF433086

WHISPERS, WHISKEY, AND WISHES

Book Two in
The Skye O'Shea Cozy Mysteries

Rowan Dillon

Green Dragon Publishing

Published 2024 by Green Dragon Publishing
Beacon Falls, CT
www.GreenDragonArtist.com

This book contains words and names from other languages, and the pronunciation of such words are different from English. I have included a Pronunciation Guide in the back of this book for your guidance on these.

CHAPTER ONE

Ballybás, County Cork, Ireland, September 22ⁿᵈ

Numbers on the hand-written ledger danced in front of my eyes, like some surreal production of the *Sugar Plum Fairy*. I hated numbers, accountants, and all things related to taxes. A huge mess of financial statements, spreadsheets, and half-finished tax returns were scattered across Gran's antique kitchen table to create my own personal purgatory.

Despite that, it gave me a thrill to see my name. *Skye O'Shea, O'Shea Family Discretionary Trust.* The amount at the bottom, which was the only part of it I could understand, already showed half what it had been when I moved to this seaside village in Ireland just five short months ago.

I missed Gran terribly, but she'd left me her little farm, with a pub and B&B attached. All I had to do was get it up and running again, if the owner of the other pub, O'Leary, didn't get in my way. Despite the steadily dropping balance in funds, the pub was nowhere near ready to open and start earning money again.

Leaning forward, I rested my forehead on the dining room table. Then, I lifted it and dropped it a few times. *Thud, thud, thud.* Maybe I could knock some financial sense into my thick skull this way. I doubted it, though, as I'd never been particularly good with money.

I wasn't a horrible gambler or anything, just couldn't seem to make good choices. Like eating out way too often and buying pre-packaged food rather than learning how to cook for myself.

With barely a whisper, a huge black cat with a white diamond under his chin leapt onto the table and planted himself in the middle of my spreadsheets.

"Faelan! You scared the heck out of me!"

Gran's fairy cat just let out a growl and swiped his tail, sending one of the unfinished tax forms floating to the plush Turkish carpet.

I wrinkled my nose and leaned over to retrieve it. "Thanks so much. Your help is invaluable."

"Of course, it is. That goes without saying."

The first time he'd talked to me, I almost jumped out of my skin. Now, it was more of an annoyance. Raising my eyebrows, I said, "Oh, you're talking today? To what do I owe this honor?"

His tail swept a few times more, but I managed to catch the papers before they fluttered away. "You have failed to feed me in a timely manner."

"Oh. Right, just a sec."

In the kitchen, I pulled out a few cans, peering at the labels. He preferred the seafood options, but I was out of those. "Chicken?"

"If that is all you have, it will suffice."

I dumped the contents into his bowl and mashed it with a fork. He wouldn't eat if it was still a can-shaped mold. *Finicky jerk.*

The cat in question leapt off the table. Since he had been standing on a stack of papers, they slipped out from underneath him. He did a creditable imitation of Scooby Doo by trying to run but staying in place. The papers flew *everywhere.* Finally, he regained his aplomb, sauntered into the kitchen, and started eating his food.

Definitely a jerk.

With the fairy cat suitably occupied, I let out an enormous sigh and glanced at the clock. Five already? Well, that at least gave me an excuse to put things away for the day. I promised my doctor friend, Adanna, that I'd meet her at the pub tonight. Besides, I needed a break from this tedium.

I bent to retrieve the scattered papers, shooting annoyed looks at the oblivious cat.

As a nurse, I was used to filling out loads of paperwork, and the numbers on medication dosages were never a problem. Attach dollar signs to them, or Euro signs, and they became the worst gobbledygook, a cypher beyond understanding.

I wished I could afford an actual accountant, but the little sense I made from the statements told me I'd best concentrate on getting that stupid pub open and bringing in some cash, stat.

Just as I put the last stack of papers back in their respective folders, a knock on the door shattered the comfortable silence. I padded through the parlour, my stockinged feet making no noise on the thick carpet. Then, through the dark, empty pub, being careful not to slip on the wooden floors. I peered through the peephole to see Finn and Rory Lynch, the cousins who were doing my renovations.

I unlocked the latch and opened it with a half-smile. "It's almost half five, gents. I was about to go out."

Finn, the taller, thinner cousin with sandy brown hair, said, "Ah, that's fine, Miss O'Shea. We're just here to pick up a few of the tools we left. We need them to work on Rory's roof. The pure lashin' storm last night took some of his tiles, like."

Rory, the shorter, rounder one with a mop of dark hair, nodded, but didn't add anything.

I opened the door more and gestured for them to go inside. "Get what you need. You'll be back in the morning to do more work on the walls?"

Rory answered, "Ah, sure, it's grand, like. We won't be here until past ten, though. We've a wee job with Sean first."

I wanted to roll my eyes, but I'd learned that in Ireland, contractors weren't as punctual as they might have been in Miami. At least, the ones in this village in West Cork. Perhaps the folks in Dublin were more on-the-ball.

I'd asked them once about working the farm, but they said that wasn't their cup of tea. I couldn't blame them, as farming was hard work. Besides, I couldn't afford a full-time helper. Sean helped out now and then, but he had his own place to work.

Renovating the bar should have taken a month, tops, but it had taken three so far, with no end in sight.

The pub had been closed for over a year through Gran's illness, death, and my own arrival. It still needed repaired and repainted walls, updated kitchen equipment, several broken tables and bar stools replaced, décor updated, and the electrical to be brought to code.

Then, I'd need to buy supplies, including spirits, beer, snacks, napkins, straws, plates, and things like that. All this before I could even think of applying for a publican license.

The sheer weight of all those tasks pressed down on me. How could I possibly handle all of this? I had no idea how to renovate a pub. How would I get it all done before the money ran out?

As the cousins left with their tool bags, I shoved the panic away. *No, can't think about that now. It's time to relax and chat with my friend.* I hurried up the stairs, changed into a pair of jeans and a colorful blouse, gave my shoulder-length brown hair a quick brush and pulled it back into a ponytail. I added a few touches of eyeshadow and lipstick and ran back down the stairs.

"Don't wait up, Faelan!" I shouted as I shut the pub door and locked it. As if he cared. Still, it seemed rude not to acknowledge another sentient being in the house, even if he didn't always talk.

The other pub in town, owned by Cormac O'Leary, was beyond glitzy and perfectly decorated to attract all the tourists. Dark wood-paneled walls covered in photographs of famous people visiting the pub, antique lights, a huge mirror behind the well-stocked bar, everything the discerning visitor expected.

Luckily, tourist season had already wound down in September, and the massive crowds had thinned to mostly locals.

When I'd moved here in May, I hadn't been prepared for so many visitors. If I'd been able to open my place, I would have made bank with all the folks driving around the Ring of Beara. Visitors would come to the lovely sandy beach, buying up tourist tat souvenirs, and spending all their money on Guinness and cheese-and-onion Tayto crisps.

Next summer, for certain. I'd be ready then. In the meantime, O'Leary's was pumping with people, even in the off-season. It was only a few streets away from my place, but on the main road, while mine was off a side street.

I swung the door open, and someone slammed into me. The tall, dark-haired man in a leather jacket flashed me an annoyed sneer as I grunted and staggered back. Then, he marched away without a second glance. I scowled at his retreating back, then rolled my eyes and continued inside.

The noise of people and canned traditional music slapped me in the face. "Fields of Athenry," of course. That seemed to be the standard tune in any Irish pub, and the locals usually sang along with all the fervor of a college football team fight song. No matter that it was a poignant song about the Great Famine; the Irish loved their misery.

Scooting by a group of strangers dressed in tie-dye T-shirts and caftans, I pushed my way through the mob. The dying words of some heated argument filtered through as I went by, evidently about the guy who had just left.

Standing on my tiptoes, I spied Adanna's curly black hair at the far end of the bar. She raised her arm and waved.

Threading my way through the crowd, I hopped on the empty stool she'd been saving. "Whew! I thought you said the crowds went down during autumn?"

"More or less. These are all Irish folks, not tourists. The mob moves from area to area. In a month, there'll be half as many."

Was it a bad thing that I was looking forward to some solitude? I was a social person, if they were folks I knew and liked, but masses of strangers made me antsy.

Someone pressed against my back, and I turned to find Jess, one of the artsy residents, who had tons of wavy red-blonde hair. I gave her a quick nod, and she flashed a smile before returning to her conversation. I didn't recognize her companion, but they looked similar enough that they might be sisters. While Jess's eyes gleamed, the other woman's lips were pressed together.

"Fields of Athenry" finally finished, to be replaced by "Whiskey in the Jar." A few people clapped and cheered.

Adanna rolled her black eyes and waved at Niamh, who was working the bar. My friend gestured toward me, and I mouthed the word *cider* before Niamh disappeared again.

My companion said something, but I shook my head. I couldn't even hear her voice, much less the words. As soon as I got my pint, she hopped off her stool and pulled me toward the door. I held tight to the cider to keep it from spilling.

As we got outside and the din subsided, I let out a sigh of relief, and we perched on the picnic tables. The silence of the evening was a blessed thing, and I drank in the relative silence while taking my first sip of cider. "What were you asking in there?"

"I was asking if my husband had been by to talk to you?"

That took me by surprise. Adanna's husband, Garda McCarthy, had no love for me. "Donal? What for?"

She took a long drink before answering. "Oh, nothing, really. He just mentioned he might talk to you."

"I haven't even seen him lately. Was it urgent?"

Adanna gave a shrug. "No idea. Maybe it wasn't important. I was also wondering if the boys had finished up the wall reconstruction yet?"

I pressed my lips together, then said, "They've got the drywall up and some of the joints smoothed out, but there are still several patches they need to repair, sand, and prime before they can even think of painting."

She took a sip of her Guinness. "Have you decided on a color yet?"

Giving a shrug, I wrinkled my nose. "I'm torn between something traditional, like a wooden veneer or beige with dark wood accents, or something bolder like blue, red, or maybe green stripes." O'Leary's was wood, ceiling to floor. When it was full, the darker colors made the space seem even smaller.

"Have you thought about a stone façade on the lower half? I've seen some brilliant pubs with that."

A rumble in the distance promised rain, though the sky above was still clear enough for me to see the stars. I shivered and pulled my sweater on more tightly. "Sure, I thought of that. It's super-expensive, and I'm running on a tight budget until I can start making money."

Adanna leaned against the picnic table. "Have you done your accounts yet? You said you were struggling with them."

"No, they're still plaguing me. Are you good with numbers?"

"Ha! Not likely. You should ask Jess."

I furrowed my brow. "Jess, from the art gallery? She doesn't seem like the accounting sort."

"She definitely isn't, but her sister, Audrey, is a chartered accountant. She's just come into town yesterday. Did you not see her? They were sitting right next to you in the pub."

So, Audrey was the woman who looked like Jess. "Sure, I'll ask her. Do you know her rates?"

"No idea. She might be up for some barter."

I took a long drink of my cider. "Barter? What could I possibly trade her for?"

"Who knows? Audrey's an odd one, like."

As if being odd was unusual in this town.

That night, curled up in my Gran's king-sized bed, in her beautifully decorated bedroom, I couldn't sleep.

Well, no, that's a lie. I did get to sleep, but I kept waking up from a nightmare. And yet, I couldn't remember what the nightmare was about.

I'd had plenty of nightmares in my life, up to and including my abusive ex-husband, Armand. I'd finally managed to extract myself from his control, just as I got blamed for a death at the hospital that wasn't my fault.

So bad dreams weren't new to me. I'd had this one each of the last three nights, but I'd never had it before moving to Ireland.

Trying to get back to sleep would probably be a waste. I looked over at the window, but it was still the dark of night. Two green spots glowed in the darkness, so Faelan must be watching me.

He must be on top of Gran's antique dresser. Faelan knew better than that, but nothing I said would keep him off.

"Faelan? Why don't you come lay on me and purr? That always helps me to sleep."

He took his sweet time coming over, but as he settled on my chest and rumbled, I closed my eyes, determined to remember some details from the dream. With surprising quickness, I was dropped right into it again.

A cold, wet night. Swimming in the water. In the ocean? Yes, this was a huge body of water. No one else was there. My body slipped under the surface, again and again. I couldn't get a breath. I tried to break the surface, but there was nothing to grab onto.

The next morning, I awoke with a start, my heart racing and gasping for air. Dark water, moonlight, being unable to breathe…I ran through every detail I could remember, trying to grasp the images.

Faelan sat on the nightstand, staring at me. His eyes flashed.

"Well? Do you have something to say?"

He leapt from the nightstand onto my chest.

"Oof! Don't *do* that! I'm not your trampoline!"

"I shall do as I please, as I have always done. Yes, I do have something to say on this infernal morning."

I glared at the huge cat. "What do you know?"

"More than you could possibly fathom. But I know that the dream you had is not your own."

I rolled my eyes. "No kidding. I'd never swim in the ocean at night. I've never come close to drowning, either. So why is this haunting me?"

"You borrowed it."

I shoved the huge black cat to the side and sat up in bed. "Borrowed a dream? How the heck could I do that? *Why* would I do that?"

He let out a low growl. "It is not something *you* have done, foolish human."

I was getting tired of his half-answers. "Then who did it?"

The Cat Sídhe groomed his tail and ignored me.

"Back to being silent? Great. Thanks so much for your help." Would a can of tuna keep him talking?

I flung off the covers, and Faelan with them, stomped into the bathroom, and took care of some urgent bodily functions and splashed chilly water on my face. With a groan, I did a full body stretch.

Glancing at the clock, I grimaced. An hour before dawn. I might as well get my day started. If I tried to sleep, I'd probably just relive that dream and drown again.

A shower made me feel almost human.

By the time I was dressed and drinking my first mug of coffee, the sun had risen, and a dim sunbeam slanted into the parlour windows, making dust motes glow. It shone on one of the many old photographs on one wall. I'd looked at each of these in turn, but most were unlabeled, just old sepia-toned pictures of people who I presumed were my family.

Even in September, the sun came up later in Ireland than in Miami, and it was past eight. I had no job to go to, so it didn't matter much, especially as the cousins wouldn't be here until after ten to work on the pub.

Before they'd started, I'd gone through a long list of tasks that needed completing before I could open for business. Unfortunately, most of the things I needed to do, such as decoration decisions, buying bottles and supplies, couldn't be done until they had finished a lot of their repairs.

My need to open and start making cash was at direct odds with the sheer amount of work I had to rely upon other people to get done. And their sense of urgency was not the same as mine.

In the meantime, I'd been upgrading the bedrooms. Maybe I could open the B&B portion of the business before the pub opened. Either way, I wouldn't get many patrons until the summer season.

For now, I went to the wall-to-wall bookshelf in the parlour and pulled out my favorite reading material—Gran's diary.

When I'd first found the diary, I had examined about the first thirty pages with a fine-toothed comb, analyzing each word and nuance. I'd even thought about digitizing it, but when I tried to scan a page at the library, the scan came out all distorted and illegible. Fairy magic and technology probably didn't mix well.

I wanted to ration the remaining pages and not consume them all at once. My reasoning was that, once I'd finished reading them all, Gran's voice would be silent again.

Besides, it was more of a reference book for all the different fairy creatures than a diary.

Sniffing back a tear, I flipped through a couple of pages, searching for an entry on stealing dreams. Or borrowing them, as Faelan had phrased it.

One entry recounted the tale of Caer Ibormeith, the daughter of Ethal Anbuail. I practiced pronouncing the names under my breath. I only knew a few words of Irish but was trying to learn. My American-trained tongue had a really hard time with some of the Irish sounds.

But I could hear Gran's thick Irish accent sounding them out in my mind, and that helped.

Ethal was a chieftain of the Tuatha dé Danann, the tribe of people who had occupied Ireland before the Celtic migration of humans had come from Spain.

His daughter was a shapeshifter, and she spent part of the year as a swan, changing at Samhain.

Samhain is the Irish word for November, but also Halloween, which was only five weeks away. While the Irish didn't go all out like Americans did, I'd been noticing a few tasteful decorations of autumn colors, hay bales, and carved turnips on doorsteps.

Caer Ibormeith met her lover, Aengus Óg, in her dreams. She sang to him as he slept, and he hungered for her, losing his appetite and getting ill. After many people helped Aengus Óg search for her, he found her bathing with a hundred and fifty maidens. He had to choose her from the rest, as they were all in their swan forms.

Luckily, he chose wisely, and they wed and lived happily ever after.

I waited for the other shoe to drop, as Irish tales seldom have happy endings, but that was all Gran wrote.

Faelan chose this moment to jump on my lap. "No, it wasn't like that at all. The human scribes writing the tale were bungling idiots."

"Oh? How should it have ended?"

"That is not for me to say. Keep reading."

The tale of Caer Ibormeith was lovely, but it hadn't mentioned anything about taking dreams. *So, that was a waste of time.*

Next, I dropped down a rabbit hole on Aengus Óg then, as he was a god of dreams. Besides the first story, he dreamt of Brigid when she was a captive of a fairy queen, but that was from Scottish Lore. So, he was a dead end for my Irish dream-stealer.

The next entry I found was about the púca. I'd learned about this creature before, when I was researching the Dearg-Due in May. Another shapeshifter, the púca could turn into a horse, goat, cat, dog, or hare, as well as a human. They were just vaguely associated with nightmares. Nothing about stealing dreams.

I flipped through pages about other creatures, both familiar and strange, until my gaze fell upon an entry about receiving prophetic dreams by sleeping next to an ancestor's grave. A shiver ran down my spine as I remembered the night we found Gerald, a murderer who had been sleeping in my family's crypt.

A loud engine rattled by. Not many vehicles drove down my road. I caught a glimpse of a tractor as it passed the window, and I returned to my reading.

I found an entry for the Tarbh Feis. Not a creature, but a ceremony for prophetic dreams. Having not found much else, I read through the details. The words translated into *bull feast,* which gave the first clue as to how to prepare this ritual.

Kill a bull with primitive tools and eat it, offer some ritual objects, chant a spell, burn some herbs, lie down, and have a dream about the next king.

Could I even find bull meat in the local butcher shop? Not that he'd be using primitive tools. Cow, sure, but probably not bull. Could veal be from a male? I'd never cooked with any of them, so I had no idea.

The idea of a thick beef stew made my stomach rumble, and I decided it was time to feed the beast. I walked to the cupboard, but I knew I'd had the last of the oatmeal yesterday. No eggs left, either. If the farm still had chickens, I would probably have an endless supply of those.

I hadn't gotten up the nerve to actually keep livestock yet. Being a city girl, I didn't want to make that leap until I knew what I was getting into. I'd need full-time help if I did that.

Fine, I'd eat out. I did that way too much, and a twinge of guilt at my diminishing bank balance made me hesitate. Still, I pulled on my sweater and walked outside, shivered, and returned to grab a jacket. It would take a while for my Miami blood to get thick enough for an Irish winter. Well, an Irish autumn.

My favorite place for breakfast was the Blarney Scone, a cute café with good coffee options, run by Joshua and Emily. Their baked goods were delicious, too.

The place was only a few streets away, but the cold wind was biting, so I quick-marched down the main street and into the restaurant.

The plate-glass window was surrounded by purple and orange fairy lights, what I'd call Christmas lights. They twinkled in the gloomy morning.

Just as I opened the door and wondered why the place looked empty, the lovely aroma of burnt toast reached me. This sort of stench didn't happen with lightly toasted bread, though. Something had been absolutely charred into a brick.

Joshua was running around like a chicken with his head cut off. Gray smoke billowed from the back room and was already coloring the walls. He threw me a hasty wave, and said, "Dealing with an issue, Skye! Be with you in a minute."

As much as I was looking forward to a delicious breakfast, that scorch odor made my stomach roil, so I had to go back outside.

Maybe breakfast wasn't something I needed right now. Instead, I strolled down the main road while my stomach settled. The exercise might warm my blood.

Only a few people were braving the streets. It wasn't stormy by Irish standards, and the locals weren't afraid of a bit of wind. The early hour probably had more to do with the lack of pedestrians than the September chill.

Each streetlamp had dried cornstalks tied to them, a few with bundles of leaves in autumn colors. I hadn't expected this nice seasonal touch in Ireland. I always figured Halloween decorations were an American thing, but then again, hadn't the holiday originated in Ireland or Scotland?

I was sure I'd read something about Samhain in Gran's diary. I remembered her mentioning a type of bread baked during this time. Barnbrack? Something odd like that. I wondered if anyone around did baking like that. Was it something I should learn?

There was so much I didn't know about the culture and language of my new home. Maybe I should look into taking some Irish lessons?

Out of the corner of my eye, I spied Jess and her sister walking toward her art gallery, her mass of red-gold curls floating in the wind like a jellyfish.

The faint glow of yellow I always saw on her seemed faded. I wondered if she wasn't feeling well, though she'd seemed fine the night before in the pub. Only a few other people even had that glow, and none were as strong as hers, even Sean's.

I hurried to catch up with them. As I got closer, I called out, "Jess!"

She turned around, as did her companion. While Jess was red-gold and summery, Audrey had similar features but seemed like a cold winter's day. Their clothing even matched their personalities, as Jess wore a loose dress with amber swirling around crimson paisleys. Her sister, however, wore a buttoned blouse and pencil skirt with severe stripes in several shades of blue.

"Skye! Have you met Audrey? My sister is staying here for a few days. Or more." Jess's voice held a tinge of bitterness in the last few words.

I held out my hand. "Very nice to meet you."

With just a half-second of hesitation, she shook it. "It's grand."

After a moment of awkward silence, Jess said, "I've got to get to the shop and open up. Coming, Audrey?"

"Oh, sure! Uh, Audrey, can we chat for a moment? I understand you're an accountant."

Jess flashed me a look I couldn't interpret, but Audrey gave a nod. "Sure and I've been doing accounts for years. Do you need someone?"

Relief washed through me, and I nodded. "I definitely need help! I inherited my gran's pub. There's a trust with it to fix it up, but I'm terrible with anything numbers-oriented. What are your rates?"

The wind chose that moment to howl, and we huddled closer to the empty store front. "It depends on how much work there is to do."

Sheep nuggets. I just wanted some idea of how much this was going to cost. "The lawyers did last year's books, so there's only this year's so far. I haven't even opened for business yet."

Audrey's eyes gleamed. "Shouldn't be too dear, then. How quickly do you need them?"

I had no idea what the tax deadlines were here, but I couldn't imagine they'd be due before the end of the year. "Nothing fast."

She narrowed her eyes. "Wait, for last year? We've only a few days until the deadline. I'd have to charge extra for a rush job."

"No, I've got nothing for last year. The trust does, but the lawyers did that accounting."

Her eyes sparkled when I said *trust.*

"But I just moved here in May. No rush needed."

Her face fell as a few stinging droplets of rain hit my face. "Ah, that's grand, then. You have until the end of October to do the prior year's accounts. I could take a look at this year's, if you're up for a retainer."

"A retainer? You mean, paying up front?" I'd never heard of that from an accountant, but I'd also never had an actual business before. Maybe that was the norm.

Alarm must have been clear on my face. Audrey looked at her feet. "I normally wouldn't ask for one but, well, it's complicated."

Her voice wavered, and I wondered if she was about to cry. I glanced around, trying to find a place we might chat out of the rain. I spied a bench along the side street, under an awning. "Let's go over there."

Once we sat away from the worst of the wind, Audrey's shoulders slumped. "I hate asking for funds up front. You'd think an accountant would be smart about money, wouldn't you? But I need some cash for my boyfriend."

"What about Jess?"

She let out a snort. "That one. She wouldn't give me one Euro."

Why was this stranger spilling her guts to me? I patted her hand awkwardly. "Jess probably needs to hold on to her cash through the slow season."

"I know, I know. But he needs help and fast."

I suspected whatever her boyfriend needed funds for was on the shady side. Perhaps she wouldn't be the best person to entrust with my finances.

Audrey looked up, her cheeks red and her eyes brimming with tears. "He could pay everything off and be free!"

What in the name of all that's holy does that mean? Has he been kidnapped or something? I didn't want to get drawn into whatever drama she had going on, but I did need someone to do my books. "How much?"

"A thousand Euro would do it."

A thousand Euro? I jumped to my feet. "I'm sorry, Audrey, I can't afford that." I glanced at my phone, noting the time. "Look, I've got to get going. Good luck."

She grabbed my arm, her fingers digging into my skin. "Five hundred! I'll do them for five hundred."

Alarm bells went off in my head, and I pulled away, shaking my head. As I rushed away, Audrey sobbed into her hands. I felt like a lousy, rotten jerk, but a thousand Euro was a lot of money. Money I didn't have. She was right, too; an accountant with money problems didn't sound trustworthy.

I didn't really want to go home. That had just been an excuse to extract myself. Instead, I craved the solitude of the beach.

Slowing down to a casual pace to reduce my anxiety, I walked by the side street to my place, the empty farmhouse on the corner, and the church across the street. The only thing after that was the graveyard until I got to the parking lot for the beach.

The lot only had room for ten cars, but even in the high tourist months, it didn't fill often. We had a lovely beach in Ballybás, but it wasn't a blue flag beach, famous like White Strand or Youghal.

Today, it was almost empty, except for a couple and their two kids on the far end. They were all bundled up against the misty, cool day.

After pulling up my collar to block the chill, I headed in the other direction, staring out to sea as I walked. I tried to keep my mind clear, free from worry, free from anxiety, taxes, and everything I still needed to do to the pub.

It didn't work so well.

I found a flat rock and perched on top, still staring out at the horizon. The soothing sound of the waves breaking on the sand lulled me into patterned breathing. *Breathe in with the wave, breathe out. Breathe in with the wave, breathe out.*

For a few precious moments, I managed to keep the worry away. Then, the mist turned to a light rain. I should head back to town, but I didn't want to leave this lovely peace.

My phone sprang to life with a *Star Trek* klaxon, and I answered, "Hello?"

"Ah, 'tis herself. Finn here, just letting you know we won't be able to make it to the pub until about noon."

I suppressed a sigh. "Sure, I'll see you then."

Exactly as I suspected. At least that gave me some more time this morning.

One thing I could say for living in Ireland, is that any agenda set for the day had to be flexible. That may have been the best thing about it.

As I hopped off the rock, the wind picked up. I sucked in my breath, hastily closed my jacket, and hoofed it halfway back into town to the other end of the main street, turning right down a side road to the library.

The two shops next to it were empty, and the ones across the street weren't open yet. The road looked sad and abandoned, like it was dying.

A shiver that had nothing to do with the cold ran down my spine as I hurried up the steps and into the warm embrace of the Ballybás Library.

I was used to the huge Miami-Dade Public Library downtown. In contrast, this long, narrow building probably had fewer books than the one in my high school.

Regardless of size, this place would be the best source for any creatures that might steal dreams, other than Gran's diary.

I perused the folklore section, made a few selections of local publications, and found a cozy niche to cuddle up into.

I'd always loved libraries, but being married to Armand meant I had very little free time to enjoy them. He'd always mocked my love for reading, along with my penchant for crossword puzzles and anything with bees. Freedom from that abuse was a delicious, heady thing.

I found a couple of mentions of dream-associations from other folklore. A Romano-British god named Nodens from the Severn in Gloucestershire, who was the patron of sleep, dreams, and healing. Minerva from Catamandus, who appeared in the dream of a Gaulish king. The Welsh prophets known as Awenyddion, who would roar violently when they were consulted on any doubtful event.

By the time I'd read through the Dream of Rhonabwy, also from Wales, who experienced a dream vision about the Battle of Mount Badon and King Arthur, I was ready to give up.

Dream-bringers, dream-stealers, and dreamt prophesies—I had no idea so much folklore centered on dreams. But even after reading all that, I was no closer to discovering an Irish dream-borrower.

A glance at my phone made me realize I'd have to hurry to the pub to beat Finn and Rory.

CHAPTER TWO

By the time I got back to my house, I was panting hard. Despite their normal penchant for tardiness, Finn and Rory Lynch were waiting outside for me. *Great.* The one time I was counting on them being late, they were on time.

Finn waved as I approached, and started in before I even got my key out. "Sorry, Miss O'Shea, but we need to get some more boards. We ran out the last time."

Clenching my teeth, I said, "Did you forget you'd need more?"

Rory shook his head. "No. The DIY shop's been closed, as the owner's been on holiday. They're just opening again today."

I suppressed a sigh at the delay. "Fine. When will you be back?"

Finn rubbed the back of his neck. "Well, ye see, we'll need some more funds."

This time, I couldn't hold back the sigh. "How much?"

The two fell into consultation with each other to figure out how many more 2X4s they needed.

After several urgent murmurs, Rory finally said, "€150 ought to handle it."

I didn't have any cash, but I pulled my checkbook out of my purse, and wrote one out. Finn stared at it a moment, made a face, but then folded it into his pocket. "Fair play, like. We'll leg it and be back in a few hours."

I wondered if he had been hoping for cash, which made my paranoid mind think he wanted cash for something other than buying timber.

Just then, my phone klaxon went off. I was so exasperated, I didn't bother looking at the number before answering, "Hello?"

"So, you've moved pretty far away, Skye."

Chills ran down my spine as I recognized my ex-husband's voice. I'd bought an Irish phone when I'd arrived but forwarded my US number for any business calls. "Armand."

His sickly sweet, wheedling tone put my nerves on edge. "Who else would call you? You never were one with a lot of friends, after all. I was the only one to stick by you."

The cousins stared at me, stock still, Finn's hand over the shirt pocket he'd just tucked my check into. I kept my voice steady. "What do you want, Armand?"

His voice turned hard. "I heard you came into a bit of cash. You know you still owe me, right?"

Fear and anger warred within me. I clenched the phone so hard, my knuckles turned white. "I owe you exactly nothing. Go away."

I wish I could have slammed the phone, but mobiles didn't have that option. Instead, I shoved it into my purse, vowing to block that number when I had a chance.

Finn asked, "Was that yer auld one, like?" His tone was sympathetic, but also way too nosy.

"It was. You boys had better get going if you want to be back in time to do something today."

They hurried away and after a moment, so did I. For no real reason, I didn't want to be inside the house alone today. Armand's call had stirred up old fears, and I needed company.

Why had he called me today? He'd obviously found out where I was, or at least that I'd moved far away. Did he know where? I might have to worry about him coming for me.

But why would he? He was perfectly happy leaving me for my best friend, Marie. I could still remember finding them in bed together, her long, black hair splayed out on his chest. Good riddance to them both.

Still, worry gnawed at me and didn't want to go away.

Since I'd skipped breakfast to commune with the ocean, my stomach informed me on no uncertain terms that it needed feeding, now. Despite the chilly wind and misty rain, I headed back into town.

The Blarney Scone should have gotten rid of the scorch stink by now. Besides, they had a fantastic salad with goat's cheese, pear, and balsamic dressing that I suddenly craved.

Armand had always mocked me for eating salads, too, saying I'd never lose all that weight no matter what I ate.

Armed with determination to eat whatever the heck I wanted, I marched with purpose into the café.

Joshua usually handled the morning shift while Emily served the lunch crowd. It made me feel a little less weird that she didn't know I'd already been there today.

As soon as the door closed behind me, I let out a sigh of relief from the chilly breeze and sniffed deep of the coffee aroma. Heaven on earth, and so much better than toast burnt into charcoal briquettes.

Emily looked up from behind the counter, where she was placing fresh-baked scones on a tray. "Hey, Skye!"

"Hello! Can I get a mug for coffee?"

"Sure, there's clean ones." She gestured to the other end of the counter, where an eclectic collection of large coffee mugs was perched upside down.

Each one had a saying. The blue one had *I'm not yelling, I'm Irish.* A big white one read *Keep Calm and Drink Guinness.*

I grabbed the red one with *What's the Craic?* On it and carried it to the coffee station, thinking about how poorly that particular phrase would go over in Miami.

What was I in the mood for? I read each of the Monin bottles along the table today. I wasn't a fan of anise. Vanilla seemed too boring for my current mood. The praline sounded delicious, and would taste great with a dark roast.

I filled my mug most of the way with this selection, added cream and sugar, and nestled in my favorite booth, right against the plate-glass window. I loved people-watching as I ate lunch.

Emily asked, "Enjoying the weather, are you?" as she pulled out her order pad.

I grimaced and patted down my hair. It must be all over the place from the wind. "I'm getting used to it. Slowly."

"Fair play to you. Some folks never get used to it, like. Did you get some breakfast, after all? Joshua mentioned you'd come in this morning."

So much for stealth. I wrinkled my nose. "I've run out of bread, cereal, and eggs. I need to get to the grocery store, but I've been stuck at the pub overseeing the repairs. Can I get your goat's cheese salad?"

"Of course, be right out."

I wanted to shrink into my seat, but I still didn't know why. Then, the door jangled and Jess entered with a sunny smile. "I hoped I'd find you here. Can I join you?"

"Sure! I'd love some company." I waved at the chair.

After Emily took Jess's order, she told me about an interesting customer who had come into her gallery.

"Did she end up buying anything?"

"She did. That impressionistic painting of the stormy beach."

I knew exactly which painting she was talking about. I'd considered getting it for the pub once the walls were fixed, but it was too late now.

While I wanted to ask Jess's opinion on the pub décor, I had no idea how to ask. And after Audrey's demand for money up front, I was hesitant to request professional services as a favor.

Then, Emily came over with two plates. "You're grand now?"

Jess nodded. "We are, thanks."

As we ate, folks walked by outside. The plate-glass window was why this was my favorite seat. Máiréad's husband, Ronan, jogged past, his head down against the wind.

"I wonder where he's off to in such a hurry?"

Jess gave a shrug. "Máiréad's probably got him on some fool errand for a demanding customer. If she said jump, he'd ask how high."

I caught a glimpse of the priest, Father Fraser, dressed in dog collar and practically jogging toward the church. A few strangers, three teenage boys and a girl in a huddle, laughing at something.

I nodded toward them. "I haven't met that group. Who are they?"

"Two of the boys are Patrick's grandsons. Not sure about the girl or the other boy. I've seen her here once or twice. She sometimes runs errands for Adanna."

From where we were, just off on a side street, we could see the main road at an angle, but I couldn't catch a glimpse of the surgery where Adanna worked, nor the Garda station with her husband, Donal.

That was just as well, as he still didn't like me. I'd learned he had some sort of vendetta against my family, but I'd never been able to get the full story out of anyone.

After I chased the last bite on my plate and Jess finished her meal, we brought our plates up to the counter and paid.

Emily gave us a cheery wave as we went back outside into the windy, misty afternoon.

If I didn't ask Jess soon about helping with the pub, I'd lose the chance. "Would you mind coming back to the pub with me? I'd love your opinion on décor options. I have absolutely no talent with decoration, and less with Irish pubs."

She gave a bright smile, and her yellow glow flickered. "Sure, and that would be fun, but I can't stay long. I need to get back to the gallery before Audrey flounces out in a huff. She's not good with customers, especially those who need, well, a bit more care."

At least the rain had finally faded out.

As I fumbled with my keys at the ornate wooden pub door, Jess said, "How's the form, Sean?"

I turned to see the handsome man who had helped me with my car when I first arrived in Ballybás. He had a brilliant smile, and I still got tongue-tied around him. His black hair and jacket were wet from the rain, but his blue eyes were bright.

We hadn't seen each other much in the last few months, as he'd been in Dublin doing something with his book marketing. He'd described it as some sort of writing retreat, followed by a convention.

My cheeks were burning. "Oh, hi, Sean."

He gave Jess a hug, and I felt a twinge of jealousy. As if I had any business being jealous. I was nowhere near ready for a new romance, not with my ex-husband calling. "Any new stories with you? How's your sister settling in? I brought you some muffins."

Were they an item? I hadn't heard any gossip, and Adanna loved to chat about others.

Jess clapped her hands together. "Oh, I love your muffins. What kind are they?"

"Honey and sage. Don't make a face, you'll love them."

Then, he hugged me, and my paranoia calmed down. He smelled of honey and rain.

Once he let go, I turned to the door. The key didn't turn at first. It was always a bit sticky. I should get some lubricant for it before I forget.

I jiggled it, pushed, jiggled again. Finally, the door swung open. The day was still cloudy, and the pub was gloomy even on sunny days, so only a black maw greeted me, along with the musty odor I still couldn't get out, no matter how much I cleaned.

I reached for the light switch on the inside wall, flicked it on, and then froze.

There, sprawled out on my hardwood pub floor, was a black leather jacket. The jacket wasn't the shocking part. The shocking part was the body wearing it.

Ice flowed through my veins as I stumbled back into Sean. He automatically caught me. "Skye? What's wrong?"

Jess frowned at me, her color wavering. "You're as white as a sheet. Did you see a ghost?"

All I could do was shake my head and point. They both peered into the now illuminated room at someone lying face down, arms flung wide.

CHAPTER THREE

As we all stared at the motionless man—I thought it was a man—a junky pickup truck rattled in. Finn and Rory tumbled out, chattering about the timber they bought and having a minor argument over the type of wood.

Sean cleared his throat. "I'll go see if…uh, if he's breathing."

He stepped inside and knelt next to the man. Placing his hand in front of the mouth for a moment, he then placed his fingers on the man's neck, evidently checking for a pulse.

I should be doing this. I was a trained nurse. But my legs refused to budge.

Then, Sean turned the man over, and his eyes stared, wide open. Sean let out a sigh and said, "I'll call the Gard."

Jess pulled me to one side. "You look near to collapsing. Let me get you someplace you can sit."

She glanced around, but I didn't have any benches or tables out yet. Then, she gestured toward the low stone wall along one edge of the road. Straggling bits of determined greenery poked through the weathered stones. "Here. I'll fetch you some water. Or something stronger."

"No." My voice sounded like it was far away. What was with me? I was an experienced nurse. Death shouldn't be throwing me for a loop like this. I'd seen it hundreds of times.

But not on my own property. Again.

I cleared my throat. "No, don't go into the pub. The inspector will want to examine the scene. Sean shouldn't have gone in." My voice still sounded flat and inhuman, but at least I could speak again.

Slowly, life began to flow back into my limbs. My fingers were tingling, numb and painful.

Sean was on his mobile, speaking in low tones. The cousins were leaning against their truck, whispering to each other. Jess rubbed my back absently while shifting her gaze between me, Sean, and the road.

By the time Garda Donal McCarthy arrived and told us all to back off. Sean had also called Adanna, as she was the local doctor. I imagine McCarthy had called the inspector, as well. He didn't enter the pub but took photos of everything from the doorway.

The tall, thin Garda gave me a withering glance. "So, another body at your place? This is getting to be too much of a coincidence. We never had so many homicides before you moved here *Miss* O'Shea."

Something snapped inside of me. Both with my lassitude and my patience. "You're right, Detective, it's probably my charming personality that's driving people to murder. It couldn't possibly be your inept patrols, Garda McPetty."

His face turned a lovely shade of purple as Adanna hurried up. She took in everything, with her husband about to explode and Jess still rubbing my back with one hand.

First, she sent her husband a cryptic glare. Then, the doctor clicked into professional mode. "Where's the body?"

Sean gestured inside the pub, and she pulled a white plastic suit out of her bag, along with plastic gloves, booties, and a facemask. She pulled them all on before entering. She left the door open so if I craned my neck, I could see her and the body.

I was grateful for the interruption. My temper had been my downfall many times in my life. I'd needed to keep it tamped down for so long with Armand that it wiggled out at the slightest provocation now.

Donal glared at me as if I'd killed his favorite puppy, every muscle in his body rigid.

Adanna knelt by the body, taking pictures from all angles. She used a pen to lift the hand slightly, getting another photo. Then, she rose and came back outside. "When is Inspector McGowan arriving?"

Donal spun on her, scowling, arms straight at his side. "He's not. His assistant said he's in France on holiday. This one's up to you and me."

Oh, great. Just what I needed, for Garda Donal McCarthy to accuse me of murder again.

At least this time, I had an excellent alibi. Jess had been with me throughout lunch, and Sean had arrived before we even opened the pub.

But I'd been alone that morning on the beach. Rory and Finn hadn't even arrived until noon.

I hoped with all my heart that the pathologist would determine the time of death to be less than an hour ago.

Donal was asking Jess questions, so Sean sat next to me and took over rubbing my back. "Hey, are you grand? Do you need something to drink?"

"We can't go in the pub."

He lifted his chin. "Ah, I'm happy to go around to the house. Or leg it to Máiréad's and grab a Coke. I could even bring a nip if you need one, like."

I turned to him with a wan smile. "I doubt Garda McCarthy wants us wandering off at the moment."

The anger that had propelled my earlier rebellion faded. As the adrenaline drained from my muscles, fatigue replaced it.

We waited while Adanna made her examinations and called for transport. Peering through the doorway, I could still see the body from where I sat, as it lay just inside. Even though I didn't want to, I tried to make out some details.

He *was* a man, probably late-twenties, with wavy dark hair down to his shoulders. Handsome, or had been when he was alive. Along with the jacket, which had a triple swirling

Celtic knotwork over the front pocket, he was dressed in a gray V-necked T-shirt and jeans.

Red scratches were all over his face and neck, as if he'd been in a fight with ten cats. Had Faelan attacked him? But the scratches didn't look like a cat made them. They had a pattern more similar to human fingernails.

Another shiver ran down my spine.

The Garda finished questioning Jess, then called me over. Sean helped me up from the stone wall, but the Garda wouldn't let Sean stay while Donal questioned me.

"Do you recognize the dead man?"

I swallowed and shook my head.

"Verbal responses, please."

"No, I don't recognize him."

"What time did you leave your house this morning?"

"Probably around nine? I went to the Blarney Scone. Then, I talked to Jess's sister, Audrey, for a while. After that, I walked along the beach and had lunch with Jess."

"Did anyone see you at the beach?"

I scoured my memory. "There had been a family in the other direction. I have no idea if they saw me."

"And you found the body?"

I gave a sullen nod. "Yes, when I unlocked the door."

He raised his eyes to mine, piercing. "The door was locked?"

I rubbed the back of my neck while looking at the door, wide open. Black biker's boots were in view. "Uh…actually, I'm not sure. I turned the key, because I expected it to be locked. I don't remember if it clicked."

"Mm-hmm. And what time was that?"

"Just past noon, I think. Rory and Finn said they'd meet us here at noon, and they arrived just after I turned the key."

"When did Sean arrive?"

"Before I opened the door."

He wrote a few things before asking, "Did you notice anyone else around?"

Had I? Then, I remembered the person in the black hoodie and told the Garda.

"Male or female?"

I shrugged. "I couldn't tell. Stocky build, but about my height. The hood was cinched tight over their face. I caught a glimpse of light hair, maybe? They bumped my shoulder."

Garda McCarthy scowled at me. "The others didn't mention anyone else. Are you sure you saw someone?"

Had I imagined it? Now, I was questioning my own memory. Armand used to do that, insisting that I was making things up. "I'm sure I saw someone. I definitely didn't imagine them bumping into me! But I wasn't cataloging things for later recall, so I can't remember any details."

"Right." He wrote more in his pad, looked up at me, frowned, and wrote some more.

My knees were beginning to get wobbly, and I wanted to sit again. But I'd chew shards of glass before I would ask this Garda for any accommodation or admit any weakness.

Garda McCarthy asked me some clarifying questions and a few minutes later, he closed his notepad. "Don't leave town. Don't go into the pub. Don't touch anything in the pub."

The Garda started to turn away. "Wait! Can I go into the house entrance?"

He hesitated but then gave a grudging nod. "We'll put tape up where you can't go."

By the time everyone cleared out, the mist had turned to rain again, and I was alone in my parlour. Normally, I treasured my solitude, but the loneliness was now a stab in the heart. I both wanted to be around people and to retreat, curled into a ball.

Nestled in the overstuffed comfy chair I'd claimed as my favorite, I stared at the hearth. Bricks of peat were piled next to it, ready to burn. The house had electric heat, but the coziness of a peat fire might be just what I needed to banish the shivers.

I went through the motions of placing two bricks side by side in the hearth, with a third on top, leaving a small space beneath it. Then, I placed a block of chemicals called a firelighter in that space. I tossed on some wood shavings for kindling and clicked the long lighter under it.

As I waited for the fire to catch, I glanced at the old photos on the wall. One did have a name, Turlough O'Shea. He looked straight out of the Edwardian era, with top hat and tails. He stood next to an elegant woman, but only his name was on the frame. *Typical to ignore the woman.*

Once the kindling crackled and the brick glowed, I returned to my chair. The aroma of burning peat filled the room, earthy and acrid.

I'd only been here five months, and this was the second corpse I'd found on my property. If I didn't know any better, I would have thought myself the murderer, too.

I warned you that things like this would happen. The Fair Folk are gathering, and they'll focus on you.

I almost jumped out of my skin before I remembered Gran sometimes talked to my mind. I had no idea how that worked, or if it was my own overactive imagination, but I cherished the bits of wisdom she shared with her musical Irish lilt.

"Great, Gran. That's exactly what I needed to hear just now. Maybe I should move somewhere else, like Donegal."

You have a duty here, remember? A duty to this village to protect it from the Other Crowd.

"A duty I never asked for."

I waited for Gran to answer back but heard nothing. She must have faded back to wherever she was. Our conversations were always painfully short.

I remembered the scratches on the dead man's face. I glanced at the shadows to find Faelan, but no glowing eyes stared out of the void.

"Faelan! Faelan, are you okay? Did you see what happened?"

I still didn't understand why this incident was hitting me so hard. I was a nurse with ten years of experience. I'd seen countless people die. Sometimes from disease, sometimes from wounds, sometimes just from a broken heart. A few had died as I held their hand, with no one else to mourn them.

But this was the second body I'd found on my property in five months. That wasn't normal, by any measure. Garda McCarthy had obviously come to the same conclusion.

Opting for the hermit choice, I stared into the darkness of the pub. The bright yellow caution tape across the door kept me away, but I couldn't help peer into the gloom, if only to assure myself the body had been removed.

I had to do something other than brooding about the darned pub. With a sigh, I turned away and went into the kitchen.

Making myself some chamomile tea, I glanced at my cell phone. *No, it's called a mobile here.* How could it be only three o'clock? It felt like much later.

Just as I sat down to take my first sip, a sound came from the pub. I practically jumped from the seat, put down the tea, and crept toward the white and blue tape.

The door opened wide, and Garda McCarthy walked in, along with a shorter young woman in uniform, her blonde hair slicked back into a severe bun under her hat.

McCarthy glared at me and spoke in a cold tone. "We're here to do a catalog of items and perform forensics."

I turned to the woman and raised my eyebrows.

McCarthy scowled. "This is Garda Fitzgerald. She's training."

"Very nice to meet you, Garda Fitzgerald."

She gave me a sharp nod and turned to McCarthy, evidently awaiting orders. Great, another Garda who didn't like me. Just what I needed.

I retreated to my comfy chair and my chamomile tea and tried to ignore them. Despite my best intentions, I couldn't help but hear them.

"Make a list of the bottles and note how much is in each. I'll start dusting."

Her voice was more gravelly than I expected for such a petite woman. "By brand or by type of alcohol?"

"Brand is more precise. Also, if there are any of particular value, make note of those."

"Yes, sir."

They went quiet again. I sipped my tea and tried to clear my mind, but it didn't work very well.

Someone cleared their throat behind me, and I rose to my feet. Garda McCarthy stood just on the other side of the police tape. "Miss O'Shea? I need you to let me know if anything is missing from the pub."

I swallowed and put my empty cup down. "I'll try, but I haven't taken a full inventory yet. I'm nowhere near the point where I'll need to restock."

His tone was prim, even a little snide. "Nevertheless, please try."

"Does that mean I can cross the tape line?"

McCarthy rolled his eyes. "Of course."

I ducked under the tape and glanced at the bottles behind the bar. They'd been there since Gran shut the place, before her illness and death, and way before I inherited the pub. Most were dusty or grimy, half-empty, and likely no good.

I noticed a couple gaps. "There, there, and over there. The line of bottles had been full, so there are at least three bottles missing." I looked around the room itself, but since the cousins had been renovating, I couldn't tell what else might be amiss.

Garda Fitzgerald stood on the other end of the bar, her notepad and pencil poised. "Do you know what type? Were they expensive?"

The first gap was flanked by some Hennessy and a Jameson twenty-two-year-old single malt, but I couldn't for the life of me remember what had been there. Why should I? It wasn't as if I'd need them any time soon. Not until the boys were done with the renovations, at least.

I snapped my fingers. "Wait! I took photos before Finn and Rory started their work. Let me find them."

Pulling out my phone, I scanned through the pictures until I could find the right ones. Making one larger, I pointed at the gap. "That one was a Teeling twenty-four-year-old."

Next was some flavored gins. "Some gin from Connemara there, but I can't make out the brand."

For the third gap, the photo was a bit blurry. "Poitín here. Micil, I think? I'm not sure if that's expensive or not. The label is very plain, white with black lettering."

Garda FitzGerald held her hand out. "May I see the photos?"

I handed her my phone with some trepidation. I hated someone else having my life in their hands. She frowned at the photo, made it larger, then said, "Sure and that's Micil, a pricey one."

McCarthy asked, "And are you carrying insurance on this place?"

I shook my head. "Not on the pub, no. It's not open yet, so why would I?"

"Hmm."

He seemed disappointed in my answer. Did he think I'd concoct a murder as some elaborate insurance fraud scheme for some pricey liquor?

My turn to ask some questions. "Do you know who the dead man was?"

He shook his head, and his voice was almost normal this time. "No, we don't have an identity yet. He wasn't a local."

I stared at the spot where the body had been, and my skin pebbled with a chill. "How did he get those scratches?"

He snapped his notebook shut. "That's our business to discover, Miss O'Shea. Thank you for your input. You may return to your house."

The ice was back in his voice. I not only ducked under the tape, I grabbed my purse and continued out the door. While they were there, I needed to be elsewhere. Not alone, but not there, either.

I wished I could visit Adanna, but she'd be busy with writing up the case. She might even be doing the autopsy, though I doubted it. The last time, the pathologist in Bantry had to do that.

I could have spilled everything to her, my best friend since I arrived. However, she'd pulled away from me lately.

To be fair, she'd been taking trips to Dublin at least one day a week. Conferences, she said, but that was a lot of conferences in a row. Maybe she was behind on her continuing education?

Or she was just escaping her husband. Adanna and Donal always seemed to be angry at each other, and I might have been one reason. That piled on the guilt, but also left me without a close friend when I needed one.

Instead of going to Adanna's surgery, I headed down the road to Jess's gallery. She'd been there and would be understanding company. Besides, she was a comforting person in general. Something was very warm about her, like her yellow glow.

I wondered why I noticed her color so much. Adanna's was more of an olive green. Donal didn't have much of a color, maybe a hint of mud brown here and there when he got angry, but nothing strong.

Even Sean had a faint dark blue glow, but only when the sun was bright. I hadn't noticed anything about Garda Fitzgerald, but it had been dim inside the pub.

I'd long since learned to shut up about seeing those glowing auras because most folks didn't. Gran used to see colors, too, or at least she wrote about them in her diary.

The rain grew heavier as I walked down the street, and I hurried as the drops pelted down. I pulled my jacket over my head and turned the corner. By the time I got to the gallery door, I was a sopping mess.

Trying the best I could to shake off the excess water, I opened the door, making the bell jangle. Jess looked up from her desk, a momentary scowl transforming into a sad smile. She removed her glasses and opened her arms.

I was never much of a hugger, but I needed one now. Jess understood exactly what had just happened, the best sort of comfort.

We held each other for a long minute before I let go.

Gripping me by the shoulders, she examined me with frank assessment. "How are you holding up, Skye?"

I gave a shrug and dropped my gaze. "Not so great, honestly." I wanted to let it all out, but I didn't know Jess well enough.

"Have a seat. Would you like some tea? I just put the kettle on."

"Thank you. That would be lovely."

Jess went back into the kitchen, and I heard the clink of china. I glanced around the gallery, though I'd been there a few times before. The walls were absolutely covered in paintings, prints, and wall sculptures of all types.

Glass cases along the wall held jewelry and smaller sculptures. Several racks held fiber arts, both wearable and hangable. Mobiles and wind chimes hung from the ceiling.

How did the saying go? You couldn't swing a cat without knocking something over. I always walked through the narrow aisles carefully. The aroma of sandalwood and patchouli emanated from a huge pillar candle on her desk.

In a few minutes, Jess emerged with a steeping teapot and two cups, complete with matching saucers. "There's milk and sugar on the table over there. I usually have a cuppa for visitors. You'll want plenty of milk and sugar after a shock like that."

I shook my head and clasped my hands in my lap. Why had I come here? Did I just need company? I wished my psyche would make up its stupid mind.

Fermented sheep nuggets, wasn't I a hot mess?

Jess broke the awkward silence with her sales voice. "How are you doing on the redecoration? Are you ready to shop for some art for the pub walls?"

"Ha! I'm nowhere near that yet. When I am, I'll come see what you've got."

The door jangled again, and in walked a petite woman with jet-black hair in a pixie cut. She couldn't have been much older than twenty, and barely topped five feet.

Jess flashed her a smile, but the customer just gave a nod and started perusing the art on the wall. She paused at a shelf of pottery, then touched an elegant abstract sculpture.

She turned to us, her gaze shifting from me to Jess and back again, evidently not knowing who to address. "Are these locally produced?"

Jess answered in a professional tone. "All the work is from artisans in County Cork, though we do have a few Irish artists who live here part of the year. Is there anything in particular you're searching for?"

The woman literally sniffed, her nose rising at least an inch. "Local artists shouldn't be priced nearly this high."

Jess's yellow glow flared so bright, I had to squint. This wasn't a happy flash; she exuded anger. She kept her expression pleasant, though, and I admired her control. I'd never had great luck hiding my own temper.

"My artists are all quite skilled and command high prices in galleries in Dublin, Cork, Galway, and London. If you don't see anything which appeals to you, perhaps you'd prefer to patronize a different gallery."

She sniffed again and predictably demanded, "I need to speak to your manager." I was just guessing her name was Karen, though maybe there was an Irish version, to match her accent. Caireann, perhaps?

Jess's tone remained calm but firm. "I am the manager and the owner of this gallery. If there's something you wish to discuss, I'd be happy to help."

Though she said this with confidence, there was something in her expression that told me she didn't want to run the customer off. During the tourist season, Jess probably did very well in her gallery. The winter months were likely much less profitable. She'd need the business, even if the woman was ruder than rude.

As the customer continued examining each piece on display, Jess whispered to me, "I don't want to toss her out, but I wish she'd buy something and leave."

"Maybe she'll trip and be too embarrassed to stay?"

Jess shook her head. "No, she might fall on one of the sculptures. With my luck, she'd take down the entire pottery shelf."

"Maybe someone else will come in and get her."

Jess turned to look at the customer again, an intense stare that might have shattered the woman if looks could kill. Her yellow glow flickered madly. "I doubt she has a lot of friends."

The sound of ripping fabric cut the silence. The customer stared, horrified, at a huge tear in her fashionable, expensive-looking dress, evidently caught on a metal swan sculpture.

Her face turned scarlet. I worked hard to hide my smile.

Then, a man with black, curly hair and olive skin rushed into the store. She glared at the newcomer, but he opened both of his hands, palms up, as if asking a question.

The woman scowled at the newcomer. She whispered something to him, the harsh sounds punctuated with anger. She flashed a few resentful glances toward Jess during her discourse. He responded in calm tones, his hand on her arm, as if trying to calm her.

She turned on the ball of her foot and fled into the now-pelting rain. He let out a deep sigh and followed her.

Jess and I exchanged a glance and burst out laughing. I wasn't sure what was so funny, but I needed that release. It was a salve to my prickly soul.

As our mirth faded, Jess placed a gentle hand on my forearm. "Your laugh reminds me of Saoirse's so much."

I looked down at my teacup. "I didn't get to speak to her a lot. We mostly wrote letters. She didn't like phone calls."

"Sure, and that's true enough. Saoirse preferred to see expressions when she talked."

I cocked my head. "Did Gran visit you here often?"

Jess shrugged. "Now and then. She was part of a group who met about once a month. I attended a few times."

"Really? What group was that?"

This time, Jess looked embarrassed, fiddling with her teacup handle. "Well, a bunch of folks who like New Age things."

My skin prickled at her words. "New Age? Like magic and stuff?"

"Sort of. Tarot cards, crystals, Wicca, spiritual faff, like."

That sounded innocuous enough, and I could see Gran being into that sort of thing. She had a penchant for folklore, fairies, and magic herself, though I knew first-hand that her powers were no stage tricks.

Adanna seemed to take the existence of fairies and otherworldly creatures as a matter of course. Perhaps Jess was the same.

I wondered if Jess had magical powers like Gran and I did. Is that why she glowed so strongly? Only a few people had them, and even then, they could fade to nothing, depending on their mood. I'd never been able to figure out all the rules, if there were any.

But no matter how much I suspected, I couldn't make myself ask such a weird question to someone I'd only known a few months. Instead, I asked, "What was the group called?"

Jess downed the last of her tea and poured more into her cup. "She was part of a group called Mystic Moon Meadow. They met at a stone circle up the road, usually just to sing around the fire. Sometimes they did something more substantial, but mostly it was just social."

Something more substantial. Questions crowded in my head, shoving and pushing to get out, but my mouth refused to form them.

It shouldn't have surprised me that they were using a stone circle. After all, they were a New Age group, right. It just struck something cold in my heart.

Instead, I gave a smile. "I'm so glad I'm learning more about her."

She held up her cup. "Would you like some more?"

I didn't want to overstay my welcome, so I said, "No, I think I need to get back. Thank you, though." Awkwardly, I rose and excused myself, exiting into the now sprinkling rain.

Maybe another time I'd have the courage to ask more questions.

CHAPTER FOUR

Sleep did not come easily that night, not until Faelan hopped up and laid on my chest. His purrs rumbled and lulled me into a deep slumber.

Which meant that I dreamt. However, rather than the horrific dreams that a dead body in my pub might inspire, I found myself sitting in a field of wildflowers. The surrounding landscape was splattered with white, yellows, blues, and purples.

Butterflies and dragonflies flitted by my head, and a yellow one landed on the daisy beside me. I swatted at it, but it fluttered away into the bright sun. I dropped my black paw with disappointment.

Everything smelled of spring, fragrant perfumes from the blossoms, the fresh green grass, all the summer smells.

I spied something small moving in the grass a few yards in front of me. I crept forward, careful not to disturb whatever it was, step by step. Crouching out of sight, I was about to leap when the creature beat me to it.

A tiny, fuzzy black kitten leapt into the air to catch a dragonfly. Adorable and clumsy, he missed his target and fell back into the grass. I giggled, but it came out more like a rumble.

Past the kitten, off in the distance, a tree rose. I swore it hadn't been there before but, for some reason, I needed to get closer. I waded through the tall grasses, the kitten following me and attacking my ankles. It took only a few steps to close the distance to the enormous hawthorn tree.

Thin bits of fabric and ribbons were tied to every single branch. I'd heard of wishing trees or fairy trees. Maybe a clootie tree? That may have been a Scottish name. Tie a ribbon, make a wish.

A wishing tree like this was hidden behind the empty farm across from the church, diagonally across the road from my house. I could just glimpse it through a hole in the stone fence if I stood on my tiptoes.

I wanted to make a wish, but I didn't have anything to tie on it. I looked down at what I was wearing, some sort of black fur coat, but I couldn't focus on the cloth.

I twisted and turned, but the fabric always seemed to sway out of view. Then, I just started spinning just for the joy of it, like Sister Maria on an Austrian hillside.

In a moment of genius, I stared at my arm. I had a sleeve! Ripping a small piece from the edge was easier than it should have been, but I didn't question it. Tying the black strip on a branch, I made a wish.

Before I could complete the thought, a horrible klaxon shattered the peace.

I sat straight up in bed. Faelan growled and hopped off. I grabbed my phone and shut off the Star Trek klaxon. Then I glanced at the time, blinking to clear my vision. *Who the heck is calling at three in the morning?*

"Hello?" My voice croaked with sleep.

"Hola, mi corazón. ¿Qué pasa?"

Armand. Sheep nuggets.

I was too groggy to come up with a clever or biting response. Instead, I snapped, "What do you want?"

"Now, is that any way to greet your loving husband?"

I wiped at the grit in my eyes, trying to gather my senses as the dream faded. "*Ex*-husband. What do you want."

"Just to talk to you. Where are you now?"

No way, José. If he didn't already know where I'd moved, there was no way I was giving him any clues to my new location. If we had been in the same room, his charm might have worked. He had an incredible physical charisma. But across an ocean, on a phone line? Nope.

My eyes were getting used to the darkness, and I made out Faelan's eyes glowing from his perch on the dresser. "Away from you."

His tone turned to silk, that perfectly reasonable rhythm that was so hard to argue with. "You're not being fair, Skye. I just need to talk to you."

I should just hang up. Why wasn't I hanging up? But he was fantastic at putting me in a defensive position. "I don't need to talk to you."

Faelan jumped back on the bed and began kneading onto my pillow. It soothed my ruffled temper back to normal.

After a few heartbeats, I had the strength to hang up and block that phone number. Blocking this number wouldn't stop him for long; he'd always been good at hacking. But it might give me some peace for a while and, in the meantime, he couldn't mess with me.

Closing my eyes again, I wanted to get back to the dream. It had been so peaceful and sweet. I could just catch a glimpse of the field of daisies, a fuzzy kitten, and a wishing tree…but I couldn't even remember what I'd been wishing for.

I was grasping for that moment between dreaming and waking up, when everything could still be possible. I needed to hold onto that magic so hard, but it dangled just out of my reach, like Tantalus and his tempting fruit.

A feeling of intense emptiness washed over me at a wish forever lost.

Images of the field flashed in tantalizing flickers. A vague glimpse of a black kitten running through the grass, and it was gone.

With a sigh, I gave up trying to sleep, as I was way too awake to get any rest now. So, I did a full-body stretch, showered, and dressed. Plodding down the carpeted stairs, I went through the motions of making coffee and toast, though dawn was still far away. The quiet hours of the morning always made me wistful.

What I wanted was an everything bagel, but I hadn't been able to find any bagels in the grocery store. Adanna claimed there was a bakery in Cork City that served them but nothing nearby.

I had, however, managed to find some things for Faelan to enjoy. Well, if he had been a normal cat, he might like them. A laser pointer, a catnip mouse, and a bag of treats. I planned to parcel these out slowly to gain his trust and cooperation.

The wonderful aroma of dark roast coffee filled the kitchen, shortly joined by burnt toast. I cursed and pulled the toast out, dropping it on the plate and scraping yellow butter over it.

An image from my dream came back to me, a yellow butterfly on a daisy. No, not my dream, someone else's. It sounded crazy, but it must have been a cat's dream.

Maybe Faelan? Was that why I'd gone to sleep so easily? Cats never had problems with getting to sleep.

Wait, did Faelan have a kitten?

I looked around for the Cat Sídhe, but I hadn't caught a glimpse of him since I was so rudely awakened. Many of the corners in the parlour were dark, and he could be hiding anywhere. "Faelan! Are you around? Do you want some breakfast?"

I grabbed the can opener and cat food. That sound usually brought him running, but not this time. *Drat that cat.* It was just like him to be difficult.

Finally, I caught sight of his fluffy black tail in the pub. "Faelan! Come out of there."

He sauntered into the kitchen, sniffed the cat food, and twitched his tail three times. "Have you anything other than this pitiful offering?"

I never knew when he'd disdain cat food. Some days, he would devour it. The next day, the same food was beneath his dignity. Then, I remembered my notion about bribing him. "Some tuna fish?"

"That is much more acceptable."

I tossed the stinky cat food, cleaned out the bowl, and opened a can of tuna, which was equally stinky. After I placed his bowl on the floor, he devoured it, making little growling noises as he inhaled the treat.

I chuckled as I tossed the empty can. Once he finished, he strolled over to the sofa and started grooming his paw with feline nonchalance.

"So, Faelan. You mentioned that I had borrowed a dream before, right?"

He paused and glared at me. "That is correct."

"I think I borrowed yours last night."

Letting out a hiss, he backed up, his hackles raised. "That should not be possible!"

"Oh? I was in a daisy field with butterflies and a clumsy black kitten. Do you have a kitten? If not yours, whose dream was it, then?"

The fur settled, but he still looked spiky. "The dreams of a Cat Sídhe are not for others. You have committed a grievous trespass!"

"Hey! I didn't do a thing. *You're* the one who was lying on my chest and putting me to sleep."

He glanced back and forth, as if searching for someone eavesdropping. His voice was low when he spoke. "I do not lend my dreams. The dreams of the Fae are nearly impossible to steal. It should be clear, even to you, that something powerful must be involved. Something close by."

Then, the huge black cat with a white diamond on his chest darted out the cat door and disappeared.

Great. Off to do fairy cat stuff. He didn't even answer me about the kitten.

I really didn't want to contemplate what it might mean to be sharing dreams. Or if there was some fairy creature out there messing with dreams, as Faelan implied.

Instead, I spent the hours until dawn working on a cryptic crossword puzzle. I was getting used to this style of clue. There were several layers of puns and sometimes the clue to solving the word was baked inside the description.

After the sun finally rose, someone knocked on the pub door. Since I was still forbidden from passing the police tape, I pushed back from the kitchen table, ran out the back door, and hurried around the building, only to find Garda Donal McCarthy. His trainee, Garda Fitzgerald, stood behind him.

I placed my hands on my hips. "You know I can't enter the pub. Why did you knock on this door?"

He gave me a nasty smirk. "To see if you were obeying the rule."

Clenching my jaw, I said, "Obviously, I passed your childish test. What do you want now?"

"Just to take the tape down. Your place is cleared, but I may have more questions for you later."

Garda Fitzgerald's gaze shifted between us.

I ran back inside, grabbed the keys, and walked to the tape. I hesitated, still feeling squeamish about the dead body.

But I was a nurse, and that was silly. I'd taken so many classes on learning how to keep people from dying, but none on how to keep living after encountering death, literally on my doorstep.

With a deep sigh, I ducked under the tape. Then, I strode through the pub to open the door from the inside, giving the Garda a glare. My scowl might have been lost on him in the dim pub, but it made me feel better.

As Garda Fitzgerald removed the tape, someone else knocked on the door. I was still standing next to it, so I flung it open to reveal Sean.

Determined to temper my dislike with McCarthy and be pleasant, I said, "What a nice surprise! Would you like to come in? I can make us some tea."

Sean entered with a smile and a nod, and we both sidled by the Gardaí. The frown on McCarthy's face was worth it all.

By the time I got tea things going, the Gardaí had left, and I could be myself again. I sat in the comfy chair as the teapot steeped, suddenly awkward again with Sean.

He glanced at the table, where my cryptic crossword still lay open, half-completed. Then, he sat on the chintz sofa, his hands held awkwardly in his lap. "I'm sorry to barge in on you, like. It looks like you're busy, but I need to know what your next project is on the house."

Sean had been doing the minor repairs on the house portion of the building, while Finn and Rory worked the bigger jobs on the pub. They had all the equipment and, supposedly, more experience, though I was still reserving judgment on that. Also, they said they were registered, and the pub had to pass inspection.

"Is there a way to replace those horrible fluorescent lights in the bathrooms with something kinder on the eyes and the environment?"

He let out a chuckle. "Brilliant, I can work on that. Do you have any particular design in mind? Have you chosen a decoration theme?"

I wrinkled my nose. I hated decorating and had never been good at it. My style could best be described as college student hoarding shabby. I *did* collect things with bees on them, and perhaps that would be an idea for the B&B theme.

As I poured the tea, I suggested, "How about something bright and cheerful? Blues, whites, and yellows with bees? I can put out some of my trinkets as finishing touches."

His eyes lit up, and I was almost knocked back at his smile. "That's pure deadly! You know I'm a fan of all things related to bees. You could even call it the Buzzy Bee & Bee B&B! I'll see what I can find at the DIY shop in the city next time I go."

The city, I'd learned, meant Cork City, as opposed to County Cork. One of the largest cities in Ireland, that's where people went for anything beyond the basics.

"If you like, I could sell jars of your honey, too. A souvenir for all who visit."

Sean beamed. "Fair play to you. You've a marketing head on your shoulders."

Another awkward silence descended upon us. I sipped my tea, then grimaced, as I'd forgotten to add any sugar. I remedied that and took a second sip, feeling the silence grow heavier each moment.

Despite the silence, I had a sudden itch to find out all I could about the dead man, but I couldn't just rush off now. I had a guest and the obligations that came with that. Also, he was lovely to look at.

After I drained my cup, I poured the last bit of tea from the pot. I held it up in question to Sean. "I can brew some more, if you want?"

He shook his head and placed his cup down. "No, I'm after getting back to my farm. I may be back later today, but that depends on if I can get the right fixtures in the city. Will you be fine on your own, like?"

I had no idea if I would be anywhere near *fine* on my own, but I didn't want him to know that. Years of shielding my inner emotions was a hard habit to break.

Regardless, I had no intention of staying in an empty house where someone had been murdered. "I've got some things to research."

Sean's eyes shone with eager interest. "What sort of research?"

Giving a shrug, I hastily ordered my ideas into something resembling cohesion. "The man who was killed. Someone must have seen him in town. Did he have friends? Family? It's not like there are so many visitors that it would be hard to discover, not in September."

"Shouldn't you be leaving that to Donal?"

"Well, yes, I *should*. But, if I don't keep myself busy, I'll fall into a pit of madness, and no one wants that mess."

I'd said it with a good dose of self-loathing, but Sean took it as a joke and laughed. "Ah, well, I always appreciate a good puzzle to keep the mind going strong. Let me know if I can help."

He rose and carried his cup and the empty teapot into the kitchen. When the tap started running, I realized with horror that he was doing the washing up. I couldn't allow him to do that!

I drank down the dregs of my cup and hastened to join my guest. "Here, let me do that."

"Ah, no, I'm happy to wash dishes. It's calming, almost meditative." He held out his hands for my cup.

With narrowed eyes, I handed my teacup and saucer to Sean. Armand would have eaten rusty nails before doing something he considered a woman's job.

"There, that's done. So, where are you going to ask about your man? We don't have a name yet, do we?"

"No, but I figured O'Leary's is the most likely place to start. I'll head there in a few."

"Aye, fair play. I'm off to walk Sétanta. Let me know if you need some backup, Detective O'Shea." He gave a jaunty salute and left through the pub.

I had to sit down and collect my thoughts. Why *was* I so interested in finding out about the dead man?

Was it just that yet another stranger had died on my property? Or that I needed something to keep my mind occupied? I didn't want to fall back into a pattern of solitude and paranoia, especially with Armand sniffing around. Working out a puzzle would help keep my mind off that.

Fine. I *would* go to O'Leary's and find out what I could about yesterday's dead stranger.

CHAPTER FIVE

I left the house only a few minutes after Sean, but I waited until he was out of sight. Why was that important? I had no idea. It just was.

The day seemed brighter than yesterday had been, but some gray clouds lingered. The wind had lessened to just below gale force and was chilly, rather than biting cold.

I finally understood why Gran always talked about the wind. It never seemed to stop, at least here on the coast. Perhaps farther inland there wasn't a constant blow from the Gulf Stream.

My thin, yellow cardigan was sufficient, at least for now. In an hour? Who knew?

I strolled down my side street, past the empty farm, and around the corner, heading for O'Leary's pub. One aspect of living in Ballybás I absolutely loved is that I could walk places. I didn't have to get in a car every single time I left my house.

It was almost midday, and I could do with a spot of lunch despite a stomach full of tea. My finances wouldn't be happy with my decisions to eat out again, but right now, I didn't care. Besides, this was a fact-finding mission.

O'Leary's pub served soup and sandwiches during the day. He didn't run a gastropub with gourmet burgers and fancy fry-ups, but the food was tasty and not overpriced.

When I entered, I paused in the doorway to let my eyes adjust to the interior. The huge mirror behind a phalanx of glittering bottles took one whole wall. A polished wooden bar divided the room, with a dozen tables in the outer section.

There were about ten customers in the pub. A few sat at the bar, including Patrick, the old sheep farmer that no one could understand.

Three tables held people, all staring at menus. I took one of the smaller tables, put my purse down, and grabbed a menu from the polished wooden bar.

A grilled cheese sandwich and some tomato soup would hit the spot, even if the Irish did call it a toastie instead. Alas, they only had leek and potato soup, so I had to make do with that. I gave my order to Niamh, behind the bar, thankful not to have to deal with the owner. Cormac O'Leary and I had gotten off to a rocky start.

After my ordeal with Gerald in the bog last May, I'd finally figured out why O'Leary was so angry with me. He thought I was going to swoop in and make Gran's pub into some plastic American tourist tat atrocity.

I'd heartily assured him that wasn't my plan, but our truce was tentative, at best. He'd still lose business once mine was up and running, and Cormac O'Leary wasn't one to ignore a rival for his profits.

As I sat back at my table, I studied the others in the pub. Most of them were familiar faces, both at the bar and the tables.

O'Leary's daughter, Niamh, worked behind the bar. She did some shifts at the local radio station, too, an Irish language show. That reminded me of my idea to take some lessons.

She was leaning on the bar, chatting to the town mechanic, Ciaran. When I'd first driven to town and promptly got into a fender bender, he'd repaired my car. My mood went down a notch, remembering Brian and his nastiness. Brian had been the first body I found on my property. I clamped down on the shiver that memory summoned.

Father Fraser and two older church ladies sat at the round table closest to the front door. I didn't know the women's names.

The next table had a tall, older man with glasses. The primary teacher, I thought. Brendan, perhaps? He ate alone, reading the newspaper.

A new group came in, talking and laughing. They were dressed in colorful outfits, sort of like hippies, and looked vaguely familiar.

Niamh walked over with my soup and sandwich. "Hot off the sandwich press."

"Thanks! Hey, do you know anyone around here that gives Irish language lessons?"

Letting out a snort, she said, "Labhrás'll be your man. He delights in schooling us."

"Oh?"

Before she could elaborate, one of the men at the hippie table called her over. She flashed me a smile and moved on to them. A moment later, Jess's sister, Audrey, sauntered in, resplendent in a bright pink and orange dress that could flag down airplanes on a dark night. A fabric belt in the same paisley print was tied around her waist with a bow.

For a moment, I tried to make myself small. I didn't want her coming to sit with me. That would be horribly awkward after our conversation about money. Luckily, she joined the table Niamh was standing beside.

Her new companions were three men and a woman. One man was lanky and blond, while the next had sandy-brown hair and a stocky build. The third man had darker skin and short hair, perhaps some middle-eastern ancestry.

Next came a woman with a pixie haircut, and I suddenly recognized her as the angry customer in Jess's shop. Something shiny flashed on her hands, and I stared at her long nails, painted with metallic silver polish. The darker-haired man was the one who had taken her away.

The others were scooting over to make room, five people around a table made for four. I stared at my table, shutting out distractions so I could eavesdrop on their conversation.

Audrey spoke first, addressing the blond man, "Have you prepped the site?"

He shook his head. "Not yet. I don't have all the supplies." He turned to glare at the other man.

"Don't look at me, Marcus! I brought everything I was supposed to. Tara, here, she was to bring the meat."

Tara glared at him, but her eyes were red. She rubbed her nose with the back of her hand and sniffed. Had she been crying?

I couldn't make sense of their conversation, but at least I was learning some names. Desperate Audrey, Blond Marcus, and Pixie Tara.

I had no idea if they had anything to do with the dead man, but they weren't locals and at least they were distracting me.

The other man, with the sandy-brown hair, rolled his eyes. "Tara told me she wasn't able to get the right kind. She said as much last week! I thought you were making other arrangements."

Audrey drew herself up. "You do not speak to me like that, Liam. You are still an acolyte."

"Chill, Audrey! You're harshing my mood."

An acolyte? Wasn't that something they called monks before they took vows? Or was that just in medieval times? I pulled out my phone to look up the word.

Acolyte: A person assisting the celebrant in a religious service or procession.

Okay, well that was interesting. They sure didn't look like a bunch of monks, but maybe some other religious group. From Tara's goth dress and Liam's tie-dye pants, maybe they were part of a pagan group, like Jess had been talking about.

What had she called her group? Something with a bunch of Ms. Was it Misty Mountains? Meddling Moonies? Murky Midnight Marsh? Oh, right, Mystic Moon Meadow.

If Audrey was a member, maybe it *was* the same group Jess used to be part of. And Gran.

Suddenly, these people seemed too close to home.

The Madcap Moonlit Mystics got up shortly after that. They hadn't even eaten anything, just sucked down a few sodas. I wanted to follow them, but I also wanted to finish my lunch.

By the time I came to a decision, they'd gone.

Niamh came to the table and asked, "Would you like another Coke, Skye?"

I shook my head. "Hey, do you know those folks who just left?"

She glanced over her shoulder at the door. "They came into town a few nights ago. One of them is Jess's sister."

"They've been in the pub before, then? Do you know their names?" I had Desperate Audrey, Blond Marcus, Pixie Tara, and Hippie Liam, but I hadn't caught the other man's name.

With a conspiratorial wink, she said, "Sure and there were mad ructions when they got pished last night. The little one, Tara? She had a go at the shorter man, I think his name is Liam, the one with light brown hair, like."

"She actually hit him?"

Niamh let out a low chuckle. "She didn't hit him. She jumped on his back and started pummeling his head, like. Pure feisty one, she is. After that, they all took off. The strange thing is, they didn't go in the direction of their lodging."

"Where are they staying?"

"At the B&B across from the school, the one Eileen Donovan owns?"

That means they went down to the beach, and my house was between O'Leary's and the shore. I thought briefly of Pixie Tara's long nails.

For the life of me, I couldn't think of any defining characteristic of the dead man, other than the scratched face. Was he tall? I hadn't seen him standing up, so I had nothing to compare him to, but I had to give it a try. "Was there another guy with them? I'm trying to find out information on a man with black hair."

Niamh let out a rueful chuckle. "Jaysus, that describes half the men in Ireland, pet."

I remembered another detail. "He wore a leather jacket."

She frowned, but then her eyes danced. "Yes! Your man was here a few nights ago, with your feisty one there."

"He was?"

"Sure, and the one named Liam? He started in on your man with the leather jacket. I thought he was after biting the guy's head off! Something about stealing his woman."

"Tara? Or someone else?"

"Liam screamed several names, so I'm thinkin' it's a habit."

Tara and the dead man, then. And Tara had a demonstrable temper. If she'd leapt on Liam's back, that could have been a jealous rage. Maybe they were an item? Where did that leave Leather Jacket Guy? A third wheel? An ex-lover? Competition?

If Liam was getting in his face about womanizing, it made sense he had a few folks angry with him.

Another patron came in, and Niamh left to attend to them. I finished my lunch, paid, and went outside. Looking back and forth on the street, the group were nowhere to be found. They'd had plenty of time to disappear, so that wasn't a surprise.

I needed to get a few things from Máiréad's store, so I walked to her shop. Her windows were plastered with posters for various brands, obnoxious sale signs that were way out of date, and announcement flyers for local events. They covered so much window that I couldn't even see through the plate-glass.

When I opened the door, she gave a wave, then went back to reading her magazine. Her store was chock full of things from floor to ceiling, with aisles barely big enough to sidle through, but she stocked the basics, from fresh fruit to paper towels. Anything past the basics I'd need to head into Schull or Bantry for.

I grabbed some jam and peanut butter, as well as a loaf of bread. Máiréad had been kind enough to start stocking peanut butter once I asked her to. I wasn't feeling up to cooking much right now, but I needed to eat. PB&J sandwiches were easy and had protein.

As I brought my choices to the counter, Máiréad looked up. "Good afternoon, Skye. How's the form? Any stories?"

I'd learned the embarrassing way that these questions were the rough equivalent of *what's up?* and she wasn't actually asking me to relate a fairy tale. "Not much here. How about yourself?"

Of course, dreaming someone else's dream did sound like it came out of a fairy tale. I wondered if it was just me getting these dreams.

As we completed the sale, I wanted to ask Máiréad if she'd had someone else's dreams, but I was too nervous. I didn't know the older woman very well, and she always seemed so prim and proper. In addition to running the store, she played the organ at church and provided flowers. Having some fairy-controlled dream shenanigans would be too weird.

I turned to leave and caught sight of a colorful poster half-obscured by an announcement of a music festival from last June. Blues and purple letters promised a spooky time at a Witch's Ball.

If Máiréad allowed such a poster in her shop, perhaps I'd misjudged her. Before I could think better of it, I turned back and asked, "Máiréad, you haven't heard about anyone having weird dreams lately, have you? Like, dreams that might belong to someone else?"

Her eyes grew wide, and she drew back a moment. "Now, that'll be an odd question, to be sure."

Which wasn't an answer to my question. I lost whatever shred of nerve that had prompted me to blurt out that question, and mumbled, "You're right, sorry."

As I turned to leave again, Máiréad's husband, Ronan, shouted out from somewhere in the back of the shop. "You know you've been having my dreams, Máiréad! Just tell the girl about it. It won't hurt your immortal soul, I promise!"

Stifling a laugh, I waited for the shopkeeper's answer.

After a deep sigh, she gave a sharp nod. "Sure, and I was just having one last night. I was in hospital, rushing from patient to patient, never having enough time to sit or even spend a penny!"

That gave me a jolt, and my heart raced. This wasn't just my imagination, after all! Someone else had been swapping dreams. As a nurse, that was a very familiar dream. Not in a vague, philosophical way, either. "I've had that exact dream too many times to count. And the reality, come to think of it."

She raised her eyebrows. "That'll be your dream, then? Which dream did you have?"

After a nervous swallow, I said, "I was drowning in the ocean at night. I haven't gone swimming in the sea more than a dozen times in my life, and I'd never gotten close to drowning."

"Night? You were drowning at night?" she tapped her fingernails on the glass counter. "I know someone who nearly drowned at night. That would be the doctor, your friend Adanna."

Adanna had nearly drowned? I knew she was leery of the bog. "So, I know this sounds whacky, but I think dreams are being mixed up. Have you heard of anyone else?"

Máiréad gave me a long, searching look, but then gave a sharp nod. "Aye, well, we've a few strange things about now and then in this town. Saoirse always managed to be in the thick of them, so it's little surprise you're doing the same."

Huh. I supposed that made sense. At least Gran's reputation for meddling in things might make my investigations go more smoothly. "Do you know of any local legends that might have an answer? I've searched through all sorts of books, but can't find anything that might relate."

She paused a moment, staring at the ceiling, but then shook her head. "No, nothing I can think of. Sure, the Good Neighbours have lots of creatures, but this seems like something new."

"Did Gran ever mention switched dreams?"

"Not that I remember, no. Adanna told me of a dream about working a busy pub. That might be O'Leary's or Niamh's dream."

If I had borrowed Faelan's dream, and Máiréad had borrowed Ronan's, was proximity a factor? But I'd taken Adanna's dream, and Máiréad had borrowed mine, so that didn't track.

I felt like someone had pulled a finished jigsaw puzzle apart and was hiding all the pieces. My muscles twitched and my calf tried to cramp. "

She shook her head.

"I want to find out if anyone else has had issues like this. What's the best way to do that?"

The older woman gave me a sly smile and a wink. "You might ask others about their dreams?" Her tone rose to make it a question.

Ronan called out from the back again. "For the love of Jesus, Mary and Joseph and the wee donkey, just call a town meeting!"

For some reason, that prospect filled me with dread. I was a newcomer here, a blow-in from America. What right did I have to summon everyone to a town meeting? That seemed like the height of *throwing my weight around,* just the sort of thing the locals would hate. Just the sort of thing O'Leary had expected me to do.

I clenched my hands together. "Maybe I should talk to some other people, first. You know, build up a list? Some sort of proof that something was happening."

Máiréad shrugged. "If you like. Everyone's already talking about it, so your job is well-begun."

With a half-smile, I said, "And well-begun is half-done?"

"That's the job."

As I left the shop, my thoughts raced. Did I have the cheek to call a town meeting? Maybe I should play it safe and ask someone else to do it. Who would be the best option?

Father Duncan Fraser would be highly respected. Or Cormac O'Leary. If Adanna had stolen his dream, perhaps he'd stolen someone else's.

However, while O'Leary had eased off on his hatred of me barging into his town. I'd had the temerity of wanting to open a competing pub, and he still nursed a lingering resentment. Asking him to call a meeting for me might fan that flame back into a bonfire.

With a left turn, I headed down the main street. I glanced at my phone to check the time. How did it get to be three already? The priest had confession in the early afternoon, but since I didn't partake, I didn't know the precise times.

As I strode toward the spire reaching above the other rooftops, a stiff ocean breeze hit me. The wind almost knocked me over and was considerably colder than it had been earlier. I pulled my sweater around me more tightly and pushed through.

Passing the font with holy water, I reached for the church door handle. But before I could touch it, the heavy door swung open, and someone almost ran into me. I stumbled back, startled, as Blond Marcus stomped out, his fists clenched. He shot me an angry glare as he passed.

I stared as he hurried down the street, wondering what had gotten him in such a huff. He was almost running, as if the Devil himself was chasing him. Did he have a guilty conscience? I'd already put Tara and Liam on the suspect list, but maybe I needed to add Marcus, too.

When I entered the church, I halted to admire the sheer beauty of the interior, as I always did. The lingering aroma of incense, the ornate altar, and especially all of the stained glass. I wasn't Catholic, nor was I very religious in anything. If the Catholics had done one thing right, it was magnificent architecture.

Though the sun wasn't bright, a few brave sunbeams filtered through the stained glass, dappling the pews with color. Dust motes danced in the beams in a delicate ballet.

After I breathed in the wonder and almost sneezed from the dust, I walked quietly toward the front, where a few people sat near the confession booth.

How long did these sessions last? Until the last person had availed themselves of the Father's services, or did he stop at a set time? As I approached, I recognized the people waiting. My very favorite person, Garda Donal McCarthy, sat closest to the booth.

Farther down sat Jess, which surprised me. I figured she'd be far more into New Age spirituality than Catholicism. Still, a lot of Celtic Christianity had kept elements from the old pagan ways.

I took a seat on the pew next to Jess. She flashed me a friendly smile, then whispered, "I didn't know you came to confession."

With a shrug, I admitted, "I don't. But I wanted to ask Father Fraser something. I figured this would be the best place to wait and see him. Do you know when he's finished?"

"Whenever he's done with those waiting. He never cuts anyone off just because confessions run late."

"That's very kind of him."

I'd suspected as much. Curiosity burned in me, wondering what Jess needed to confess. Her yellow glow was waxing and waning in a heartbeat rhythm. Something must be bothering her.

Almost as if I'd asked her out loud, she rose and gestured toward the front doors of the church. "Can we talk for a moment?"

Giving a startled nod, I followed her outside, both being careful to keep our steps from echoing.

I blinked a few times as the sun was brighter now, and Jess let out a sigh. "I don't normally make confession, but something happened with my sister, and I'm having a hard time dealing with it."

I understood the psychology of confession. A guilt shared and absolved was a huge burden lifted from the shoulders. Sometimes, though, sharing with a friend was better. "Is there anything I can help with?"

She stared at her feet for a few moments before speaking. "Audrey came into the shop a few days ago. I thought she was there to help, but she…well, she asked me for money."

Since Audrey had spilled her story to me, I already knew she needed funds, so I just nodded.

Jess gave a shrug. "She was asking for her friend, Declan. He's been in a bad way with gambling, see, and was trying to climb out."

"Declan? Is he part of that New Age group in town?" Was he the other dark-haired man at the pub? But that man had looked more middle eastern than Irish, and Declan was a very Irish name.

Then again, Adanna had been born in Ireland, even though her darker skin shone with her Nigerian ancestry.

The church door opened, and a local man stepped out, but I didn't know his name. He must have been the parishioner inside the booth when I entered.

"Aye, Declan is in the Mystic Moon Meadow. Well, he was. And I told her no because this is the slow season, and I need to make sure I have enough cash to pay the bills through the winter. I told her that Declan was pure trouble, even though I've never even met the man. Audrey always chooses the bad boys." She looked at me with pleading eyes, as if begging me to understand.

"Of course, that makes perfect sense. Did she get mad?"

"She did, yeah. She yelled and threatened me, then stomped off in a rage." Another image of those nails flashed through my memory, along with the scratches on the dead man's face.

I gathered her in a hug and held her, trembling, for several moments. "I'm sure she'll come to her senses."

Jess pulled away and shook her head while staring at her feet. "Now, she blames me for Declan's death. She said if I'd just given her the money, he wouldn't have died."

Aha! Declan *was* the dead man! Both dread and sympathy washed over me. Did Tara know? Is that why she'd been so angry? Now things were clicking into place.

But I had to get back to Audrey and Jess. I recognized emotional blackmail when I saw it. At least, now I did. Armand had given me plenty of education. "That's a horrible guilt trip she's taking you on, Jess. Did she at least buy you some new luggage?"

Jess let out a mirthless snort. We stayed silent for a moment, each lost in our own thoughts as the wind rose around us, playing with our hair. Then, I said, "We'd better get inside. The only other person in there was McCarthy, and once he's done, if no one is waiting, the priest will shut down for the day, right?"

"He will, true enough."

We went back inside, the still silence of the church a welcome respite from the wind. Our footsteps echoed as we returned to the front pew.

Sitting quietly, Jess fumbled for my hand, and held it for a while. Tingling energy passed between us, and I made a mental note to ask Faelan about it. Could Jess be sensitive to the Good Folk, too?

She had something magical going on, but asking outright seemed ridiculous, even for someone who had already admitted she was part of a new age group with Gran.

Especially while we sat in a Catholic church.

But there was something I could ask her. I kept my voice to a whisper and asked, "I was talking to Máiréad about some strange dreams we've all been having. Ronan suggested I call a town meeting about it. What do you think?"

She gave a startled nod, but before she could say anything, the booth door opened, and Garda McCarthy emerged. As Jess rose to replace him, he shot me an angry glare. When the booth door closed again, he spoke in a harsh whisper, "What are you doing here, Miss O'Shea? You aren't Catholic."

While I didn't like his accusatory tone, I also didn't want to get into a fight in a church. I might not be Catholic, but this was sacred space.

And yet, even with all that in mind, I'd promised myself to stop cowering before bullies. "I need to talk to Father Fraser about some things."

His scowl deepened. "What sort of things? Is this to do with the murder investigation? Is that why Adanna keeps pushing me to talk with you?"

I didn't want to get into it here and clamped my lips shut.

His frown turned into a nasty sneer. "If you've found anything pertaining to my investigation, you're obligated to report it to me. Otherwise, I'd be thrilled to bring you in on obstruction. It wouldn't be the first time someone from your family fell into that."

Now, he had my hackles up. Despite my resolution to keep the peace, adrenaline rushed through my blood, and I had to work hard to keep my voice low. "I don't think it has anything to do with the murder. So, why don't you just leave me in peace and go do your job?"

His face turned dark red, and he opened his mouth to say something. A murmur came from the confession booth. The Garda stared at the door for a second, then turned and marched down the aisle, his anger clear in every step.

Once the doors shut again and silence prevailed, I heaved a sigh of relief and tried to get my temper under control.

Jess emerged from the booth, flashed me a quick smile, and left. The light on the confession box turned from red to green. After a few long minutes, the light went out, and Father Fraser emerged from the booth.

As soon as he saw me, a flash of confusion colored his expression. "Skye? Were you wanting to make confession?"

I rose, shaking my head. "No, I just wanted a chat. I'm not into the whole confession thing."

"I hadn't thought you were, but there's always room to change your mind." He gave me an encouraging smile, then sat next to me on the pew. "How can I help you?"

Suddenly, it felt incredibly silly to speak of magical dreams to a priest. But he was in the business of believing in miracles, right? What were miracles but magic created by God?

I cleared my throat, which sounded horribly loud in the empty church. "Well, you see, I had a few weird dreams. Dreams I'd never had before and had nothing to do with my past. I'm thinking they might be from other people's stories."

I paused, waiting to judge his reaction. He looked thoughtful, as if puzzling something out himself. "That might explain a few things. Go on, tell me some details."

Encouraged, I related the dreams I had and then shared what Máiréad had said about Adanna's dreams and her own.

Once I finished and fell silent, Father Fraser gave a slow nod. "I had a dream just last night. I was running down a Dublin street, chasing someone. It was dark and raining, and the person I was pursuing was a criminal. Somehow, I knew that."

He raised his eyes to lock gazes. "I've never been to Dublin overnight. I do know, however, that Garda McCarthy trained there for several months, as did Garda Fitzgerald."

Curiouser and curiouser, as Alice in Wonderland would say.

"Ronan had an idea about calling a town meeting. But I just moved here in May, and I don't feel right doing that. I figured I'd ask some people one on one first."

Father Fraser stared at his hands folded in his lap for a few long moments. Still looking down, he said, "'If there be a prophet among you, I the Lord will make myself known unto him in a vision and will speak unto him in a dream.'"

That didn't sound like casual chatting. "What?"

"It's a verse from Numbers. Which means I probably shouldn't dismiss this out of hand."

I had no idea how to answer a Bible verse, so I went back to the dream. "Your Dublin dream sounds terrifying."

Glancing up, he gave a sheepish grin. "It was. I usually dream about standing on a Scottish mountain with a claymore held high."

"So you're a true romantic?"

He gave a shrug. "I'm always shouting 'There can be only one.' More like a Highlander fan."

We shared a laugh that died pretty quickly. "So, that's another name for the borrowed dream list. Does that mean we should call a meeting?"

The priest pursed his lips. "I'm not certain Bishop MacNally would be pleased with the idea of me calling a meeting to discuss magical dreams."

I hadn't yet met the bishop, but I imagined he was a stickler for protocol, as most bishops seemed to be. "How about backing me up when I call it? Or would that still be too much?"

He gave a shrug and raised his eyebrows. "We can try and see!"

CHAPTER SIX

The next day, I woke with my stomach in knots. I had never been great at public speaking.

The village community centre was commandeered for the town meeting. The empty space bounced every sound around like a basketball as we pulled chairs from a pile and unfolded them. I stared up at the posters plastered all over the walls, advertising coffee mornings, dance classes, language classes, and even hot goat yoga, whatever the heck that was.

Both Father Fraser and I sat behind a table in the front, facing several rows of chairs. He smiled or nodded at each person as they came in. I tried to remember everyone's name, but was too embarrassed to ask the priest on those I didn't know. I kept folding and unfolding my hands, and then wiping the sweat off my face.

How ironic that a Miami native was sweating in Ireland in September.

And here I was, a nosy interloper throwing my weight around and demanding attention. Everything Armand used to accuse me of. I spared a glance at my phone, but it didn't show any calls.

So as not to interfere with Mass, we set the meeting for 2 pm. People were still filtering in ten minutes after the start time. Máiréad and her husband, Ronan, sat proudly in the front row of chairs. He had brought a novel and was reading it while Máiréad spoke to him.

Jess was a few seats down from her, but Audrey, was conspicuously absent; not that she lived in the village. She was probably off with her Dublin friends. I wondered if she had ever found anyone foolish enough to give her the money. With Declan dead, she probably didn't need the funds anymore, unless the people he owed came after her. A shudder ran down my spine.

You're being silly, Skye. This isn't the movies. There isn't any mafia in Ireland.

To my surprise, both O'Leary and his daughter, Niamh, came in, chatting in low tones. Adanna and Donal entered after them, the latter wearing a deep scowl. He glared directly at me, so I gathered he wasn't peeved with Father Fraser.

More people came in groups. The older sheep farmer, Patrick, came with Finn and Rory Lynch. Sean came in chatting with Eileen. She was dressed in a prim, dark blue business suit and sat with excellent posture. She ran the B&B at the other end of town, as well as the local Irish language radio station.

There were several people I didn't know, including a glowering man who stood in the corner, despite several empty chairs. He wore a dark jacket and kept his arms crossed. He wasn't watching me, though. Instead, he studied each person as they came in the door. Maybe he was another Garda trainee, or even McCarthy's boss.

Someone coughed at one end of the room, and a chair clattered to the floor at the other end. Everyone stared as Finn glanced up with a sheepish expression and picked it back up.

Ciaran entered with Labhrás, an older man with glasses and a receding hairline, he was the Irish language teacher Niamh had recommended. I mentally added calling him to my to-do list.

The trainee Garda Fitzgerald entered last and pulled the door shut behind her with a thud.

Father Fraser cleared his throat as he stood, nodding to all assembled. "*Dia daoibh!* Thank you for taking time from your Sunday afternoon to join us."

O'Leary stood with his chest puffed out. "Here now, what's all this about?"

The priest glanced at me, so I stood with my hands on the table to balance my wobbling knees. "I've heard of some things going on and wanted to get everyone together to discuss them rather than rely upon hearsay and rumor."

Garda McCarthy growled, "What sort of things?"

"Dreams."

Everyone started murmuring, though a few people hushed their companions. The room fell silent again.

I felt like a prime idiot. What was I thinking? They must consider me insane, but I had to push through. "Has anyone been having odd dreams? Of things they don't remember doing or situations foreign to them? I'm not talking about the strange, surreal dreams we all have, but something that *seemed* like it was a memory, but not your own."

A few attendees chuckled. Others murmured. Someone in the back let out a bark of laughter, but I couldn't see who it was.

I took a deep breath. "For instance, I had a dream about drowning in the ocean at night. Now, I've gone swimming in the sea maybe a dozen times in my life, always near shore and always during the day."

I watched Adanna as I spoke, and her eyes grew wide. She grabbed Donal's hand and squeezed it. He murmured something to her, perhaps a reassurance, as he patted her arm with his other hand. Then, he smiled, the first time I'd actually seen him do that.

Adanna got to her feet, her expression blank. "That's my dream. A recurring nightmare since I was a child."

Labhrás gave a firm nod. "Aye, I can remember that day quite clearly. Half the village was at the beach, and Ciaran here swam out to fetch her." He rolled his Rs and enunciated as if he was in a Shakespearean play.

Ciaran ducked his head and rubbed the back of his neck. "The lass needed help, was all."

I said, "I understand there have been other instances of swapped dreams. Máiréad dreamt of being a nurse in a busy hospital, which is a dream I've had too many times to count. Anyone else?"

A woman yelled, "No one wants these silly fairy stories, girl! Go back to America!" I couldn't see who said that. A few people looked around, but no one refuted her. A ball of fear formed in my stomach.

Jess reached behind her, patted Adanna's hand, and rose to her feet. "I've been dreaming of thousands of bees. Nothing scary, now, just clouds of them surrounding me. It was almost soothing." She nodded at Sean and flashed a smile.

The beekeeper took her place, cleared his throat, and said, "I've been experiencing some very strange, abstract dreams, unhinged and terrifying. Like something out of a Salvador Dali painting. But they stopped a few days ago."

I wondered if he'd been exchanging dreams with the dead man, Declan. Or someone who took drugs.

When no one else spoke up, I cleared my throat. "So, we've been trading dreams somehow. Does anyone have any idea how this might be happening? Have you ever experienced anything like this before?"

More rumblings spread through the room, but no one offered any comments. After a few moments of this, the priest held his arms up for silence. "You probably think it strange that

I'm here for something like this, but I, too, have been having what I must believe are someone else's nightmares. They involved running down a street in Dublin on a rainy night, chasing a criminal."

The scowling man in the back corner looked interested. My theory of him being a detective of some sort just went up a notch.

He stared at Garda McCarthy as he spoke, and the officer squirmed in his seat. He mumbled something, cleared his throat and croaked out, "Aye, that's mine."

Adanna patted him on the shoulder and said, "We haven't experienced anything like this before, so far as I know." She turned to look at the ancient sheep farmer in the back corner. "Patrick, can you remember anything?"

The man grumbled, totally incomprehensible to me, but Adanna nodded. "There, he can't recall anything, so we've a few generations covered."

Eileen stood with a mighty scowl. "This is pure bollocks. Do you expect us to believe in this fairy tale?"

Labhrás pulled his companion back down into her seat and whispered in her ear. The older woman's eyes grew wide, but she stayed silent. Maybe he'd had someone else's dream, too.

With a look at Sean, I asked, "You said your dreams stopped a few days ago. Was the last one the night before the murdered man was found?"

Another round of murmurs swept through the crowd, and Garda McCarthy leveled an evil glare at me.

Sean gave a shrug. "Sure, and that's the truth. That might be a coincidence, like."

Adanna and Donal exchanged glances. I wondered if they'd figured out who the dead man was and just wouldn't tell anyone else, or if they were still searching. In truth, I was only guessing that he was Audrey's Declan.

Now, I had to bring up the fairy part. Would they all think I was bonkers? I had the overwhelming urge to run out of the hall, but I gripped my hands together and stayed put.

I cleared my throat again, and plunged in. "So, I've been doing some research into some, uh, Good Folk who might be related to dreams. I haven't come up with much, I'm afraid. Does anyone have any suggestions to help my research?"

Someone asked, "What about a púca?"

"A Leannan Sídhe?"

"The Muirgen!"

"Is it Aengos Óg visiting us, like?"

Father Fraser raised his hands. "Settle down, the lot of you! Miss O'Shea was just going to tell us what she found."

"Well, I haven't really found anything conclusive. However, I do think we need to do something."

Joshua called out from the back row. "Like what?"

I glanced at the priest. "Honestly, I have no idea. Does anyone have any suggestions?"

Father Fraser said, "I think the first thing we should do is pray for a solution. After that," he had to raise his voice as a few people groaned and others chuckled, "after that, we should document all the incidents. I'll keep a list, and then we can meet again after a few days. Maybe we'll see a pattern."

As a general murmur of agreement swept across the assembly, the doors burst open, and Audrey marched in, her face set in an expression that suggested someone had set fire to her new Persian kitten.

She halted in the middle and jabbed a finger at Jess. "You! What sort of kin are you, then?"

Jess drew back and her glow dimmed to nothing. "What are you talking about?"

"It's all your fault! You're the reason Declan's dead! You might as well have killed him yourself!"

Jess turned as white as a sheet. My heart sank as the words sunk in. My friend couldn't be guilty of murder, could she?

I jumped to my feet, as did the priest and Garda McCarthy. The man in the back corner finally uncrossed his arms, suddenly looking alive.

Audrey let out a yowl and leapt toward her sister. The two Gardaí moved toward Audrey, but Joshua and Sean were closer. They took hold of her arms and pulled the angry woman back toward the doors.

Father Fraser caught up to them, speaking to Audrey in a low, soothing tone. I hurried to Jess's side, putting my arm around her shoulders.

She was trembling and looked as white as a sheet. I tried to guide her to one of the side doors, away from the public gaze. "Come on, then. Why don't we go into another room? Somewhere quiet."

The other woman pulled back, her eyes glittering with moisture. "No, no, she's right. She asked me for money to help him and I told her no and now he's dead and it's all my fault."

Maybe there *was* a mafia in Ireland, after all? No, that was ridiculous. Declan must have been killed by someone else.

My response was interrupted by a woman's high-pitched scream. It wasn't Audrey, whose voice was lower. This screech could have shattered glass. The doors were wide open now, and I caught a glimpse of Pixie Tara.

The dark-haired woman jumped on a man's back, the one named Liam. He ducked and spun, trying to dislodge her, but she clung like a monkey, still screaming.

I stepped back, trying to make sense of all this anger. Where was it coming from? She couldn't be that filled with rage all the time, could she? She would drop dead of a coronary by the time she was thirty.

Garda Fitzgerald shouted at her to stop. Garda McCarthy strode toward them and wrapped his arms around Tara's back to pull her off, but the woman clung on like a barnacle.

After a few moments of shouting and cursing, the Gardaí managed to separate the two. She was screaming obscenities and struggling against McCarthy's grip as he pulled Tara away from the doorway, and out of my line of vision.

Several people rushed outside, thankfully leaving the auditorium mostly empty. Only Máiréad and old Patrick remained.

The shopkeeper stepped closer, her hand out. "Can I help, pet? Would you like me to fetch some tea?"

Evidently, tea fixed everything in Ireland. Especially if it was sweet and milky.

Jess shook her head. "No, no, that's much too far. I just need to get back to my shop. Skye, can you help me there?"

Máiréad took one arm, and I took the other. Her balance wobbled as we led her out a side door, down the hall, and out of the school. That way, we skirted around the fight outside, as I didn't want any part of that mess.

As we walked away, more shouts hung in the air.

Luckily, Jess's gallery was only a block away. When we got Jess back there, and Máiréad insisted on staying and making her milky tea. After about an hour of soothing Jess, the older woman shooed me off. "I'll be grand, Skye. You're knackered. Go home."

After a token argument, I left. I glanced at my phone. How was it already past four? I noticed I had a message, but when I saw the number was from the States, I just deleted it.

The sunlight was already fading and every muscle in my body ached as I trudged home. Why was I so tired? Speaking in front of others definitely drained me, but not usually this much.

So many people had been having stolen dreams. From the reports, they'd started just a few days ago. What had happened a few days ago? Audrey and her friends had arrived, and they were the ones to interrupt the meeting.

Could they have something to do with the dreams? Why would they want to swap dreams out? I couldn't think of any advantage. It certainly wouldn't get them money to pay off her boyfriend's debts. A incongruous image of a mafia boss with fairy wings flashed in my mind, and I let out a chuckle.

I shuffled down the long main road, past O'Leary's pub, then turned down my road, past the empty farm.

A streak of black darted past me and by the time my exhausted brain recognized Faelan, he'd leapt over the stone wall and into the empty farm's garden.

Growls and hisses told me he wasn't having a fun time. Crap, I couldn't catch a break today.

The bleat of a goat joined his complaints, and I wondered what in the world my cat had gotten himself into. Could I get into the garden to help him? Did he even need help?

Faelan was a huge fairy cat and could take care of himself, but a goat might make him very unhappy. I didn't want him to get hurt. He was Gran's cat, and I had to take care of him. I had to make sure he was okay. She'd never forgive me if I let Faelan get hurt.

I walked around the stone wall, searching for a gap in the overgrown vines. While I found nothing around the back or one side, as I got near the house, there was a wooden gate beneath the fading foliage.

There might have been a lock there once, but only a scrap of rusty metal remained. I had to tug vines off it before it would budge. I yanked it out and creaked the rusted hinges open.

Faelan was screeching and yowling. The goat was still bleating. I couldn't see either animal. Wild vines and bushes blocked the path, with autumn-bare branches poking up here and there. This place was a jungle, and as the sun was setting, visibility faded.

I crept in, worried about trespassing even though I knew this place had been empty for years. Adanna told me the old owner had died, and he'd had no relatives to inherit. No one wanted to invest in a crumbling farmhouse that ought to be condemned, or a garden with precious little arable land.

As I pushed past a large hedge, a huge hawthorn tree came into view. Dozens of fluttering strips of fabric decorated the branches. It looked just like the one in my dream, though it didn't shimmer with light.

The strips weren't in any order or pattern. Most were faded and weather-worn, all but rotted away, but a few of them looked brand-new. One near the trunk was bright white, while a scarlet piece dangled from the branch next to that. A neatly cut piece in various shades of blue stripes flickered right next to my face.

Faelan hunched next to it, facing off against the biggest billy goat I'd ever seen.

The cat hissed and spit, slashing his paw toward the goat.

How did the goat get in here? He couldn't have belonged to the prior owner. "Faelan! What are you doing? Leave that poor goat alone!"

The cat sídhe growled and said, "This isn't a goat, you human fool! Can't you see it's a púca?"

I stared at the animal. Was it a shape-changer? An evil spirit? It was jet-black with enormous, curved horns. His eyes glowed red, and a chill ran down my spine as I backed away.

I didn't want to be anywhere near another fairy creature, especially one Gran's cat was so intent upon fighting.

With no warning, Faelan leapt at the púca's face, clinging on with his claws, while the fairy goat swung his head back and forth, trying to dislodge his attacker.

An unholy cacophony filled the garden and must have been heard all the way to Killarney.

"'Ere, now, wot's dis?"

I spun to find Patrick, the old sheep farmer. "You gi' me goat back, ya wee mog!"

I backed farther away, almost disappearing into a bush covered with yellow leaves. "You want to get between that cat and your goat, you be my guest."

Faelan leapt off his prey and scrambled up the fairy tree, making the ribbons and strips of cloth tremble. Twilight was creeping up on us, and I could barely make him out in the gloom.

The goat bleated and butted the trunk. Everything fluttered, and the tree creaked.

Patrick approached the goat, his hand out. "Calm yer fool head, ye pure eejit. C'mere to me, I'll get ye hame."

Gashes covered the huge goat's face and neck, his black fur glistening with blood. His eyes no longer glowed red, and he looked like a normal goat now. I blinked several times. Had I been hallucinating?

As Patrick pulled the goat past me, he glared. "Ye owe me for the damage, ye gombeen!"

CHAPTER SEVEN

As Patrick led his goat through the foliage and out of the gate, I stood next to the trunk and scowled into the branches. "He's gone now. Will you get down here?"

Faelan let out a long, mournful howl, a sound I'd never heard from a cat before. Not even a Siamese cat in heat.

Just as his cry faded, a gust of wind swept through the wild garden. All the overgrown weeds rustled and whipped and the strength of it almost pushed me over. I kept my balance on the trunk of the wishing tree.

Another shriek, not from Faelan, followed the wind. The unearthly noise rattled my bones. Electric shock made every nerve in my body tingle. With a shout, I jumped back from the tree. Though I examined my hand for burn marks, I found nothing. My palms itched, and I rubbed them on my thighs.

I glared at the tree. "What in all that's holy was that?"

Faelan's voice turned timider than I'd ever heard. "Something is awake."

"The púca? Didn't that just leave?"

"Not the púca. Something else."

Before I could ask more questions, rustling in the foliage behind me made me turn. Pushing through the vegetation, someone asked, "Hey, are you hurt?"

I turned to find Blond Marcus and Hippie Liam emerging from the overgrowth, white faces glowing in the dusk. Marcus said, "We heard a terrible noise. Did that man attack you?"

Shaking my head, I said. "No, no, I'm fine. But his goat chased my cat up into the tree, and now he won't come down." I eyed Liam carefully, remembering Niamh's story about him getting into Declan's face. If he was capable of that much anger, I didn't want him finding a reason to yell at me.

I could just about make out Faelan's hulking black form against the darkening sky. I had no idea if they'd accept my mundane explanation for that horrific sound. So, I clenched my fists, anticipating a barrage of uncomfortable questions.

Marcus followed my gaze, then looked at the branches. "A clootie tree, huh? I'd say leave the cat there for a while. Maybe he'll become a fairy cat!"

I turned my laugh into a cough. *If only he knew!* But I wasn't about to reveal Faelan's nature to strangers. Jess was the only other person alive who suspected what he was. Even Adanna didn't know yet.

I put out my hand. "I'm Skye. I just moved to the area from Florida about five months ago."

Marcus's handshake was warm and firm. "I'm Marcus, and this is Liam. We're from Dublin, but we're in the area for some celebrations."

We shook hands all around. "I've seen you in the pub, I think." I didn't want to appear nosy, but if they knew Declan, maybe I should delve more. "What sort of celebration?"

Liam jumped in before Marcus could respond. "Just some stuff we're doing outside of town. Savage stuff." He added a saucy grin.

After an awkward moment of silence, I began to get concerned about being alone in this secluded spot with two strangers. Just as I was about to craft my escape, Marcus and Liam exchanged a cryptic look.

Then, Liam said, "I'd better get on to the Garda station. Tara will be simmering mad." He gave a cheery wave as he walked back out of the garden jungle.

Now it felt even more awkward with just Marcus. But Faelan would protect me, wouldn't he? He'd just proved he could be vicious. I stared back up at the tree. "Faelan, are you ever coming down?"

Marcus lingered, and out of the corner of my eye, I took a better look at him. I couldn't tell what color his eyes were in the low light, but he had a cheerful smile.

His lanky build towered over me, which made me recoil. I told myself firmly that he didn't remind me of Armand, not in the slightest. Really, he didn't.

"Are you sure you just moved here from the states? I swear you look familiar."

"I used to visit Gran, but that was years ago."

Marcus narrowed his eyes. "Who's your gran, then?"

"Saoirse O'Shea. Well, she was. She passed away about a year ago."

He snapped his fingers. "You're Saoirse's granddaughter? *That's* why you look familiar! She used to be a leader in our group! That's why we use the stone circle here."

His smile was so wide it almost broke his face in half.

"Stone circle? For some sort of ceremony?" I wondered if it was the one Jess had mentioned before.

He rubbed the back of his neck and ducked his head. "Sort of related to it, yeah. And to the fairy tree, here."

Peering into the branches, I noticed that strip of cloth with blue stripes on it. The pattern looked familiar, but I couldn't remember from where. Then I gazed back at the black spot that was Faelan. Two emerald eyes glowed back at me, then blinked once. "Is it a wishing tree or a fairy tree? What do you know about them?"

He gave a rueful laugh. "You can call it either, or even a clootie tree. It's a complicated story. Why don't we have a seat?"

I settled on the chilly grass facing the trunk of the fairy tree, strips of cloth fluttering gently in the breeze. I didn't want to touch it again in case it let out another horrid screech. Earthy scents tickled my nose to the sound of the soft rustling of leaves.

Marcus had a twinkle in his eye. "You see," he started, his Dublin accent lilting and musical, "trees like this are deeply rooted in ancient Irish and Scottish traditions."

I glanced up at the colorful strips. Some were faded and tattered, while others looked freshly tied, vibrant against the fading foliage. "So, what's the lore?"

"Well, it's said that these trees are sacred to the Fair Folk. The Good Neighbors, aye? People come here to make wishes or ask for healing. They tear a strip of cloth from their clothing, ideally something they've worn, and tie it to the tree while focusing on their wish or prayer."

I recalled my dream of trying to rip a piece of black fabric from my dress. Had I ever completed that wish? I couldn't even remember what I'd wished for.

"As the cloth disintegrates, the wish is gradually released into the world and fulfilled by the Fair Folk."

That sounded so silly, but my experiences since I arrived in Ballybás had given me a stronger belief in the supernatural. Marcus touched one of the strips, his fingers brushing it gently.

I murmured while staring at the dangling wish. "Do you believe in all that?"

He chuckled, his eyes finding mine. "I like to think there's a bit of magic in the world, sure. Whether it's the Fair Folk or just the power of belief, who knows? But there's something deadly precious about the old ways. They connect us to our past and to each other."

Deadly precious. I knew it was Irish slang, but it sounded ominous.

Marcus placed his hand on the tree trunk, almost caressing it. Then he turned to me, his eyebrows raised, as if daring me to do the same.

Instead of risking that electric shock again, I asked, "Have you made a wish?"

The corner of his mouth quirked up as he shrugged. "Maybe I have, maybe I haven't. The Good Neighbors like their secrets, they do."

My gaze drifted again to that strip of blue-striped fabric. My memory clicked into place, and the image of Audrey wearing her business-style pencil skirt flickered in my mind. What would she be wishing for?

Faelan chose that moment to leap from the branches into my lap. I jumped up with a cry. "Ow! Fiendish jerk!"

The black cat streaked away while Marcus unsuccessfully tried to muffle a laugh. "That was a huge cat! Are you sure it's not one of the Fair Folk already?"

"I'm sure of very little." I leaned my chin in my hands with a huge sigh, all my energy drained. "It's been a rough couple of days."

His voice turned kind. "Want to talk about it?"

Did I want to talk about it? With a stranger, alone, at night, in an abandoned garden?

No matter how pleasant he seemed, self-preservation alarm bells started ringing in my head. I was still too much of a Miami girl to feel safe in that situation, even in a quaint Irish village in the hinterland of County Cork.

And, while I'd been bone-tired, something really bizarre was going on, and I needed to figure out what. Besides, Marcus might be more willing to divulge details if he had some alcohol to loosen his tongue.

"I wouldn't mind chatting to someone, but not here. Want to go for a pint?"

As I tucked into a corner table at O'Leary's, Marcus brought me a pint of cider and Guinness for himself. Once we settled with our drinks, he asked, "So what's happened the last few days that's left you so rough?"

While I wasn't sure I wanted to share, I felt obligated after he bought libations. "It started when I found a dead man in my pub."

He let out a laugh, but after seeing my expression, sobered. "Wait, are you serious?"

I nodded and took a long pull of my cider. "Yup. Dead as a doornail, and the pub hasn't even opened yet. I've still got renovations going on. The killer seems to have taken some pricey bottles of liquor, too."

His forehead wrinkled. "Wait, you already have bottles, but you aren't open yet? Something isn't adding up here."

"It was Gran's pub. She shut it down when she got sick. The bottles are from when she ran the place."

"Ah, that tracks." Marcus glanced around the room, then whispered, "Who was the dead man?"

"I'm not sure. He had dark hair. Might have been tallish? He wore a gray T-shirt and jeans. Oh, and a leather jacket with some sort of Celtic knot on the front pocket."

Marcus's face turned pale, evident even in the low pub light. "Jaysus. I wonder if it's Declan."

So maybe my guess *had* been correct. "Declan? Is that someone from your group?"

His voice went flat. "Yeah. He headed back to Dublin after Tara got into a row with him."

I narrowed my eyes. "Tara seems to like fighting. Actual physical brawls. Is she prone to anger issues?"

Marcus shook his head, but his voice was still flat. "Not normally. But after she started dating Declan, yeah. He called it quits before we came out here, but she won't leave well enough alone."

I took a wild stab at the rest. "And she's with Liam now?"

He'd just taken a sip of his Guinness and almost did a spit-take. "Ha! No, but she wants to be. But she's been too upset to get with anyone."

I let out a bark of laughter. "Upset is a bit of an understatement."

His grin faded. "No, really upset. Like, bawling her eyes out upset, since they learned about Declan. I think she really loved the jerk."

I filed that tidbit away for later use. "Tell me more about Gran in the group. When was she active?"

Marcus pursed his lips and considered for a few moments. "Feck, it must have been three years ago, at least. She had a dustup with another member."

"What happened?"

After another drink of Guinness, he gave a half-smile. "Aidan was a right eejit, even to me, and we're second cousins. He thought he was our fearless leader, barking orders left, right, and center."

He paused to sigh and wrinkle his nose. "Most of us were new at the time and kept shtum, but Saoirse, she wasn't having any of it. Got right up in his face and tore him a new one."

I had to chuckle at the visual. "That sounds like Gran, all right. Then what?"

He gave a shrug. "They both legged it. Never did see Aidan again. The rest of us scrambled together and formed a new group with no leaders."

Someone at the bar let out a loud laugh, and I glanced over, but it wasn't anyone I knew. "And how's that working out for you?"

Marcus cocked his head and gave me a huge grin. "Why don't you come and see for yourself? We're having a gathering tomorrow. Come along, it'll be pure craic."

Alarm bells rang in my head again. They were really annoying, but seldom wrong. *Don't go with the strange man to a lonely place!*

He must have noticed my dismay. "You can bring a friend, if you like. If it makes you feel safer."

"It would, actually. Are you doing some sort of ceremony? I don't have much religious faith."

He waved his hand. "No, no, we're just going to sing and dance and talk. Typical bonfire fun."

Typical bonfire fun. Which could have meant anything since I never did such things. That's what I got for being a city girl. "Thanks, we might. Where'll you be?"

"We meet about ten minutes out of town on the north road. It's called Scánnatrumloo Stone Circle. We'll be there after sunset, so about seven?"

Once I got back to the house, I had a hard time getting to sleep. The screech from the tree haunted me most of the night.

By the time I finally found sleep, I had a recurrence of the dream where I touched the tree. The branches were laden with tied wishes fluttering in the breeze. However, when I placed my hand on its trunk, it screamed and tore me to bits.

The confetti that had been me floated gently to the ground. For once, there was no wind.

Once I woke the next morning and had coffee in hand, I pulled out Gran's diary, caressing the embossed leather cover with its Celtic knotwork, and nestled in my comfy chair.

I flipped through, trying to find any mention of dreams, nightmares, or screaming wishing trees. Each page felt thick beneath my fingers as I turned them, emitting that lovely odor of old books.

I didn't linger on any entry this time. Instead, I went page by page, looking for something that might catch my eye. Something that might jump out at me. I did find a description of the local stone circle, and I read through for any clues. She only listed the name and location, nothing juicy or interesting.

I wondered if I should ask Gran. Occasionally, she would speak to me, or at least, I imagined she spoke to me.

Are you there?

Silence answered me. She must be on some afterlife tea break.

Just as I'd scanned through the whole book, Finn and Rory showed up.

I let them enter, and they carried in tools and a sawhorse. I tried to read again, but their chatter kept distracting me.

"Does that go there? Are you sure?"

"Sure, I'm sure, you bleedin' eejit!"

"Hand me that, will you? No, ya gombeen, the hammer."

Despite the bright lights in the pub, their presence kept reminding me of the dead body. Every time I glanced at the room, I could see him lying there.

That memory drove me to the library for some peace. I pulled on my jacket and high-tailed it down the main street.

The Ballybás library was smaller than the Miami-Dade Public Library had been, but they made up for it in an extensive section on local folklore. This section was tucked away in its own alcove the back corner with a reading nook next to it.

Tall shelves reached the ceiling, forming a cozy corridor that smelled of antique curiosity. I adored this quiet space, filled with charm and the love of books.

Once there, I continued my quest for any legends that might help. Fair Folk, Good Neighbors, Tuatha dé Danann, whatever might fit the bill. I looked up púca for good measure. A few of the illustrations were scary enough to haunt my nightmares, and I'd had a difficult time sleeping as it was, so I halted that search.

So much for my vaunted research abilities. And asking Gran wouldn't do much, I'm sure. Did she really exist? Probably just my overactive imagination.

No, mo chroí. I'm truly here, her lilting accent assured me.

I halted mid-page, glanced back and forth to make sure no one was nearby, playing a cruel prank. However, I was alone in this section. No one stood close enough to whisper in my ear.

"Gran?"

Of course, Skye. I'm here.

I had dozens of questions to ask her, but I couldn't choose one from the crowd Finally, I asked, "Do you know what's affecting my dreams?"

I do, but I cannot tell you directly. That's against the rules, you see. Strictures are tight on this side.

Well, that was interesting information. "Is it a creature of the Fair Folk?"

That, I can verify, yes.

"And what happened with this group you were part of? Was this after Grampa Seamus died?"

That elicited a chuckle in my mind. *Oh, the Mystic Moon Meadow folks? Long after, my dear. The group had some fun parts, and some not so fun parts. When the latter outweighed the former, I made tracks.*

The librarian walked past, a finger on her lips. I swallowed and bent as if studying my page. However, once she was out of sight, I spoke in sotto voce, "What was that thing at the fairy tree? Why did it scream?"

That's another forbidden bit of data. Faelan can't tell you, either. However, you have a big battle coming up. Be wary. I must go, but I will be watching over you.

A shiver ran through me. I shut the book, replaced it on the shelf, and exited the library.

Should I tell Donal about the tree? No, he'd laugh at me. Adanna might have believed me, but she was off to Dublin yet again.

Which meant, if I was going to find a companion to go to this stone circle party tonight, Jess was my best option.

I halted. What about inviting Sean? No, no, he was much too attractive. I would never be brave enough to ask him out, and I was still nowhere near ready to start riding the romance train again.

As I passed the side street Jess lived on, I called the gallery. I ought to visit, but I was chilly and frustrated and just wanted a warm cuppa by the fire. The phone clicked. "Ballybás Gallery."

"Hey, Jess? It's Skye. Have you got anything going on tonight?"

"It sounds like I'm about to." Laughter bubbled in her voice, and I had to smile in response.

"A guy from that new age group asked me to the stone circle tonight. They're doing music and singing and stuff. Would you come with me?"

Her voice was muffled, as if she was covering the phone with her hand. "Thank you, come again!" The jingling bells indicated someone had just left, and her voice was stronger now. "Was it that fit blond, Marcus?"

I almost tripped along the road as I coughed. "It was him, yeah. Will you be my safety net?"

She raised her eyebrows. "Will Audrey be there?"

I shrugged. "They didn't mention her. Would that be a deal-breaker?"

Jess hesitated a moment, and then shook her head. "Ah, sure. I'll be there with bells on, like. Come to the gallery first, and we'll get you kitted out. I've loads of appropriate garb for this sort of thing."

As I clicked off, another call came in, but I messed up and hung up on it by accident. I didn't recognize the number, but it was from the states. Was Armand still trying to find me?

Rain drizzled down and I hurried, hoping to get home before it came down in earnest. Would it be too wet for a bonfire? Or to be out at all on a September night in Ireland?

Just as I got inside the pub, I had to wonder what Jess meant by *appropriate garb for that sort of thing?*

CHAPTER EIGHT

Around six, after several cups of coffee to ensure I stayed awake long enough to have fun, I hurried down the road to Jess's place. The rain had stopped, though mist clung to everything. She lived above her gallery, conveniently, and the store lights were all on when I pushed the door open. "Hello? Jess?"

"Upstairs!"

I peeked through the beaded curtain into the back room, and spied a set of narrow stairs, each one painted in a different vibrant color. I couldn't figure out any pattern, but that seemed on brand for Jess.

Once I reached the top, I gasped. Jess's place seemed like something out of a movie set. The cloying scent of sandalwood incense tickled my nose. Rich-colored fabrics were draped everywhere. Crimson and mustard, royal purple and emerald-green.

Every piece of furniture wore a different texture; paisley and brocade, corduroy and velvet. Thick Turkish rugs covered every inch of the floor.

Jess poked her head out. "Come on in! Have a seat. Would you like a cuppa? I just made some matcha."

"Sure." I'd never tried matcha, but there was a first time for everything. Low instrumental music was playing, with drums and tambourines, rhythmic and almost primal. It made me want to dance.

I chose the closest seat, a huge, overstuffed armchair that might swallow me whole if I leaned back. Not wanting to be eaten alive by random furniture, I perched on the edge.

My friend emerged from another room and did a twirl. "Well? What do you think?"

She wore at least three shawls. A red one around her shoulders with miles of fringe, and two around her hips in sapphire and olive, each with little gold coins tinkling.

Underneath those, somewhere, she wore a gold and silver sari. I felt like I'd popped in for a tarot reading. "Uh, I definitely wouldn't lose you in a crowd."

She burst out laughing, her head flung back in unfettered delight. "Ha! That's your polite way of saying I'm loud and unhinged. That's the effect I'm going for. Here, go through these and choose some while I'm making the matcha. At least three pieces, mind you!"

Jess threw an armful of garments over my chair and disappeared into another doorway.

I lifted the first garment, an African-print blouse. The fabric felt thick and might keep me warm enough on a chilly night.

Next was a skirt made entirely of different types of ribbons in all the colors of the rainbow. That definitely wouldn't keep anyone warm.

Then, I found a brown suede skirt that flared out from the hips, but other than that, was relatively subdued. Underneath that was a soft green angora shawl. I grabbed both of those.

I set aside a tie-dyed sundress in green and yellow, a Bohemian maxi dress covered in giant purple paisleys, and a brown fringed vest.

The last item was a flowing caftan, patterned with Celtic knotwork in dark blue and purple. It might clash with the green shawl, but it would keep me warm. Besides, it wasn't nearly as outlandish as the other items.

Just as I set aside my selections, Jess emerged with a full tray with cups and a teapot, and placed it on the low table between the chairs. "This will keep our bellies warm on a chilly night! Now, show me your choices."

She held up each piece, and I found myself silently praying my friend wouldn't urge me to be bolder. To my relief, she said, "These will suit you wonderfully. Good picks!"

Jess took the discarded items back into her bedroom and I poured two cups of matcha. Once she returned, she plopped into another chair. "Whew! It's been a whirlwind of a day."

"If you're too tired for this…"

After a sip, she shook her head. "No, no! This is brilliant. I'm looking forward to the craic, like. Did you bring an instrument?"

My eyes grew wide. "Was I supposed to? I can't play anything."

She let out a laugh. "Ah, no worries! I'll fetch a bodhrán. Those are easy enough to play the basics. Besides, I've got the one your gran liked to use."

I took a sip of the matcha, but it was still scalding hot, so I sucked in some air to cool the liquid. It tasted like burnt grass. "Gran used to play the bodhrán?"

My hostess disappeared again and emerged with a round, flat, hand drum, painted with a Celtic cat knotwork in blue and green. She handed this to me along with a little wooden stick with knobs at each end.

Taking them from her, I stared at the two objects. "I have no idea what to do with these, Jess. I'm serious about having zero musical ability. Even with singing, I can barely carry a tune in a bucket."

"There's nothing to it. Here, hold it like this in one hand. No, where the crossbars meet inside. Right. Now, take the cipín. Yes, that's what they call it. Hold it loosely, like you were twiddling a pencil. Exactly!"

The drum seemed warm in my hands, almost comfortable. A whisper of Gran's voice echoed in my head, a pleased sound but without words.

I twiddled the stick, as Jess directed, and almost accidentally coaxed a fluttering beat from the drum. With a huge grin, I glanced up, proud of myself.

Jess picked up a tin whistle and tucked it into a fabric sheath, tying that to her belt. "You'll be brilliant. Now, finish your drink, have a crack at the loo, get dressed, and we'll get going."

While Jess drove the lonely, country road, the twilight still held enough light for me to glimpse the countryside. Still, I could only make out the shape of hills and the occasional copse of trees. She pointed out a few places where people lived, but the names wouldn't stick in my mind.

As promised, the stone circle was only a ten-minute drive away. We parked in a tiny dirt lot below a hill. No other cars were there yet, so we must have been the first to arrive.

I peered up the pale path leading to the crest. "That's where we're going?"

"Bundle up, the wind's always strong there." Her yellow glow almost faded into nothing tonight. I wished I knew the rules, but I'd never been able to figure out patterns. Only a few people had the auras, and I'd never lived with any of them.

I pulled my borrowed shawl around my shoulders. I grabbed my coat, too, just in case.

The rain had stopped earlier, so everything smelled of pine needles and damp earth. The ground was still squishy. I worried about the path being muddy, but it had been lined with rocks.

By the time we reached the top, the wind had indeed picked up, despite the surrounding trees.

Five irregular stones stood in a small circle, the largest one to the east, opposite from the last vestiges of the dying sun. One was lying down. A lying stone? A dying stone? Oh, wait, recumbent. That was the word.

Wind rustled the leaves in an autumn melody. The air smelled of the sea and rain. I shivered and draped my coat over my shawl.

Jess sat on the recumbent stone. "No one else here, yet. I'm going to do some practice trills." She pulled the tin whistle out and played a few scales, occasionally squeaking when her fingers didn't quite cover the holes.

Putting the drum on the stone next to Jess, I went to explore the site. With slow steps, I circled the stones along a rutted path, trodden by generations of visitors.

Somewhere in the back of my head, I remembered that going against the direction of the sun was important in pagan rituals. I had no idea if that was true, or some weird myth I made up, or if it even applied to this group.

I noticed scorch marks where someone had built a fire. A few broken twigs stuck out of the soft earth. Farther along, I spied something bright. When I picked it up, it looked like a fabric belt. It was brown with dried mud, and I couldn't tell what color it should have been. Underneath that, a shell poked out. How had a shell made it to the top of this hill?

Something pale glinted and I bent to examine it. I wiped the mud off the long, thin item, prying one end free. Carefully, I pulled it from the damp soil, brushing off the clinging bits.

A necklace. One of those surfer necklaces, strung with cylindrical beads made from shell. I couldn't tell the color in the twilight. Maybe pale pink?

A pretty thing, but not my style. Maybe it was from one of the Mystical Meddling Moons mob. I tucked it in my jacket pocket.

Jess's whistle screeched, and the sound grated on my nerves. Maybe if I distracted her, she'd squeak less. "Hey, can you show me some more ways to play the bodhrán?"

"Sure!"

I picked the drum up and held the cipín loosely in my hand, as she'd described before. "Like this, right?"

Jess's long, wavy hair whipped around her head with a sudden gust. She grimaced as she pulled it back and tied it in a loose knot. "Almost, but not quite. More like you're holding a little bird. Gentle, but firm. You don't want to let it slip out of your fingers while you're drumming and let it go flying into someone's head. Here, let me adjust your grip." She reached over and helped position my hands.

It felt weird, almost as if I'd drop it. "Okay, I think. Now what?"

Jess teased, "Now, you summon the rhythm gods and pray they don't laugh at us."

Rolling my eyes, I let out a snort. "Great, so no pressure at all!"

"None whatsoever! Just start with a simple beat, like." She demonstrated a basic rhythm.

I tried to follow along but ended up creating a series of awkward, off-beat thumps. "I think I just summoned a rhythm demon instead."

"The rhythm demon! Quick, we must banish it with music!" She played the tin whistle up and down the scales quickly, and we both laughed.

I beat a rapid tattoo along with her scales. She switched to a jaunty tune, something I'd heard dozens of times before but couldn't remember the name. Maybe "Mairi's Wedding?"

I did my best to keep up with her, though I missed a lot of thumps.

Jess paused for breath. "Perfect! You're getting it! Just feel the music, don't overthink it. Remember, this is for fun. You aren't being judged." Then, she kept playing, switching to a different tune. This one was slower, more melancholy.

I closed my eyes, trying to feel the rhythm. I started playing a slightly more coherent beat. "Okay, okay. I think I'm getting the hang of it."

Jess smiled proudly. "There you go! Now we're ready to make some magic. The others should be here soon, and they'll be so impressed."

I laughed. "If by *impressed* you mean they'll laugh themselves silly, then yes, totally."

Jess grinned. "We're here for the craic, not to win a contest."

Murmuring voices came from below, and my hand halted mid-beat. The others must be coming.

"Hey, look who finally decided to join us!" Jess called out, waving.

Marcus was the first to crest the hill. "Grand evening to you, ladies," he said, his eyes lingering on me. "Miss me?"

I had to admit, he was charming. I couldn't help but smile. "Just in time to save us from the rhythm demon, Marcus."

Tara appeared next, carrying a flashlight and her demeanor so frosty, I pulled the shawl tighter. I caught a brief glare from the woman before she turned her attention to Jess. Liam and the dark-haired man followed. Both carried grocery bags filled to the brim.

"Good evening, everyone," the stranger said, "Skye, Jess, welcome to our group. I'm Nabil, and I believe you've met the others, right?" A lilting middle eastern accent added a rich texture to his words. "Ready for a night of singing and stories?"

"You bet!" Jess replied, standing up to help them unpack. "Let's get this shindig started!"

Liam passed out several bottles. Beer, cider, wine; they seemed to have raided the off-license. A few bags of Tayto crisps came next, mostly cheese and onion flavored.

I chose a bottle of cider and twisted off the cap. The cool, sparkling sweetness felt wonderful.

As each new arrival chose a spot in the circle, the surrounding stones seemed to pulse with ancient energy. I glared at my cider. I'd only taken a sip. Surely, I couldn't be drunk yet?

Marcus plopped down next to me, closer than necessary, and started unpacking his guitar. "So, Skye," he began, tuning his strings, "have you been to one of these before?"

I shook my head. "Stone circles are a bit thin on the ground in Miami. You would more likely find remnants of Santeria rituals." As if Armand would have let me go off camping, anyhow.

Marcus strummed a few chords. "You know, your gran used to lead the singing here. She had a voice that could charm the Fair Folk, they say. Everyone in the groups knew her."

"Groups? Plural?"

He waved his hand, as if encompassing all of Ireland. "Sure, the different pagan circles. Each one has different belief details, but we get together now and then for some grand craic."

A pang of loss squeezed my heart, thinking of Gran. "I wish I could have seen her in her element."

A whisper in my head said, *I was something to behold, no doubt.*

I stifled a giggle as Jess smiled at me. "You've got her spirit, Skye. And in those clothes, you could be the spitting image of her. I should have got you some jewelry, too. She loved the bold bling."

"Oh, jewelry! That reminds me!" I reached into my jacket pocket and pulled out the shell necklace, along with the strip of fabric. "I found these earlier. Do they belong to any of you?"

Tara's eyes widened, and she reached for the necklace, her hand trembling slightly. "Th-this was Declan's."

A chill ran down my spine. Everyone else grew silent. "I'm sorry. Here, take it."

Tara clutched the adornment, her expression hardening. "How did you get this? Did he give it to you? Did you…did you *ride* him, you manky wagon?" The atmosphere grew heavier with the weight of her biting words.

"Whoa! Slow down, sweetie. I found it over there, tonight, before you got here. Near the stones, along the outside path." I modulated my defensive tone. She'd just lost someone she cared for. "I didn't realize it was his. I'm so sorry, Tara."

She stared at the necklace, then at me, her eyes filled with a mix of anger and sorrow. "This place has always been special to him."

Marcus asked, "Wasn't he wearing it during the ceremony the other night? I remember you were playing with it at one point, and he told you to back off."

Tara just growled at him while she stared at the jewelry clutched in her hand

Remembering his V-neck T-shirt, I was certain Declan hadn't been wearing it when I found him in the pub. Which meant that either he'd come up here again after their ceremony, or someone had planted it after they killed him.

Tara mumbled. "Maybe it's a sign."

What if the killer had been watching them during the ceremony? What if the killer was watching us now? I itched to search for footprints, but any trace would be well-trampled by now.

What if the killer were around the fire already?

Liam let out a snort. "Sure and it's a sign. A sign that he was dead tired of you. He broke it off, remember? You shouldn't be touching that."

Tara shot him a glare fit to make him burst into flames. "Keep your gob shut, Liam!"

The other man shot back, "Audrey must have treated him better, like. After all, she actually has curves."

I glanced at Jess, who looked pale. Tara snarled and clenched her fists.

Nabil gently took the adornment from her grip. "It seems as if the necklace wanted to be found. If that's the case, our new friend, Skye, should decide its fate."

My mind was racing with possibilities. I probably should take it to the police as evidence, right? But Declan couldn't have been wearing it when he was killed. I remembered the V-neck on his shirt. Nothing but scratches.

Still, I didn't want to piss these people off. Tara had already proved her willingness to physically attack someone, and she obviously had a bee in her bonnet about me. I wanted to throw the necklace off the side of the hill and never to see it again.

Gran's voice whispered in my mind again, *If wishes were horses…*

That gave me a glimmer of an idea. "The wishing tree! We could tie Declan's necklace to the wishing tree and ask for his killer to be found."

Nabil beamed. "Excellent notion. Tara, what do you think?"

She gave a noncommittal grunt and stalked off to the farthest standing stone. Leaning against it, she crossed her arms, probably sulking. Had I ever been that young and temperamental?

I glanced down at my hand, still holding the muddy strip of fabric. I felt foolish asking about that. Who knows what other fights it might cause? At least the mud was all dried, so I stuck it back into my pocket.

Marcus squeezed my shoulder while Liam pulled out a drum. Not a bodhrán, but I recognized the style. A tall, thin drum with a flared top, designed to hold between the knees. A dumbek, I thought. "Now that that's settled, let's have a song. Something to lift our spirits high."

While I picked up my bodhrán and Jess grabbed her tin whistle, Nabil and Marcus began building a campfire just outside the circle.

I turned to Jess, still pale in the light of the full moon and the fire. "Why don't they build it in the middle of the stones?"

Her eyes grew wide. "That's sacred space for the Fair Folk! Never do that. Look, even the grass doesn't grow inside."

For a moment, I'd forgotten that I was in Ireland and some people truly believed in the Other Folk.

Skye, darling, your cat talks! Stop being so obtuse.

So, I had firsthand experience in the Other Folk. But it was still new experience, different from what I'd known all my life.

Besides, Jess was right. Inside the perimeter of the stones was only packed earth. Not one blade of grass dared to grow inside that boundary.

I held the bodhrán awkwardly in my hand, but Liam helped me adjust my grip. "Just so, like. Hold it loosely, as if it were made of clouds."

Tara, still sulking by the far stone, glowered at me. I tried to shrug it off. Didn't Marcus say she was interested in Liam now? She seriously needed to get her emotions under control.

Liam looked into my eyes. He spoke in a tone so low, I barely heard the words. "Remember, she just lost someone she loved. Cut her some slack, aye?"

I gulped and nodded, shame making my cheeks burn.

He continued in a normal voice. "Now, just brush the stick against the goatskin. Super-light touch. No banging; that's for other types of drums. You just need a flick of contact. Right, exactly like that. Try again."

Liam's voice was calm and soothing, and he was a patient teacher. We worked out a few basic beats, and by the time the fire had been coaxed into life, I felt less self-conscious.

Marcus picked up his guitar, and Liam tapped a rhythm on his dumbek. Nabil joined in with a few scrapes of a bow across his fiddle.

Tara, still next to the stone, uncrossed her arms and stood tall. Then, she began to sing.

She had a gorgeous voice, sweet and soft and mournful. The words were familiar to me, as no one who has been to an Irish pub can mistake "Fields of Athenry." Her pathos and longing were so strong, tears pushed against my eyes.

I became entranced with her melodic voice. Goosebumps rose along my arms and I rubbed them. I didn't even remember to play my bodhrán as I sniffled back unexpected tears.

"That was beautiful, Tara," I managed to say, my voice thick with emotion. She gave me a sad smile, her earlier temper evidently softened.

After that, Liam and Jess did a duet, singing a rousing tune called "The Foggy Dew." Then Nabil sang one from Syria, where he was born. Marcus chose a bawdier song called "Biddy McGrath," where a woman defended her honor by strangling her attackers with her bra. Jess accompanied him on the tin whistle with only a few sour notes. As he sang, I grabbed a second bottle of cider.

The first few songs were hesitant and soft, as if everyone was trying out the audience, finding where the sweet spot was. As the night wore on and the drink flowed more freely, the tunes became more spirited.

While they took a break, I laughed at a joke Marcus told and felt more relaxed than I had in a long time. I might have been on my fourth bottle of cider by then.

Alcohol blurred the edges of the night. Marcus stood up and offered me his hand. "Come here to me, Skye. Let's see if you can handle a bit of trad dancing."

The four—or was it five—ciders I'd had by then made me much bolder than usual. I laughed, taking his hand. "All right, but no promises. You may want to put on some steel-toed boots first."

He led me through the steps, which reminded me of square dancing, but my feet refused to cooperate. I stumbled and fell, landing on my backside in the soft grass. Everyone erupted in laughter, including me.

"You've got to be more like a feather not a rock!" Marcus teased, helping me back to my feet.

After I got up, I waved him off. "That's all I can do with this much cider. See if Jess will dance with you. I need a rest."

Marcus took Jess's hand, and I sat while Liam handed me a bottle. This one had no label and bore a metal cage flip top, the sort that could be resealed. I raised my eyebrows.

Liam said, "Some of my own alchemy. Don't worry, it doesn't have a high alcohol content. It'll get you closer to paradise, though!"

I took a cautious sip, and the lovely taste of honey, rose, and mint accompanied the aroma of lavender. I took a deeper drink and passed it back. "Thank you."

Tara said something to Liam, but I didn't understand a word of it. I wrinkled my brow, trying to decide if they were speaking in code or if I was just drunk.

Marcus whispered to me, "Do you have any Irish?"

I shook my head. "Just a few words here and there. I'm hoping to learn."

He gave an approving nod. "Aye, that'll go a long way. The folks around here love their Irish."

I thought about love, my abusive ex-husband, and wondered if I'd ever be ready for romance again.

As the others continued to dance and sing, strange whispers came from the surrounding trees. The stones appeared to shine. The drink must have been playing tricks on me, or I was more exhausted than I'd thought.

Eventually, my eyelids drooped, and I kept rubbing my face. My skin felt numb and my fingers tingled.

I stood but swayed slightly and grabbed one of the stones for balance. "I think I've had enough for tonight."

Jess looked at me with concern. "I'll drive you home, Skye. You look pure knackered." She didn't shine yellow now. Rainbow colors flickered around her like an aurora borealis.

Marcus squeezed my shoulder, then let it slide down my spine, seductive and warm. "Ah, stay a while longer, Skye. The night's still young."

I pulled away from him, suddenly feeling uncomfortable. Armand always made me stay, even if I was asleep on my feet. "No, I need to go. Thanks, Marcus."

With a quick glance at the others and my panic rising, I stumbled down the hill to Jess's car. Jess followed and helped me inside. "Are you well enough, Skye?"

"I'm fine, I'm fine. I just need sleep. Are you okay to drive?"

"I'm grand. I didn't drink six bottles of cider." As she started the car, laughter and music tumbled down the path, distorted and surreal.

While Jess drove me home, I gazed out the window at the dark countryside, the night's events swirling in my mind. The landscape seemed to pulse and breathe.

After we got back to town, she pulled into my pub's parking lot. "Are you sure you'll be grand? I can come in and make you some tea."

I waved away her offer. "Don't be silly. I'll be fine."

The truth was, I needed to clear my head. Spiky sounds were pushing in on me, and I wasn't certain it was all from the alcohol.

As I got out of the car and watched Jess drive away, whispers in the back of my mind itched at my skull, and they didn't sound like Gran. Flashes of color out of the corners of my eyes kept distracting me.

A streak of black shot past me, yowling like a banshee. "Faelan?"

What the heck was my cat up to now? I glanced back at the house, warm and inviting. My bed would feel like Heaven right now. But Faelan sounded like he was in pain. I had to see if he was okay.

I stumbled to the end of the block, looking back and forth for any sign of the fairy cat. It was full night now, near midnight. No one was out and about. The drizzle had returned, and everything sparkled in the few lights along the street.

As I glanced at the empty farm with the wishing tree, I hesitated. I needed to do something here, didn't I? Through my muzzy mind, I remembered Declan's necklace. I promised I'd give it to the tree and ask for the killer to be found.

When I patted my jacket pocket, the piece of shell jewelry was gone. I didn't remember giving it back to Tara. Had I dropped it during the dancing? Or on the way back? I still had that bit of muddy cloth.

I glanced along the road behind me but didn't see anything. That necklace could be anywhere by now.

With a shrug, I decided that if the Fair Folk wanted the necklace to be hung on the wishing tree, they'd give it back. In the meantime, I longed for my bed. Besides, the back of my shoulders tingled, as if someone was watching me. Or something.

Feeling like I was wading through molasses, I trudged down the side street to my place and fumbled the key in the lock. Once inside, I caught a glimpse of Faelan running through the parlour.

Oh, good. I'd totally forgotten to find him. I was glad he was safe, and I wanted to know what happened, but I had no energy to call him.

Everything swayed as I climbed the stairs, dragging myself up step by step. The banister felt odd, slick and soapy under my hands. The carpeting seemed thicker than usual, like I could bounce on it. I did that for a while, delighting in the sensation, before heading to the bathroom.

Even brushing my teeth felt hyper-real, as if I could discern each and every bristle on my gums. Staring at my face in the mirror, I saw every single pore, like craters on the moon.

Once I climbed between my sheets and pulled up the duvet, I was shivering and sweating at the same time. Was I coming down with something? No, this was something else. Liam must have put something in that drink.

The room started spinning, and I grabbed onto the edge of the bed, worried I might fall off. Sound pushed in on me, covering me like a blanket. I wanted to scream and cry, but I also wanted to run through the rain and jump into puddles.

"Faelan? Faelan, are you there?"

Glowing eyes blinked from the doorway.

"What's wrong with me?"

Instead of answering, he jumped to the bed and settled on my chest. His purring eased my frantic mind, and the spinning slowed.

I must have gotten to sleep because what happened next had to be a dream. A shadow chased me through the darkness. I tripped on roots and bushes, falling on my knees as a creature followed. I couldn't see a thing, not even moonlight. It was worse than the night we found Gerald last May.

Every muscle screamed. My skin was scratched and torn. My heart pounded, and I couldn't catch my breath. The growls of my pursuer were loud in my ears, but I still couldn't see what chased me.

Pressure on my chest made me gasp, and I woke with a start. Faelan was curled up on top of me, purring like an outboard motor. He said, "You have returned."

The world was spinning again, but not as fast, and it felt less dangerous. "Returned? Where did I go?"

"You went to another dream. You had help this time."

I scowled at the Cat Sídhe. "Help? No one was helping me. I was alone in the darkness."

"You had help getting there."

"Huh. With help like that, who needs hindrance?"

"I helped you return."

I pet his fur, silkier than it looked. "Thank you for that. *Go raibh maith agat.* Is that the correct Irish?"

"Good enough for a human."

Though I could barely make out any details in the darkness, the cat's face distorted into a caricature of a feline, with ears longer than a rabbit's and whiskers reaching out two feet.

There was definitely something other than botanicals and booze in that bottle Liam offered me.

As Faelan's features ballooned out and shrunk again, I remembered the only time I'd willingly taken drugs. Well, I say willingly, but Armand had bullied me into saying yes.

The party had been awkward from the beginning. I didn't know anyone there, other than Armand. He was having the time of his life, flirting with the other women, putting on displays of bravado for the men.

A typical night for Armand, in other words.

When his friend came by with little squares of paper with a cartoon rat badly printed on them, he took two. He turned to me, offering one. "Put this on your tongue."

I eyed it suspiciously. "What is it?"

"Just something to help you relax, *mi corazón*. Don't worry, I'll be with you."

That early in the relationship, I believed his assurances. I still thought he loved me. I was also worried about my job as a nurse. "They can test me at any time, you know. At work, I mean."

"*No problema, mi amor!* LSD doesn't show up in those sorts of tests."

I had no idea if he was right or not. I stared at the little piece of paper for a few more moments.

Armand caressed my cheek. "You aren't afraid, are you? It's an amazing experience, especially with a lover. Do it for me, Skye. If you love me, you'll do this with me."

Red flags were popping up all over the place, but I hadn't recognized any of them. With extreme guilt and reluctance, I took the drug and placed it on my tongue.

Nothing happened at first. I'd heard wild stories about tripping on acid, and stared at everything, waiting for chaotic hallucination. After about fifteen minutes, I figured it had been a dud or that Armand had been duped.

The walls started breathing.

I wasn't sure at first, but when I stared, they definitely bowed in and out.

Armand had turned his attention to an elegant blonde woman, his hand stroking the small of her back.

Not wanting to look at that, I glanced up at the popcorn ceiling, and it seemed to have thousands of little things crawling across it.

I let out a yelp and stumbled back.

He turned to glare at me. "Be quiet, will you? You're causing a scene."

Then, Armand reached for me. So did three of his friends. So many arms grabbing me, pulling me, shaking me. Strangers all around me.

I had to get away. I pushed and shoved and yelled, but no one helped me. Attacked by a monster with too many arms, too many hands, touching me everywhere.

I screamed.

The entire party went silent for several heartbeats. Then someone laughed. More laughter filled the room, and I wanted to run and hide, but Armand kept a firm grip on me. "You're an embarrassment. Come with me."

He shut me in a dark bedroom and locked the door. I couldn't find the light, and the darkness pressed in on me.

Creatures crawled out of the gloom. Tendrils tickled every inch of my skin, and I rubbed and scratched and sobbed, trying to get away from them.

After an eternity of fighting the madness, the door opened again, letting in blessed light. I had no idea how long it had been, as my sense of time was completely wonky. All I knew was that the light had returned. I ran into Armand's arms a sobbing mess.

He took me home, then showered me with apologies and kisses. The next day, he brought me flowers and chocolates, and like a fool, I forgave him.

I vowed never to do drugs again. And I hadn't until last night.

Liam *must* have put something in that drink he shared with me. What was it he said, it didn't have a big kick? That was a lie. Unless he meant the alcohol level. It hadn't been high proof. It had something else. Perhaps a hallucinogen?

CHAPTER NINE

After I rose and took a shower, I felt almost human again, though I still caught things moving out of the corner of my eye all day. The house seemed unusually peaceful, a safe space after a night of anxiety. I hadn't had so many safe spaces in my life, and I was grateful.

As I finished my first cup of coffee in my comfy chair, someone knocked on the pub door. I shuffled to open it, still in my robe and slippers. I avoided looking at the floor where the body had been found, so I wouldn't see him again in my mind's eye.

When I opened the door, Finn peered at me. "You look the worse for wear, Miss O'Shea. We heard there was a big hooley up at the stones. D'ye want us to leave you for the day?"

I shook my head, squinting against the morning glare as my head began to pound. "No, no, I need the pub finished. Go on in, boys."

Just as I turned away from the door, someone called my name. I recognized Adanna's voice and smiled in relief.

"Skye! Can I join you for a cuppa?"

"Sure, come on in. When did you get back in town?"

She waved to the cousins as we walked back through to my parlour. "Just last night, and I slept like the dead. Nothing like a medical conference to cure you of insomnia!"

I could detect no lies. I'd always had a love/hate relationship with nursing conferences. They were great for meeting others in the field or learning new medical techniques and technology, but the required continuing education on law and procedure was mind-numbing at best.

Adanna preferred tea, so I made us a pot. I chose Barry's, her favorite. "Did you learn anything interesting?"

She gave a shrug as she settled on the sofa. "A few good things here and there, but nothing earth-shattering. What's been going on here? I heard you made some new friends."

I'd learned that gossip tore through this village at light speed. If Adanna had come home late last night, the only person she would have talked to would be her husband, Garda McCarthy. If he knew, everyone probably knew. Obviously, Finn and Rory had learned something, too.

I detested being the subject of rumor. It was a far cry from the relative anonymity of a big city like Miami. But if I wanted to live in a charming Irish village in west Cork, I'd have to deal with the back-stabbing that came with it.

"Yeah, some of Audrey's friends from Dublin. Evidently, they knew Gran, too."

She let out a chuckle. "Sure and your gran was their leader for a time. At least until…" She trailed off as she poured her tea.

"Until? You can't just stop there."

With a wry grin, she said, "I'm not sure what happened, but they say one of the other members took some liberties. She told him to keep his hands off her or she'd blast him into Tir na nÓg. The group split up for a while after that."

That sounds like Gran, all right.

"They've evidently gotten the old band back together. There's still a lot of drama, though." I wondered if Tara *had* been in the group with Gran. Those were two fiery personalities that would likely have either clashed or ruled the world together.

That reminded me of the necklace I'd found. Had Marcus taken it while we were dancing? That stuck him back up on the suspect list. Then I recalled that strip of fabric. It must still be in my pocket. I'd have to clean it to get a proper look.

We both sipped our tea as a moment of silence filled the room. Then, the peace was shattered by Rory laughing at something Finn said.

Thinking of Tara reminded me of Declan. "Adanna, did you find out anything more about the dead man?"

She pursed her lips, and I guessed that, as a doctor, she couldn't disclose the details. I felt bad for asking, as I knew she took her professional duties seriously. I was about to recant when Faelan jumped on her lap.

Startled, the doctor put down her mug and began petting the huge black cat. "Faelan, you almost gave me a coronary!"

Faelan's purr was loud enough for me to hear from across the coffee table. As Adanna stroked his back, it got even louder.

In the past, Faelan had 'helped' Adanna divulge information with this technique. I wondered if it would work again. "Can you share anything you found?"

"Well, I could share a few things. For instance, we found his own DNA under his nails."

That was very odd. "So, he scratched his own face up? Why would he have done that?"

Or something non-human scratched him. Did fae creatures possess DNA? I kept that notion to myself. Adanna had a greater belief in the Fair Folk than most, but I didn't want to push my luck.

"Some people do that if they've had a psychotic break or anaphylaxis."

I furrowed my brow. "Like to a medication? A drug?"

Per Adanna's expression, drugs seemed like the answer. My memory of last night crowded into my mind so fast, I almost gasped.

Before the doctor could respond, another knock came from the door. I had just gotten out of the chair when Rory said, "Jess! It's grand to see you. They're in there."

Jess's red-blonde mass of hair looked like a lion's mane. I smiled and asked, "A wee bit windy out there?"

"It's pure gale force, like."

We shared a laugh while I poured a cup for Jess, then I prepped another pot. After she sat next to Adanna, she asked, "So, what have you two been chatting about?"

Adanna and I exchanged a glance. She said, "I'm afraid we were talking about drugs."

"Oh, like last night?"

The doctor's eyes narrowed and looked between me and Jess. "What about last night?"

I rubbed the back of my neck. "I'm pretty sure that we took something without realizing it. Something in the drink. I was pretty high when I got home. How about you, Jess?"

"I wasn't as bad off as you, but I felt a twinge surreal, aye."

Jess didn't seem upset by the prospect, but my sense of betrayal was morphing from fear to rage and back again.

Adanna scowled. "What sort of drug?"

Shooting a look of concern to me, Jess gave a shrug. "I'd guess LSD or magic mushrooms. There were some gorgeous lights in the sky, but I'm sure they were of my own making."

Adanna pursed her lips. "That's a serious crime. Have you reported it to Donal?"

I shook my head. "I just got up!"

Jess gave a half-smile. "Is it a crime if I had fun?"

The doctor let out a long-suffering sigh. "Yes, it's still a crime. I'm surprised at you, Jess. You should know better. You're leading Skye into a bad crowd." Adanna's tone grew sharp, like a teacher disciplining a student.

Jess raised her eyebrows. "The last I checked, Skye is a grown woman, and these aren't strangers. Saoirse used to lead this same group, and they're friends with my sister. You can keep your puritanical nose out of my business, now."

A heavy silence fell upon us.

If I didn't want to be refereeing a fight, I needed to change the subject. "If they were all playing with hallucinogens, could Declan have had any? Is that why he scratched his own face to bits?"

Adanna shot a glare at me, evidently channeling her irritation with Jess, but nodded. "That's entirely possible. LSD isn't in the normal testing spectrum, but I can call and have them add it to the blood panel."

I thought about the others in the group. "If he tests positive, do you think he would have taken it knowingly? Or been given the drug without knowing?" Liam had seemed super-casual with his special drink. Tara seemed more like the sort who would take the problem head on rather than drug someone on the sly.

Jess said, "Maybe he took something on his own, not part of the group?"

Faelan chose that moment to jump on her lap. Jess let out a grunt. "Goddess bless! This cat is huge. How old is he now?"

I glanced at Adanna. "I have no idea. Gran had him a long time."

She furrowed her brow and stared at the cat. "I don't ever remember him being a kitten, but I lived in Dublin for a few years. I think she had him before that."

Jess petted him and scratched under his chin, making him purr. "He's been around at least fifteen years, but he doesn't act like an older cat."

I had the sudden urge to ask Jess about her glow, and if she could see it, but Gran's voice whispered to me to wait.

I let out a huff. "No, Faelan's still beating up púcas in his spare time."

After Jess and Adanna left, I ran upstairs to find the clothing I'd been wearing at the stone circle. When I finally dug into the pocket and pulled out that strip of fabric, I grimaced as flakes of dried mud scattered.

I rinsed it out in the bathroom sink and by the time I could make out the colors, a horrible idea bloomed. I'd seen this orange and pink paisley pattern before, on Audrey's dress. And it had been found next to Declan's necklace.

Was Audrey the killer? She didn't exactly have a sunny personality, and seemed anywhere from desperate to unhinged, but was she capable of murder? I wasn't sure, but I hoped for Jess's sake, that wasn't true. Still, I added her name to the suspect list.

My mind was already reeling, so I needed a distraction. I treated myself to another look in Gran's diary. This time, I lay on the sofa, the book perched on my chest. At this point, it had become a comfort activity, like listening to a nostalgic song or re-reading a favorite book.

In what had now become a ritual, I caressed the cover of the big book. My fingers ran over the tooled leather with swirling Celtic knotwork and inset crystals in a rainbow of colors.

With a sense of reverence, I opened to the first page. Instead of looking for dream creatures, this time I wanted to search for any mention of the Mystic Moon Meadow.

I drew in a deep breath and flipped each thick, cream-colored page, searching for mention of ceremonies, standing stones, or drug use.

I felt guilty searching for that last one, but I had no idea if Gran had indulged in substances. After all, she'd been alive in the 1970s, so I had to entertain the notion that she'd tried some, at least once. If this group did so on a regular basis, she probably had, too.

Heck, knowing her, she'd probably started it.

About halfway through the book, her voice said, *stop here.*

I did stop and scanned the page. The phrase *standing stone* jumped out, so I went back to the top and read it more carefully.

Dear Diary:

I met up with the MMM today. Aidan wanted to move to a standing stone circle closer to them in Dublin, but I stood my ground. This circle is where we've sunk all our power and prayers. This is where we should remain.

He didn't like that at all, and his great-niece took his side. She's a feisty one, I'll give her that. With the right guidance, she could become a fantastic warrior. Not a physical fighter, though she has the temper, but a warrior for causes.

Ireland's always needed more than their share of such warriors. I miss my days on the frontlines. Sure, I made enemies. But the thrill of victory was worth it!

In the end, Aidan wouldn't listen to me. Most of them took his side, so I washed my hands of the group. I'll be sad to lose the community they offered, but perhaps I'll be better on my own. I can do what I like and not participate in some of their more outlandish practices.

Saoirse, September 10th.

I wondered what year she wrote that entry in. I flipped a few pages forward, trying to find a notation. The next January was dated to six years ago.

So, more than six years ago, Gran was part of MMM and had some sort of argument with the leader, a guy her age named Aidan. I wondered if the feisty great niece was Tara, but it could have been someone no longer involved.

And what sort of outlandish practices did Gran not want to be part of? Did they involve taking drugs? I went to the next page, but she'd switched subjects and had written about having dinner with Máiréad and Ronan.

What had gone on in that group? Did Gran know Declan, Tara, and the others? Or had they joined later?

Come to think of that, I still wanted to figure out who killed Declan, and why he'd been in my pub. As a nurse, I'd learned that most murderers know their victims, and other than Gran and Audrey, the Mystic Meadow Moon were all from Dublin. No one else in town seemed to know them.

Then, I remembered that scowling man from the town meeting, who stood in the corner. I'd thought he was some undercover detective, but what if he was a hit man? Or a money collector?

I had already chalked Tara up as suspect number one, especially if there was some history between the two.

What about Liam? Was there some rivalry between them, either for affection or power? Tara had seemed to glom onto him in Declan's absence, whether he returned the affection or not. I didn't know enough about him to come to any conclusions.

Then, there was Marcus. His aggressive flirting made me uncomfortable. Did that make him suspicious enough to consider him a murderer, though? He didn't seem like he had the necessary guile.

Nabil seemed incredibly even-keeled and calm. That made him the least likely to be a suspect on the surface, but possibly the most likely in reality. It was always the quiet ones, right?

A shiver ran down my spine as I remembered the person I'd bumped into before I found Declan's body. Had I touched the murderer? He'd had blond hair. Could it have been Marcus?

Or was it someone else entirely? A killer lurking in the shadows, watching them at the stone circle, picking off a victim once they were alone?

Or stealing their dreams.

I needed to find out exactly what Gran had done in that group, and what they were getting into now. And if they had anything to do with the dream-stealer.

What if there wasn't some Fae creature switching our dreams around? Could it just be drugs? Had the MMM found a way to administer drugs to the village, and that was messing up our dreams? That didn't seem possible or logical.

But, then again, stranger things had happened in this town.

CHAPTER TEN

That afternoon, Finn and Rory had started up with the nail gun. The constant loud shots frayed every nerve in my entire body, and quite a few I didn't even have.

Still, I was trying to conserve cash flow, so I ate a bowl of soup at home rather than splash out for a meal at the café or pizzeria. I needed to keep a tight rein on my spending if I was going to last until the pub opened again.

At the rate the cousins were working, that might be months from now. I didn't want to get to the ramen noodle stage. That was all fine and dandy during college on a twenty-something stomach, but mid-thirties stomachs were pickier.

Once my soup bowl was empty, washed, and in the drying rack, I needed to escape the constant pounding of nail guns and the witty banter of my contractors. I might have found some quiet spot on the farm, but the only place to sit without getting muddy or wet was the bench in the garden. The pounding would still be audible.

Instead, I grabbed my jacket and headed down the road, finding myself in front of O'Leary's.

While I didn't want to go in, I sat on one of the benches outside. The day wasn't too chilly, and the sun was shining.

Once the pub opened, I'd likely be working inside from noon to midnight. If I wanted to relax in the scarce Irish sun, I'd better do so now.

I knew the months ahead would be dark, cold, and wet compared to what I was used to in Miami. Adanna had warned me that the sun would set by 4pm in the winter and wouldn't rise again until 8:30am.

Miami had much longer days, even in winter. But Miami had Armand and Ireland had Gran's pub, so here I was.

A cloud passed across the sun, and the warmth instantly cooled. I pulled my jacket tighter.

A figure came pelting headlong from the church end of town. Was that Nabil? His face was bright red and streaming sweat.

I hopped off the bench and put out a hand. "Whoa, Nabil! Where's the fire?"

He paused, panting, his hands on his knees. "It's Tara… She's hurt…I need the doctor…"

My first instinct as a nurse was to run and help. But the doctor was just down the street. Besides, I had exactly no first aid supplies with me, not even a bit of gauze. "Right. Stay here and catch your breath. Have you called emergency services?"

He shook his head. "I left my mobile in the B&B."

I pulled mine out, but the battery was dead. "Sheep nuggets. Wait here, I'll grab Adanna."

I ran down another street to the surgery and tried to open the door, but it was locked. Pounding on it, I yelled, "Adanna! Someone needs you!"

I peered into the window, but nothing stirred. So, I went next door to the Garda Station. Donal and I hated each other, but that didn't matter when someone was hurt. If I was in luck, Garda Fitzgerald would be there, instead. "Garda! We need you!"

Just as I reached for the door handle, it swung wide. Instead of Donal's sour face, I saw Adanna's dark skin. "You! You're the one I need. Grab your medical bag! Tara's hurt."

Her eyes grew wide, and she gave a quick nod. Then, she rushed to the surgery and, a few moments later, emerged with her bag. As we quick-stepped back to the pub, she asked, "What happened? Someone's injured?"

"Tara's hurt. That's all Nabil told me."

Nabil was still in front of O'Leary's, bent over with his hands on his knees. He was badly flushed, but he sounded like he'd finally caught his breath. "This way! She's knocked out and bleeding and I didn't see who did this. You've got to help her!"

His words were all jumbled together. I hoped we were in time.

As we turned the corner onto the side street near Máiréad's store, Tara's prone form came into view. Her short, dark hair was sticking out at all angles. Blood dripped onto her forehead from a scalp laceration. I couldn't bring myself to examine her, since Adanna was here.

She was lying so motionless, I held my breath. My instincts screamed at me to get a gurney, a crash cart, something, but I had to let the doctor assess her first. As if I had a gurney or a crash cart.

In that moment, I truly missed working at the hospital.

Adanna knelt beside the woman, took her pulse, and checked her eyes and breathing. "She's alive."

I let out a worried sigh and clenched my fists. Then, I forced myself to emerge from my funk. "Adanna? I can help. I'm a nurse."

"I'm fine. We'll have to take her to the surgery. Nabil, is it? Do you have any friends to help carry her?"

He gave a startled nod and rushed off in the other direction. In a few moments, he returned with a very worried-looking Marcus.

Together, the two men lifted Tara. Luckily, she probably only weighed a hundred and twenty pounds soaking wet, so it wasn't difficult, just awkward. I could see the wound on her head more clearly now, as well as a few contusions that might become bruises.

Tara might not have been my favorite, but she'd never done anything to hurt me, either. She just had a prickly personality and a bad temper. Depending on how Declan had treated her, she might have every reason to be raw. She didn't deserve this sort of pain.

By the time we got her into the surgery with Adanna, the doctor shooed us out. "Go! Go! I'll come out with any news."

We milled about in the lobby for a few minutes before I asked Nabil, "Did you see who did this?"

He shook his head and shrugged. "I found her that way. We were all going to meet for lunch at the pizza place."

Nabil turned to Marcus. "Have you seen Liam? She was supposed to be with him."

Marcus rubbed the back of his neck. "No, he mentioned something about going out of town today, but he didn't say why."

Adanna came out. "Do either of you have Tara's handbag?"

We all exchanged glances. I hadn't seen anything on the ground. "What does it look like?"

Marcus answered, "One of those little shoulder bag things that can barely fit a credit card. It had a thin strap. Bright green."

Adanna scowled. "Well, it isn't on her shoulder now. Go look for it." She went back into the surgery.

Nabil gave a nod and rushed out. Marcus and I sat to wait.

"Who do you think did this? We don't get a lot of muggings in a place this size."

He shrugged. "I can't even imagine. I mean, I know she has an ill-set mind, but who'd actually hurt her?"

I held my peace. Armand hurt me, and I had never deserved it. Merit didn't have a thing to do with it.

I was about to ask about Liam again when the door burst open. Expecting Nabil, I halted mid-greeting at Garda Donal McCarthy's angry face. "You beat someone up? Moving to a new hobby, are you?"

My surprise melted into simmering rage. "Sorry to disappoint you. I was just helping her get to a doctor. Would you be happier if I hadn't gotten help?" I gestured with my thumb at the inner office.

Donal growled in my general direction and stomped into Adanna's office.

Marcus stared after the Garda. "Wow, what's his major malfunction?"

I gave a tired shrug. "He's got some ancient vendetta against my family and won't give me any clues. I'm very much over it."

A few awkward minutes later, Garda McCarthy re-emerged. He pulled out a little notebook and pen and opened his mouth to ask a question when Nabil came back in, out of breath again. "I couldn't find her handbag anywhere."

McCarthy raised his eyebrows. "And you are?"

"Nabil Khaled. Tara's my friend."

"Did you see who attacked her?"

The dark-skinned man had regained his usual serenity. "No. We were supposed to meet for lunch. I was headed to the café when I found her lying on the pavement." Now, his face flushed again, and his calm façade crumbled. "I-I thought she was…was like Declan." He swallowed.

I wanted to comfort the poor guy. Garda McCarthy, however, continued to drill him, evidently not believing his story.

Marcus whispered, "I can see why you haven't taken a shine to the local Garda."

"Shut your gob! You're next."

Marcus clasped his hands in a prim gesture, the very picture of a model suspect. Except the corner of his mouth quirked up a few times. I almost let a giggle escape.

It seemed disrespectful to find anything funny when someone had been attacked, but Marcus, for all his forwardness, made me laugh. Laughter soothed the soul, and I had been deprived of it for too many years.

The door swung open again, and Tara stumbled out. Her face had multiple contusions, and she was holding her scalp where a bandage indicated some damage.

Her skin was so pale, she might have been made of paper. Freckles stood out in stark relief.

Adanna helped her to a chair. "She'll be grand. Just a few bumps and bruises. However, she really should go to the hospital in Cork and get a CT scan."

Tara waved her off. "I will not."

With a scowl, the doctor said, "Then you lot keep her awake. I'm not convinced she doesn't have a concussion."

Marcus knelt beside her. "Tara? Did you see what happened?"

McCarthy said, "I've already questioned her. Go sit down and wait your turn."

After a few more growling questions to each of us, the Garda finally left, and we escorted Tara outside.

Marcus asked, "Are you hungry?"

She gave him a weak smile. "So starving I could eat the whole bull!"

That sounded odd to me. Wasn't the expression to eat a horse? Maybe it was some Dublin slang I hadn't heard before.

Because it was right across the street, we settled for fish and chips. After settling Tara in a booth, Marcus and Nabil went to get orders for all of us.

"I'm sure the Garda asked, but did you see who hit you? Did you have your handbag when you were attacked?"

She shook her head, more subdued than I'd ever seen her. She spoke so quietly I had to lean closer to hear the words. "No, they came behind me. I tried to get at them, scratch or kick, but I-I don't remember anything after that."

A few tears dripped down her cheeks. Grabbing a napkin from the dispenser, I offered it to her. Then, I took her hand in mine and squeezed. "It'll be all right. They'll find who did this."

Glancing up at me, she caught my gaze. The contusions on her face looked much worse close up, glistening with the antiseptic Adanna had smeared on them. Then she dropped her eyes again. I found it hard to believe this feisty warrior woman had been reduced so easily to this meek child.

The boys returned with four orders of fish and chips, steaming and covered in salt and vinegar. That brought everyone's spirits up, even Tara's. I boggled at the fact she was so hungry, as a concussion usually left one nauseous. By the time we finished eating, she was even smiling.

I cleared my throat, not wanting to give up a chance to get more information. "Tara, can you think of anyone who might want something in your handbag? Did you have a lot of cash?"

She nodded, her lips pressed thin. "I'd just gone to the ATM to buy supplies for our next ceremony."

"Supplies? Like drinks?" As Tara nodded, I thought back to the stone circle incident, and Liam's bottle of homemade whatever. I'd almost forgotten that he must have been the one who drugged me. Where had he been through all this?

Had I been wrong in my assumption? Maybe I'd gotten drugged some other way. Or I was just terrible at reading people, which was entirely possible.

Then, I remembered that Audrey had been asking Jess for money, because Declan needed it. Obviously, Declan was beyond caring about money now. Still, that could have been an excuse. Audrey might have needed money for some other reason. "Have you seen Audrey lately? I didn't see her at the stone circle."

Tara's scowl returned with a vengeance. I wondered how jealous she felt about Audrey and Declan. Nabil and Marcus exchanged a glance. Nabil shrugged. "She acts as if she's too posh for the likes of us, sometimes."

Not too posh to be begging money from a stranger, though. Suspicion loomed high in my mind.

Then Marcus said, "Uh, I think she said she was going to Cork."

He was staring at the table, unwilling to meet my gaze. Was he lying? Why would he be covering for Audrey? My head was spinning, trying to make sense of all these relationships.

I needed to get away and think things out. "Right, well, I've got a project to work on. You're okay with them, Tara?"

I felt weird saying that, since they were all friends, and I was an interloper. But I was also a woman. We women had an unspoken bond that you didn't leave someone vulnerable with just men, if there was a hint of danger.

Tara nodded. "I'll be grand. Thank you." Her voice was still so subdued, I could barely make out the words.

Once out of the chippie, I headed to the library once again. I was beginning to feel very comfortable in that space, somewhere I could retreat to when I needed some peace.

With the attack on Tara, I was seriously reconsidering her being at the top of my suspect list for Declan's murder. She was five-foot nothing, after all. To overpower a big guy like Declan would require a lot of strength. Still, she had a nasty temper and a violent streak.

Unless he'd been drugged, of course. Like Jess and I had been the other night.

A tiny voice whispered in the back of my head, *Or someone had used magic.*

It didn't sound like Gran's voice, but at this point, I was questioning everything and getting nowhere.

Too many ideas swirled in my head as I climbed the three concrete steps into the building. The normal librarian was in the back and gave me a wave. I headed straight to the folklore section.

This time, I searched not only for creatures associated with dreams but also hallucinations. I found one that used sleep paralysis, but that was more of a nightmare type of creature, not specific to Irish lore. Someone might have been trying to create nightmares in everyone by dosing the whole town. But how would they share dreams? That seemed too specific.

A few entities were associated with hedonistic pleasure. That could be close enough to taking drugs and hallucinating. The *clurichaun* was known for his love of drinking and causing mischief. The leprechaun was related, but preferred gold and fine clothes. He got his jollies in drink, too. Definitely several possibilities there. I made notes and kept going.

Just as I was about to put the book away, I flipped through it, stopping at a few random pages. Some described holy days, rituals, and one had the Tarbh Feis. I'd seen that one before, so I read more closely. That wasn't a creature, but a ceremony, literally translated into a bull-feast. Participants would eat the flesh and drink the blood of a sacrificed bull, chant a truth spell, and then dream prophecies of who would be the next king.

That was definitely magic associated with dreams. The Mystic Mob kept mentioning their ceremony. Could they have been working divination magic? LSD wouldn't be out of line for helping with that.

It seemed pretty far-fetched. Why would they have killed Declan? Was he trying to be king, and someone objected? King of what?

A niggle of doubt crept into my mind. Was that what had happened to Aidan, when he'd tried to take over? Gran had been part of the group then. Had she done something to him?

I shook my head. Gran's drama happened years ago and wasn't any business of mine. Besides, I had my own puzzle to solve. I kept reading but didn't find a lot of other possibilities.

I didn't want to think that any of those folks—Tara, Marcus, Liam, Nabil, even Audrey—were capable of either beating someone up or killing them, much less dosing innocent people with dangerous drugs.

But I'd learned from working in a hospital that killers don't look like killers. They don't come with *murderer* stamped on their forehead, though that would make things so much easier. Also, the most likely killer was someone who knew the victim.

I turned back to my research, looking for murderous creatures. Here, I found a wealth of information about too many fae. I'd already read about many of them when I was researching

Brian's death last summer. The dearg-due, the banshee, the dullahan, and the púca.

The dullahan did have some aspect of foretelling, but he predicted someone's death. None of them had anything to do with dreams.

Pulling out my mobile, I tried a few searches, but most of the things I found were new-age claptrap, complete with flowers and rainbows. I was learning the hard way that real fae were not the cutesy Victorian cherubs everyone adored. I growled in frustration.

I rubbed my temples, trying to sort out all the variables, but nothing was untangling. I needed to clear my head.

Maybe I could find something up at the stone circle. Not that it was the scene of a crime, but it was where Gran's group of hippies had held this mysterious ceremony. Perhaps there'd be some clues left. That's where the necklace had been, after all.

Besides, a walk in the countryside could be helpful.

I hurried back from the library to my house, noting that the pub was empty. Finn and Rory must be done for the evening. The sun was already hugging the horizon, and my phone said it was close to four.

The drive to the standing stones seemed longer this time, but maybe because it wasn't fully dark yet. I could see the fields and farms I passed, so it seemed like there was more land.

I parked in the tiny lot and climbed the hill. The sky, for once, was perfectly clear, but the light was quickly dying with the sun.

As I approached the ancient stone circle, my breath hung in the air, mingling with the dampness that seemed to seep into my bones.

The standing stones loomed above me, silent sentinels bearing witness to countless ceremonies and rituals over the centuries. Their presence was comforting yet unnerving. I stepped into the circle, my boots squelching in the dewy grass. The fading sunlight bathed the stones in an orange glow.

I walked around the stones first, searching the ground for anything strange. I found an empty beer bottle and picked it up. There was nothing unusual about it, but I didn't want to leave litter in a sacred space, so I placed it near the path, where I'd remember it.

I didn't find Declan's necklace, either. Had I lost it? Maybe Tara had second thoughts about keeping it and had taken it when I wasn't paying attention? If so, more power to her. She certainly had more claim to it than I had.

Something rustled in the trees behind me. I spun, my heart leaping into my throat, but nothing appeared.

Continuing my search, something caught my eye. A faint, unusual pattern in the damp grass. Kneeling, I traced the lines with my fingers. The grass had been subtly scorched, forming an elegant geometric pattern that was almost invisible. A shiver ran down my spine. Three Celtic spirals, like the ones on the back of Declan's jacket. This couldn't be random from our party the other night. This had to be deliberate.

Standing up, I dusted off my hands. Near the base of one of the stones, I found a tiny pile of burnt remnants. I knelt and picked up a few pieces. The scent of burnt sage and lavender, mixed with other herbs, tickled my nose.

These were residues of offerings, but why were they here? Had the group done it after Jess and I left?

Something wasn't making sense here, but I needed to gather the puzzle pieces to figure things out. Searching for a large leaf, I bundled up some of the charred bits and stuck them in my purse.

As I stood, a glint from the last rays of the day caught my eye from the ground nearby. I walked over and found a shard of a mirror, half-buried in the dirt. I carefully pried it free, and a strange, cold energy swept through me. The edges were sharp, and it seemed out of place in this ancient setting.

The trees rustled again. This time, I was done being afraid. "Who's there? Show yourself!"

Only silence greeted me, and I felt foolish. I was just shouting at the wind and jumping at shadows. Maybe I was going off the deep end, after all.

I spied something next to another stone and bent to examine it. A piece of leather? It still had fur on it, so not a tanned hide. It looked like cow or horse hair, but I wasn't an expert. The edges looked ragged, like it had been hacked with some crude tool.

I didn't find a knife, but I did find some sharp bits of gray stone. When I rubbed my finger along one edge, it felt bumpy, with white spots as if someone had struck it several times. Wasn't that called knapping, to shape stone into a knife? An ancient art form that very few modern people would know.

If you don't have home-made, flint-knapped tools, store bought is fine. That thought made me giggle.

I glanced up at a rustling sound, and two glowing eyes peeked out from the darkness. My heart skipped a beat, but then I recognized them.

"Faelan," I called with some frustration. My fairy cat materialized beside me, his emerald eyes smoldering with an otherworldly light. He purred and rubbed against my leg, a comforting presence amidst the strange findings.

"Are you following me? Or just out and about on a ramble? We're at least ten miles from home."

He didn't answer, and I rolled my eyes. "Silent time again, huh? Fine. Be that way."

I returned to examining the piece of mirror. Then, I placed the shard into my purse next to the leaf of burnt offerings and took a deep breath, a growing sense of unease tickling my spine.

Something had happened here, something beyond our simple celebrations. As I pondered the implications, a crackling sound from the edge of the circle attracted my notice. I turned sharply, frustrated and tired of these shenanigans. "Faelan! Stop that!"

But the cat was still sitting near my feet.

I swallowed down a sudden surge of fear. The sun had dipped well below the horizon now, and twilight had engulfed us. "Who's there?"

A shadow stepped out from the mist, cloaked in blackness. I couldn't make out their features, but the glint of red eyes beneath a hood was enough to tear the last shreds of courage from my heart.

I turned and ran, the mist thickening around me as I fled down the hillside. The sound of howling followed closely, a relentless, inhuman cry that matched the pounding of my heart.

I glanced back once, and the dark figure was gaining on me. My foot caught on a root, and I stumbled, falling hard. Pain shot through my ankle, but adrenaline forced me to my feet.

"Faelan!" I gasped, desperation in my voice.

The Cat Sídhe darted towards the figure, growing in size and ferocity. The form hesitated as Faelan's eyes blazed with green fire. He hissed, his fur standing on end, and the figure took a step back.

Seizing the moment, I pushed forward, ignoring the pain in my ankle. I headed down the narrow path toward the parking lot and the safety of my car.

Faelan stayed behind, confronting the creature with a growl that echoed through the woods. I didn't dare look back. I hoped I wasn't leaving him to be killed.

My hands shook so much, I couldn't fit the key into the lock. I glanced up several times, which didn't help my dexterity.

"Holy sheep nuggets! Get in, will you?"

Finally, I got the stupid thing in the lock, flung open the door, and hopped inside. I slammed it shut and clicked the power locks.

Then, I gave in to the shakes.

I wanted to get the heck out of there, but I didn't feel right leaving Faelan to take care of…whatever that had been.

Minutes passed, feeling like hours, until I heard a soft meow. Faelan jumped on the hood, his green eyes burning. He looked unharmed, but his fur was ruffled.

I opened the door and coaxed him inside. To be fair, he didn't require that much coaxing. As soon as he was safe, I locked the doors again and started the engine.

The drive home seemed even longer than the trip out had been. After I pulled into the yard and parked, we ran inside the house.

I locked all the doors. I checked the windows, too. Then I collapsed into my comfy chair in the parlour.

As I lay there, trying to calm my racing heart, the pieces of the puzzle began to fit together. The scorched patterns, the burnt offerings, the shard of a mirror. The bits of stone and scrap of animal skin. They all pointed to a ritual. Perhaps a ritual gone wrong?

"Faelan? Are you ready to tell me what the heck is going on yet?"

No answer. I wished I knew what the rules were on him talking. He never seemed to be able to when I actually needed information.

"Gran? Are you there?"

More silence. I was on my own for this one.

The items I found, the mirror, bit of hide, all those pointed to some sort of ceremony. I flipped through my notes, as those things sounded familiar. I stopped at the page I'd just been writing at the library that afternoon.

Kill a bull with primitive tools and eat it, offer some ritual objects, chant a spell, burn some herbs, lie down, and have a dream about the next king.

They *did* match up with the description of the Tarbh Feis. Someone must have performed the ritual to divine the future.

Whether it had given them the answers they sought or not, the ceremony seemed to have summoned something dangerous. Whether it was on purpose or by accident, I couldn't say. But now, that thing appeared to be haunting the villagers' dreams.

A sudden thought jolted me upright. I'd been assuming it was the Magical Moon Marsh behind all this summoning, but what if it wasn't them? What if someone else was responsible, trying to pin the blame on the Dublin folks?

Too many questions remained unanswered. Had this creature killed Declan? Had it attacked Tara? The latter seemed doubtful as she'd been assaulted in broad daylight. With her purse missing, theft seemed a more likely motive than a supernatural attack.

These questions whirled in my mind, but at least the panic had subsided now that I was home, safe with Faelan.

I wanted nothing more than to curl up and shut out the world. A shiver ran down my spine. That creature had frightened me more than I cared to admit.

But no matter the danger, I was embroiled in this. I'd been drugged and stalked. If Armand had taught me anything, it was that ignoring things don't make them go away. If I wanted that stuff to stop, I needed to uncover the truth. Gran had left me her legacy, and I had to honor that.

CHAPTER ELEVEN

On the plus side, I was able to sleep in the next morning. On the minus side, getting up was more difficult than usual.

After lots of stretching, a very long, hot shower, and going through the motions of preparing and eating a bowl of cereal, I finally woke up enough to feel almost human again.

Sitting in my comfy chair, I gazed out the parlour window into the back garden. While few flowers or herbs grew in September, one amazing rock maple gave a dazzling display of crimson leaves.

Sipping my coffee and contemplating the gorgeous tree, solitude embraced me. I probably sat there for over an hour, just finding some peace in the beauty.

At least, until knocking at the pub door shattered my peace and quiet.

From their arguing voices, I knew the cousins had arrived even before I opened the door.

"Morning, lads," I mumbled.

Finn touched the bill of his stained baseball cap. "Grand morning to you, Miss Skye. We'll be working on the paint this morning, so if you're sensitive to such odors, you might want to go out in an hour."

"Right. Fair warning, thanks." I glared at the cream color they were going to use. They'd suggested something darker, but that had felt so gloomy to me. I wanted a brighter space, no matter what tired tradition dictated.

They each carried several cans of paint, and once they set those down, began setting up for the project. For once, I was seeing regular progress. Still, this job had been going on for five months on just the interior of the pub. They hadn't touched the exterior or the B&B.

But I'd been warned that Irish contractors weren't nearly as fast or consistent as I would expect in America. Not that I'd had a great deal of experience with any contractors.

As I went back to the parlour, my eye caught my reflection in the ancient, streaky mirror behind the bar. Which reminded me of the strange items I'd found at the stone circle. That bit of mirror and the other things were in my purse. Declan's necklace was still missing, but even that was a clue.

I *should* bring this information to the Garda. I didn't want to, as McCarthy hated me, but I still should. My sense of duty demanded it. Besides, the dead guy had been found in my pub, so I was hopelessly entangled in the whole mess. Again.

But none of this was really proof of anything, was it? Donal had told me once that it wasn't up to me to decide that. Maybe I should err on the side of caution this time.

After I finished my coffee, I took Finn's advice and left just as they were opening the first can of paint.

The day was drizzly and cool, but at least the wind wasn't fierce. Still, I brought my jacket in case Irish weather stayed true to form and changed without warning.

It was only about eleven in the morning. The main road was busier today as I strolled down the street. Trying to find some way to procrastinate going to the Garda Station, I wondered if Jess had opened her shop yet, or if Adanna had any patients.

Almost as if in response to my need, I spied Marcus and Nabil walking toward me, discussing something passionately. Nabil halted and raised his voice. Marcus's fists were clenched, and Nabil's body looked rigid, as if he was clenching every muscle. Despite wanting a distraction, I did *not* feel like getting between two men in a fight.

I glanced back and forth, getting ready to cross the street, but Marcus must have caught sight of me. He waved and shouted, "Skye!"

With a sigh, I flashed a smile and walked toward them. "Hey, Marcus, Nabil. How's the craic?" I was beginning to get used to saying that rather than *how are you,* but it still felt odd.

Marcus placed a hand on my shoulder. "Ah, it's grand today. Will you join us for lunch? The pizza place has a two-for-one special today. Our treat!"

Which would have cost exactly the same as if I didn't join them. But he gave a silly grin, and I couldn't help but grin back. "Sure, I can't turn down pizza."

As we continued to the restaurant, which was around the corner from the fish and chips place, Nabil spoke in a low voice. "We should leave tonight, Marcus."

This seemed to be a continuation of the previous argument, so I kept silent.

The blond man gave a shrug. "I don't think we're done here yet. If you want to go back, by all means, go. I'm staying to clean up what we started."

Clean up? Maybe my theory about the ceremony going wrong had some merit. Or was I reading too much into a coincidental phrase? Most likely the latter. Confirmation bias was a powerful thing.

The pizza place had about a half-dozen people at various tables. The bright white walls almost pulsed with the overhead lights. We headed for a plastic booth along the wall.

Once seated, we ordered two pizzas with pepperoni. There was no way I'd eat two-thirds of a pizza, but that two-for-one deal would give us all leftovers.

Marcus and Nabil began talking about someone back in Dublin, a name I didn't know, so my mind wandered.

With Nabil leaving, did that mean Tara and Liam would leave, too? And Audrey? Maybe her leaving would make Jess feel better. I'd certainly feel less awkward about turning down her weird request for a retainer on accounting work.

If folks were leaving Ballybás, I would need to solve my puzzles quickly. Which meant I really did need to collaborate with Garda McCarthy.

I was definitely not looking forward to that prospect.

In fact, the thought of facing him was enough for me to want to drop the whole thing.

Sorry, mo chroí. You need to finish this.

I didn't want to speak to Gran in front of the two guys, so I spoke in my head, *Really? Why does he hate me so much, anyway? Was it something you did?*

You'll find out soon enough.

I let out a sigh. *Jam tomorrow and jam yesterday—but never jam today.*

So, at Gran's insistence, this was my duty now, to protect the village from creatures that might harm them.

Marcus was looking at me quizzically. Had he asked me something? "I'm sorry, my mind was miles away."

"I asked, how long ago did you move here?"

"In May. But I'd visited when I was a child a few times."

Nabil nodded solemnly. "This is a lovely place. I wish I could move out here. Dublin is so crowded and expensive."

"Why don't you?"

He shook his head. "My job won't allow me. I have to be in the office every day. They aren't willing to let me go remote."

I cocked my head. "What do you do?"

"Tara and I are both in IT. Normally, that would be a fine job for remote or at least hybrid. But my supervisor is a micromanager and believes if he can't see you, then you aren't getting any work done."

Marcus let out a snort. "I hate control freaks. I'm glad my boss isn't one. Mine isn't the sort of job I can do remote, more's the pity."

Nabil gave a sullen nod, but then stared morosely into his glass of water. I cocked my head. "Nabil? Are you okay?"

The other man shook his head. "He's sad about Declan. They were close."

Interesting. Close, like friends, or something more? But this wasn't the time to dig. Instead, I turned to Marcus and asked him what he did for a living.

He gave a grin. "I'm in marketing."

That sounded spot on with his easy manner, personality, and too-pushy friendliness. I rolled my eyes. "I should have guessed."

"Hey, what else would a chronic extrovert do best?"

Nabil rolled his eyes this time, just as the server brought our pizza out. We each picked a slice, and I took the first bite. Not as good as a New York slice, but decent enough.

I'd eaten here before, but they didn't sell by the slice. Eating a whole pizza by myself would result in me having to buy a whole new wardrobe, so I hadn't come often.

Marcus said, "Tara might not be able to go back tomorrow, Nabil. The Garda asked her to stick around."

I kept silent, hoping to pick up a few more clues, but Nabil just made a noncommittal grunt and reached for his cup.

I definitely needed to talk to McCarthy.

After Marcus paid for lunch, he asked me to walk with him on the beach.

I considered it, but then decided that I really didn't want to be alone with him. Not that I thought he was dangerous, but I just had an odd feeling about him. Instead, I tried to laugh it off. "In this cold? No, thanks, I've got some errands to run today. I'll catch you later?"

Marcus gave a startled nod as I rushed out, leaving them all the leftover pizza.

I shouldn't have left free food, but my stomach was roiling now, and I needed to do this now, before I lost my nerve.

With great trepidation, I entered the Garda station, my steps echoing on the cold, tiled floor. It smelled of old leather and disinfectant, the air heavy with the scent of unease.

I thought about what sort of things I could share with Garda McCarthy. The switched dreams, the ceremony, the lost necklace, a scrap of mirror, some burnt offerings, the hide, and the stone tool.

All the clues seemed disjointed, like pieces of a puzzle that didn't quite fit, but I still had to report them. I wasn't, after all, a trained detective. I might be missing something essential.

Maybe McCarthy would surprise me and offer some inspiration to solving it.

Right.

When I entered, Garda Fitzgerald was at a desk, typing at the computer. McCarthy was standing, a pad in his hand, peering over her shoulder.

Both glanced up as I came in, McCarthy's face immediately hardening. He was a lanky man with reddish hair and a scowl etched into his features, his eyes cold and calculating.

He'd been nothing but rude to me since I arrived. I'd never understood exactly why, but he'd hinted at 'never trusting an O'Shea' before. I hadn't been able to extract any details from either McCarthy. Gran said I'd find out soon enough, so I had to be patient.

"Miss O'Shea," he greeted me, his tone clipped. "What brings you here?"

His manner was already grating. I took a deep breath, trying to keep my temper in check. "I found some things at the standing stones. They might be related to Declan's murder."

His eyes narrowed, suspicion coloring every line of his face. "And why should I believe that?"

I gave a shrug. "It's the same place Declan was last seen with any people, right? With his pals in the new age group?"

McCarthy let out a noncommittal grunt. "And why are you bringing them here? Shouldn't you be at home pretending to own a pub?"

"Because it's the right thing to do," I snapped, my patience wearing thin. "Look, I don't like you, and you don't like me. This isn't about us. It's about finding Declan's killer."

He stared at me for a long moment before finally giving a sharp nod. "Grand. Let's see what you've got."

I handed him the shard of mirror and the burnt herbs. Next, the bit of animal hide, along with the sharpened piece of stone. "There was a necklace, too, made of shell beads. Tara confirmed it was Declan's, but I lost it."

He raised his eyebrows as Garda Fitzgerald rose from her desk and peered at the items. "Lost it?"

I gave a nod as my cheeks began to burn. "Sometime during the evening. We were singing around a campfire."

He gave a grunt. "Were you intoxicated?"

He had no idea. But his question was poking my temper again. "I had a few ciders, yes."

He bent to examine the piece of mirror and the burnt herbs with a critical eye. "Where *exactly* did you find these?"

"At the Scánnatrumloo Standing Stones." My American accent tripped over the Irish word. "Those visitors from Dublin are part of a group called the Mystic Moon Meadow. They held some ceremony there a few nights ago, and I thought it might be connected."

He frowned, setting the bag down on his desk. "Why were you at the standing stone circle?"

I rolled my eyes. "I wasn't there for the ceremony, if that's what you're implying. Marcus invited me to join them Monday night. We did some singing, a little dancing, some drinking. I found the necklace that night."

"Who is *we,* Miss O'Shea?"

"Me, Jess, Marcus, Tara, Liam, and Nabil."

McCarthy wrote down the names in his notebook as Garda Fitzgerald piped up. "And the other items?"

"As I mentioned, I'd lost the necklace. So, I went to try to find it the next evening. That's when I found the other things."

I swallowed, thinking of the shadow creature that had chased me away. Donal would laugh in my face if I brought that up. "I left when it got dark." There, that was true enough, if not complete.

He didn't look convinced, but he nodded anyway. "Fine. I'll look into it."

"Can you share anything with me?" I asked.

He growled. "What? What are you talking about?"

I crossed my arms and returned his scowl. "I brought you clues. I'm trying to be helpful. Can you share any with me? Like, what was the cause or time of death? Anything at all?"

His eyes flickered with something. Could it be guilt? He glanced once at his trainee, but he answered with his usual gruff demeanor. "I can't discuss an ongoing investigation with a civilian. You are not an interested party."

"Come on, McCarthy," I pressed. "You know as well as I do that I'm not just a civilian. I own the pub where Declan was killed. I found these clues. They took several expensive bottles of spirits from my pub. Don't I deserve to know if there's something I should be worried about? My safety could be at stake."

He pursed his lips but didn't respond.

Then, I took a deep breath and played my trump card. "You wouldn't want to be held responsible if someone hurt me, and I fell victim because you kept too close a grip on vital information, would you?"

He sighed, rubbing the bridge of his nose and glanced at Garda Fitzgerald again. I held onto a small hope that her presence would make him less obnoxious. "There's nothing concrete yet. We're following several leads, but it's too early to say anything for certain."

I could tell he was holding something back, but I also knew I wouldn't get anything more out of him. Not yet, anyway. "Fine. Just…let me know if you find anything, all right?"

He gave me a curt nod. "I will, yeah."

I turned to leave, but his voice stopped me. "Ms. O'Shea… Skye."

I turned back, surprised to hear him use my first name. The muscles of his jaw clenched.

"Be careful," he said finally. "There's a lot more at play here than you realize."

I frowned. "What do you mean?"

But he just shook his head. "Just be careful."

I left the station, my mind racing. What had he meant by that? Was he worried about someone at large? Or maybe something. I shuddered and shoved that notion away. Well, at least he was paying mind to my safety, even if he was being maddeningly opaque about why.

The walk back to my pub was a blur. Despite the late morning hour, the air was thick with mist, the kind that seeped into the bones.

I stopped just outside, assessing the windows Finn had installed yesterday. They looked nice enough, with simple stained glass designs. I wasn't sure I loved them, but Finn had urged me to try.

In the end, I gave in. He had far more experience with Irish pubs than I did, after all.

As I pushed open the door to the pub, the intense stink of fresh paint mingled with the faint scent of sawdust. Since they'd started this project, the interior had become a chaotic mix of old charm and new construction.

Rory and Finn were hard at work, or as hard at work as they ever got, painting the walls a warm, inviting shade of cream. The mist had finally burned away, and the afternoon sunlight streaming through the windows, a pattern I'd seen often here. The new drywall gleamed in the light, the joint compound freshly sanded smooth.

Rory was perched on a stepladder, his short, stocky frame teetering as he reached for the high spots. Finn, tall and gangly, was on the ground, stretching to reach the lower parts, his blond hair falling into his eyes.

"Oh, hello, Miss Skye!" Finn called out as he spotted me. "What d'ya think? Not bad for a couple of amateurs, huh?"

I forced a smile. "Looks good. Just be careful up there, Rory."

Rory grunted in acknowledgment, his focus entirely on the paint roller in his hand. I couldn't help but worry every time I saw him up on that ladder, wobbling precariously. After all, they were well into their forties. A fall might be dire.

These two might have been the only option in town, but they were a walking disaster waiting to happen.

As I wandered into the main house, I thought about what my next B&B project should be. I'd already replaced the sheets and duvets in the three bedrooms, each one with their color schemes of sage, rose, and periwinkle. Then, I'd stripped and repainted the dressers and conducted a thorough cleaning of everything. The shared bathroom should be next, but that required professionals.

Just as I came out of the kitchen, a sudden crash jolted me out of my thoughts. I spun around to see the ladder tipping over, Rory tumbling off it with a yelp. Time seemed to slow as he flailed in the air, his arms windmilling in a desperate attempt to grab something to break his fall.

Finn, eyes wide with panic, lunged forward, trying to catch his cousin, but it was too late. Rory hit the ground with a sickening *thud*, the ladder clattering down beside him.

"Rory!" I shouted, rushing over.

The shorter man lay on the floor, flat on his back and groaning, his face contorted in pain. Finn hovered nearby, looking utterly lost.

"Rory, can you hear me?" I asked, dropping to my knees beside him.

"Yeah," he croaked, wincing. "Jesus, Mary, and Joseph, it hurts like the devil."

I quickly assessed him, my nursing instincts kicking in. His pulse seemed fine. His heart rate was a little high. He was breathing okay.

"Where does it hurt? Finn, get me some towels and the first aid kit from the pub kitchen."

Finn nodded, dashing off and returning moments later with the supplies. I gently palpated Rory's limbs, checking for any obvious breaks. His left arm was starting to swell, but it didn't seem broken, just badly bruised.

"Okay, Rory," I said, trying to keep my voice calm and reassuring, "it looks like you've got a nasty bruise, but nothing's broken. I'm going to wrap it up to help with the swelling. You'll need to apply ice and heat in turns. Just try to relax."

Rory nodded, his breathing shallow. I carefully wrapped his arm with a towel, then secured it with a bandage from the first aid kit. He winced but stayed still, his trust in me evident despite the pain.

"Thanks, Miss Skye," he muttered once I finished. He put on a brave smile, but tension around his eyes told me he was still in pain. "Don't know what we'd do without ya."

"Let's try not to find out," I said, offering him a small smile and a baggie of ice wrapped in a dishtowel. "You need to take it easy for a bit and hold this against your arm. Finn, help him over to that chair and get him some water."

Finn nodded, helping Rory to his feet. They made their way to one of the pub chairs, Rory leaning heavily on his cousin.

I watched them, a mix of exasperation and affection filling me. These two might have been bumbling, but they had good hearts. In a place like Ballybás, that counted for a lot.

That night, just after I finished washing the dishes, a sudden knock at the pub door startled me. Maybe Marcus had arrived with some of that leftover pizza.

I opened the door to see McCarthy, his expression unreadable. I hesitated for a moment before getting up and letting him in.

"Garda McCarthy," I said, my voice wary. "Did you find out something more about Declan's killer?" I peered behind him, hoping Garda Fitzgerald was with him. Her presence seemed to soften his nastiness toward me.

"I needed to talk to you," he said, "Can I come in? Away from prying eyes."

I raised my eyebrows, my guard up, but I opened the door wider. "About what?"

He stepped inside and glanced around the empty pub, then back at me. "There's something you need to know. About me and about your family. Adanna's been pestering me non-stop to deal with this. If I tell you, she'll finally leave off."

My heart pounded in my chest. "Tell me what?"

He took a deep breath, his expression grim. "It's a long story. Could I get a cuppa?"

I couldn't figure out how to handle this friendly version of McCarthy. Keeping a wary eye on him, I gestured for him to have a seat on the sofa while I made tea.

"I know I've not exactly been fair to you since you arrived."

I let out a snort. "That's an understatement. You were going to call immigration on me!"

He waved that away. "I knew that wouldn't do anything. You're a legal citizen. I checked when you arrived and registered."

Anger bubbled up. "Then, why did you threaten me with it? Just to piss me off?"

He let out a sigh. "I guess I was testing your mettle."

That left me in silence.

"Your family and mine, they have a history. Not a nice one, either."

I set down the tea things and poured two cups. Taking a sip of mine, I waited for him to elaborate.

He stirred sugar into his own cup, then took a deep breath. "Your grandfather and my father used to be pretty close."

"Your father? Not your grandfather?"

"No, my grandfather died young, around forty. But my da was older than my ma by fifteen years, so he was closer to your grandfather's age. They were best mates."

Math wasn't my strong point, so I quit trying to figure out ages and years. Instead, I took another sip of tea and waited for McCarthy to spill the rest of his.

"So, when my da inherited a bit of land next to yours, they were excited that they'd be neighbors, like. There was confusion over where one property started, and where the next one stopped."

"Let me guess. They got into a fight about it and never spoke to each other again?"

He let out a mirthless snort. "You would think so, wouldn't you? No, they didn't bother with a fight. Not sure why, really, but it might have had something to do with a woman. Just about everything did, in those days."

I let out a sharp laugh. Things hadn't really changed all that much.

"So, they went straight to court over it, and by the time your grandfather won the case, my own da was bitter as a lemon. He left town just after I was born."

"Left without you?"

"Aye, and my ma. I have no idea where he is now, if he's even alive."

"And you blame my grandfather for him running off?"

Faelan chose that moment to jump onto the sofa next to McCarthy. Absently, the Garda stroked the cat's black fur. I could hear the purring from across the room.

The silence grew for several moments before he gave a nod. "I did, sure enough. I grew up sort of resenting your family. Ma blamed them for Da abandoning us. Once your grandfather passed, I blamed Saoirse, and you, for that matter."

"But I don't even know these people! I barely knew Gran!"

"Aye, and that wasn't fair of me. Adanna's been hammering away at me since you came, trying to get me to realize you're not to blame for the sins of your fathers. Or your grandfathers."

He smiled. It was an odd expression, as if his face might crack, but I smiled back. "What changed your mind?"

"Today. You came to me with evidence even though you knew I would be a right arse to you. That took some bravery and determination. I can admire that."

He downed the rest of his tea and slapped his hands on his knees. "Right. That's done, then. I'll be going." Garda McCarthy stood and strode toward the door.

"Wait!"

He paused but didn't turn around.

"Tell Adanna thank you for me."

"I'll do that."

CHAPTER TWELVE

A half hour after Donal left, someone else knocked at the door. Since I'd been just about ready to climb upstairs to bed, I trudged over to the pub door. Was this a glimmer of how many interruptions I'd be getting once I was open for business?

First, I peeked through the window. After all, there was still a killer out there somewhere. Then, recognizing my visitors, I opened the door. "Adanna? Jess?"

Jess said, "Well, your eyesight is fine. Come here to me, we're on the hunt for craic. You're in sore need of a night out after all that's happened."

"Uh…" I didn't want to be social, but they weren't wrong. I could use some distraction. Besides, I didn't want to piss off my new friends and lose them. I'd lost too many when Armand took control of my social life.

Adanna poked my upper arm. "You can't spend another night wallowing at home. You deserve some fun."

Maybe, if I was exhausted enough, I might actually get to sleep without nightmares tonight. "Right, what the heck. Let me change."

We climbed into Adanna's car, and she drove us to Bantry. This tourist town was almost three times as big as Ballybás, and large enough to have a choice of pubs. The centre had a huge open plaza, surrounded by narrow streets chock full of restaurants, pubs, and shops.

The wind was brisk as we made our way through the narrow streets, the salty ocean air whipping at our faces and tangling our hair. Adanna and Jess flanked me on either side, their chatter and laughter a soothing balm to my frazzled nerves.

"Come on, Skye," Jess said, nudging me with her elbow. "We're in search of karaoke. You'll feel better after a few songs."

Adanna nodded enthusiastically, her black curls bouncing. "I've been dying to see you sing."

I couldn't help groaning. While I loved listening to music, I had exactly zero talent at singing. Tonight would be a true embarrassment.

Despite my reluctance, their infectious energy was already working its magic on me. The village was alive with the sounds of the evening crowd. We passed by quaint shops and cozy pubs, their windows glowing with warm light.

Jess and Adanna walked with purpose. I had to jog to keep up with them. "Where are we going, then?"

Tossing her long, curly hair out of her face, Jess said, "O'Malley's. It's just at the end of this street. It's got a lively atmosphere and, more importantly, karaoke!"

As we stepped inside, a wave of warmth and the smell of beer and fried food enveloped us. The place was packed, with patrons gathered around wooden tables, chatting and laughing.

The stage at the far end of the room was empty for now, but the karaoke machine was set up and ready to go.

We found a table near the stage, and Jess went off to get us some drinks. Adanna and I settled in, and I let out a contented sigh. It felt good to be out, surrounded by people, even if a small part of me still wanted to crawl back into bed.

Jess returned with pints of Guinness, cider, and ginger ale, setting them down with a flourish. I took the cider, while Adanna grabbed the soda.

"To a night of fun and forgetting all our worries!" Jess declared, raising her pint.

"To fun!" Adanna echoed, clinking her glass against Jess's. I raised mine, the bubbles tickling my nose.

"To forgetting," I added softly, taking a sip. The sweet taste was comforting, and a tiny knot of tension in my chest began to unravel.

As the night went on, the pub grew louder and more raucous. The first brave soul took to the stage, a middle-aged man who belted out a surprisingly good rendition of *Whiskey in the Jar.* Cheers and applause followed, and the line of would-be singers grew.

"Are you going to sing, Skye?" Jess asked, her eyes sparkling with excitement.

I hesitated, but then Adanna grabbed my hand. "Come on, we'll do a duet! You and me, *Islands in the Stream*. You know you want to."

Her enthusiasm was impossible to resist. I found myself nodding, and before I knew it, we were signed up and waiting for our turn. Jess decided to go before us, choosing *Black Velvet Band,* which had the whole pub clapping along.

Then, it was our turn. My nerves fluttered in my stomach as we took the stage, the bright lights making it hard to see the audience.

As the music started, and Adanna gave me a reassuring smile, I found myself relaxing into the moment. She had a fantastic voice, and her skill drowned out my flat notes. Our voices blended together, and I felt a rush of exhilaration. By the time we finished, the crowd was cheering, and I couldn't stop grinning. I had to admit, I was glad my friends had dragged me out tonight.

We returned to our table, breathless and laughing. "You were amazing!" Jess said, pulling me into a hug.

"I was horrible, but Adanna carried me along," I replied, feeling a warm glow that had nothing to do with the beer.

Just as I was starting to think that maybe this night was exactly what I needed, the lights flickered. A collective murmur of confusion swept through the crowd, and then the pub was plunged into darkness. The music halted abruptly, replaced by the sounds of startled exclamations and a few nervous laughs.

"Great," Jess muttered. "Just when things were getting good."

Adanna pulled out her phone, using the screen's light to illuminate our table. "Looks like a power outage."

The wait staff moved quickly, lighting candles and setting them on the tables. Flickering flames cast eerie shadows on the walls, and the atmosphere in the pub shifted from fiercely festive to something strangely intimate.

People began to talk in hushed tones, and someone started a soft, acoustic version of *Danny Boy* from a corner.

A shiver ran down my spine, though sweat trickled down my back. Something about the sudden darkness, the way the candlelight danced, made the hairs on the back of my neck stand up.

I shook off the sensation, telling myself it was just the aftereffects of the adrenaline from singing.

Adanna and Jess were making the best of it, laughing and sharing stories, their faces glowing in the candlelight.

"So, then Audrey tells me she had been out all night! Oh, you could see the steam coming out of Da's ears!"

I tried to join in, but my attention kept wandering to the shadows in the corners of the room.

For a moment, I thought I saw a figure standing near the door, watching us. Just like the entity that chased me from the stone circle. When I looked again, it was gone.

Jess placed a hand on my forearm. "Are you okay, Skye?"

"Yeah, I'm fine," I replied, forcing a smile. "Just spooked by the dark, I guess."

Jess and Adanna exchanged a cryptic glance. Then, Adanna raised her eyebrows, her tone turned solemn. "You're wise to be afraid of the shadows."

To distract myself, I took another sip of my drink and listened to the soft music and murmured conversations around us.

The pub had taken on a different kind of charm, quieter and more introspective. It felt almost as if the power outage had cast a spell over the place, making it feel disconnected from the outside world. A throwback to an age before the buzz of electricity ruled the world.

After a while, the staff announced that they were closing up early due to the outage. People gathered their things and headed out into the night. We did the same, bundling up against the cold as we stepped outside.

The streetlights had also gone out, and the village was dark and quiet, except for the distant crash of waves against the shore and the murmur of voices as people made their way home.

As we strolled back to Adanna's car, the sky was a deep, velvety black, dotted with stars.

"Look at the stars," Jess said, pointing upwards. "Aren't they gorgeous?"

Without the usual light pollution, the constellations were clearer than I'd ever seen them.

"They are," I agreed, a sense of peace settling over me. Despite the strange ending to the night, I was glad they'd dragged me out. I felt lighter, more connected to the world around me.

After Adanna dropped me off, I stood in front of the pub door, suddenly reluctant to end the night.

The wind shifted the trees, a soft susurration caressing the night. Despite the lovely night, I couldn't shake the feeling that I wasn't entirely alone.

I'd felt that sensation before, back when Armand had been stalking me.

Shadows moved and shifted, and I caught a glimpse of something out of the corner of my eye. When I turned to look, there was nothing there.

With a shiver, I unlocked the pub and quickly got inside, making certain to lock it again. I had no energy left as I climbed the stairs and got ready for bed. It had been a very full day.

As I drifted off to sleep, I reflected that it had been a fun evening, but I couldn't shake the sense that the shadows had been watching me.

Another day, another headache. At least, that's what it seemed like. Though I went through the motions of getting ready for the day, my mind was off in Tir na nÓg.

I held my head in my hands while I stared into my coffee mug. It wasn't like I'd drunk to excess last night. I shouldn't get a hangover from two ciders. Or four.

But the cousins were busy with repairs, despite Rory's mishap yesterday, and their painting had turned to hammering. The hammering became pounding, and the pounding became pain.

That morning, I worked on my accounts again. For most of the morning, I succeeded. As noon approached, though, I'd had enough. If I didn't escape the noise, I'd commit at least two felonies, possibly more. And then, there'd be even more bodies on my property.

At least the pub was changing enough that I no longer saw Declan's body every time I walked through. Finn and Rory had definitely succeeded there.

I no longer saw it as Gran's closed pub, either. With the new windows and fresh paint, it was beginning to feel like my new place. I quickly shoved away the twinge of guilt for taking over. Gran had left me the business, after all; she'd wanted me to do this. She told me so, in no uncertain terms. Well, her ghost had. Or whatever spoke to me. For all I knew, Gran's voice was actually my own twisted imagination.

Sometimes, despite all evidence that the Fair Folk and Gran's spirit was real, I wondered if I was going mad. That didn't seem too terrible. It was a well-known secret that all the best people were.

My first thought had been to get lunch at the Blarney Scone. However, to save money, I went to make a sandwich. But, when I opened the package, there was mold decorating the edge of the bread. I tossed it with a grimace and pulled my jacket on. I'd have to go out for lunch, after all. At least there were several options within walking distance.

Back in Miami, I'd never lived in a walkable place. I relished the fact I could just walk, rather than get in a car, drive, find parking, get gas, all that hassle. Some weeks, I barely drove at all. Getting used to this change had taken some time, but I loved the freedom. Besides, I was saving loads in gas money.

The street seemed empty. Late September was firmly out of the tourist season. Sure, a few people visited, like the Moonlit Mystic Marsh Muppets, but those were Irish tourists, not visitors from another country.

That meant that a lot of tourist-funded businesses either cut down their hours or closed. Jess had told me that, starting in November, she only opened three days a week. Local services like restaurants might close for lunch or dinner.

With not much going on, I might see if Adanna had time to hang out this afternoon.

I had missed her when she had to go to Dublin, and I wanted company today. That shadow from the last few nights concerned me and I didn't feel entirely safe alone, even during the day.

As I approached her surgery, I hoped Adanna was in, and hopefully, without a patient.

The door pinged as I opened it, and after a few seconds, Adanna peeked her head out of her office. "Skye! What's the craic?"

"I needed to escape the construction noise. Care to join me for lunch?"

She hesitated for a moment. "Sure, but I've got to go discuss something with Donal. Can you wait a tick?"

"No worries."

As she went out, a file under her arm, I sat in the waiting room. The silence felt heavier than it should.

From where I sat, I could see her filing cabinet peeking out through the doorway. I wondered if Declan's autopsy report was already filed away. Maybe I could sneak a quick peek.

That was a horrible idea. It was a violation of privacy, and a betrayal of our friendship. But what if I could find something about Declan's death from her files? Something that would help me put all the puzzle pieces together? Wouldn't that be for the greater good?

The moral dilemma bounced around in my mind like a ping pong ball. But after reminding myself firmly that I was no longer a nurse, and that the dead man had been in my own pub, I made my decision.

Before I could talk myself out of this incredibly bad idea, I scooted into Adanna's office and pulled out the black metal old-fashioned filing drawer. I knew she kept electronic files of everything, but she once told me she also prefers to keep printouts, as the system had crashed frequently.

Then, I halted. What was Declan's last name? I squeezed my eyes shut, trying to dredge the information from my conversations with Marcus. Murphy? Yes, Declan Murphy. I pulled out the drawer labeled 'L-N'.

I found his file and drew it out, but then hesitated. Should I be doing this? Definitely not. I glanced at the front window, but Adanna wasn't back yet.

Well, I'd come this far, so I flipped it open and scanned the data. Name, age, place of birth, cause of death.

Blunt force trauma.

I let out a disappointed snort. That could mean anything from 'a bump on the head' to 'his chest was smashed in'. It told me exactly nothing.

The toxicology panel was done after the initial autopsy. Declan had D-lysergic acid diethylamide in his system at the time of his death, in high amounts. LSD.

Just as I finished reading that detail, a door closed somewhere. I shoved the file back into the cabinet and quickly grabbed a seat back in the waiting area.

Adanna came in again, dusting her hands. "That's all grand and done. Now, lunch. Are you up for O'Leary's? I'm a bit past pizza and fried fish, and I had brekkie at Joshua's café."

"Sure."

We exited the surgery. Just as Adanna flipped the sign to closed and locked up, her phone rang with a song from the 1980s, "Doctor, Doctor."

"Adanna McCarthy here. Right. What's the address? I'll be there in a few." She clicked off and glanced up. "I'm so sorry, Skye. Someone up in the hills needs me. Another time?"

I gave a quick nod, ashamed to admit I was relieved. I wasn't a great actor, and I didn't want to face Adanna for an hour after I'd just riffled through her files.

As she hurried off behind the row of buildings, presumably to fetch her car, I headed down the street toward O'Leary's. I was still hungry, and while I wasn't a huge fan of the man, his pub did serve a decent lunch. I was in the mood for a juicy burger.

Footsteps behind me made me turn to see Marcus and Tara. The blond man's face broke into a grin. "Skye! Where're you headed?"

"O'Leary's."

"Can we join you?"

Tara's expression looked pinched, but I nodded. "Sure."

Once we went inside, we ordered our meals at the bar and took a seat. Only a few tables were filled. I recognized most of the patrons, which gave me a warm feeling.

If I'd sat at a restaurant in Miami, the odds of me recognizing anyone were super-slim, even if I patronized a local place near my apartment. Of course, the gossip was much less rampant in Miami, too.

The three of us waited in awkward silence. Marcus broke the silence with, "We all decided to stay in town a few more days."

I gave a nod, though it was pretty obvious, since the evidence was right in front of me. "How come?"

Tara pursed her lips. "We've still got a few things we want to finish up."

I wondered what she'd meant by that. I was about to ask when my phone buzzed. The light was bright from the window, so it was hard to see my screen.

Angling it to get rid of the glare, I squinted, not recognizing the number right away. Then the gears in my mind shifted and I recognized the Miami-Dade County Library. Did I still have any books I borrowed from them? With a twinge of trepidation, I answered it. "Hello?"

"So, you finally pick up? I was beginning to think you didn't want to talk to me."

My stomach fell to the floor. "Armand."

"The one and only. Say, I have some stuff to send you. Where should I mail it?"

Nope. Absolutely not. Anything he had he could keep. Better yet, he could fold it until it was all sharp corners and shove it where the sun didn't shine. "No thanks. You keep it."

"But they're photos of you and your mom. Surely, you'll want those."

How in the world had he gotten hold of those? For a moment, I wavered. No, no, I had scanned copies on my computer. I didn't need anything from him. "No. Goodbye, Armand. Don't call me again."

I clicked off before he could draw me into a discussion. My heart raced, and my hands felt clammy, clasped in my lap. *Fermented sheep nuggets, how does he always manage to get me so upset?*

Marcus placed a hand on mine. "Are you okay?"

I gave a hasty nod while swallowing. "I'm fine, I'm fine. It was just my ex."

He picked up my hand and enfolded it in both of his. "Let me know if you need to talk things out, like."

Tara scowled at him. I had no wish to piss the violent little Pixie Tara off. Sure, I had at least seven inches on her and probably twice her mass, but she was a hellcat. and I didn't want to mess with her.

Pulling my hand away, I shook my head. "I'll be fine."

"No, really. Why don't I come back with you after lunch? I'll be a good listener, and you can have a nice cry. No judgment."

I'd never been skilled at turning men down. The danger that they'd go postal on me always lurked beneath my rejection. I'd seen the results of jealous, angry men too many times in the hospital.

Holding the image of one battered woman in my mind, I steeled my spine. "I said no."

Another awkward silence descended upon us as our food arrived. As soon as I wolfed my burger down, I gave Marcus some cash. "Thanks. I've got to get going."

I hurried out the door, but he followed, touching my arm. "Skye! Have I done something wrong?"

I pulled away, panic rising again. Armand had always been so persuasive up to the point that he didn't care anymore. "I said, I'm fine. Can you just back off? Go finish your lunch."

Tara glared at us through the window, then her expression changed to one of smug satisfaction.

CHAPTER THIRTEEN

After escaping from Marcus's attentions, I made a beeline for home. I needed to be away from people and maybe give in to the shakes.

People who wanted something from me, people who didn't like me, people who were jealous of me for no reason… just people.

Of course, as soon as I entered the pub, Finn gave a cheery wave. They had their radio up loud with some K-pop music. Not my style, but they were moving to it while they worked.

However, the pounding and screeching instruments did my head no good whatsoever. To get away from the noise, I made a beeline through my house into the back garden.

Now that the weather had turned colder, I didn't spend much time there. The house had a kitchen garden with herbs, a flower garden, and a patch for vegetables. Not that much was growing now, since Gran had passed last year.

There were also three outbuildings, mostly with gardening equipment and tools. No real farmer would say so, but this city girl considered it a farm.

I found solitude amongst the plants. I hadn't been able to do a lot with the growing things over the summer. Sean had helped me a few times with weeding and keeping the wild under control.

I truly had no idea what was a weed and what was an herb. Flowers, I could identify. Lemon basil? Thai basil? Rosemary, I knew. Garlic, only if I dug down for the bulbs. Far from green, my thumb was hopelessly black.

But I had a bench out there, in the middle of the peace of the kitchen garden. Only the bass from the lads' music came out this far.

Faelan rubbed against my leg, so I bent down to scratch behind his ears. He jumped on the bench next to me and purred.

I asked, "Is there something you want?"

He just kept purring.

Fine. If he wasn't going to talk, it was time to break out my bribes. I went back inside to the cupboard and pulled out the catnip mouse. "I've got a gift for you."

A momentary flash of something in his eyes gave me pause. Should I be giving a gift to a fairy cat? But this was *my* fairy cat. I fed him every day, right?

I placed the mouse in front of him.

Faelan sniffed at the mouse, batted it once, then stared up at me. "What is this object?"

Aha! It had succeeded in getting him to talk, at least. "A mouse."

"It is not a mouse. It is a clump of fabric. What is the stench?"

I suppressed a giggle. "Catnip. It's meant to make you happy. To keep you amused."

"I am not amused. Take it away."

Hiding my disappointment at his lukewarm reaction, I placed the mouse back into the cupboard.

Once it had disappeared, Faelan asked, "Have you discovered the cause yet?"

"Cause of what?"

His tail whipped back and forth. "The cause of the dream-stealer. The cause for the rip between the worlds."

A trickle of fear ran down my spine. "What rip between the worlds? What are you talking about?"

That maddening cat chose that moment to bound away, disappearing from sight in an instant.

Bloody animal.

But his comment inspired me to take stock of my clues so far. Declan's missing necklace, a mirror shard, some burnt herbs, a scrap of animal skin, a stone tool. These spoke of some primitive ceremony, some ritual.

A ritual for what? Something related to the dreams? And why were the Mystic Moon Meadow folks being so cagy about it?

If they'd been doing something innocent, they shouldn't be reluctant to talk about it. Then again, it wasn't my business, was it? I couldn't blame them for resenting my nosiness.

The image of the dead man sprawled out on my pub floor lingered in the back of my mind. No, Declan's body in my building had made it my business. I glanced back at the house and shuddered, even though no part of the pub was visible from my garden.

And he'd been taking LSD. Had he done so willingly? Had hallucinations made him scratch his own face? Or some creature of the Good Folks that came to drive him out of his ever-loving mind?

Were they using LSD as part of whatever ritual they were being so secretive about?

Maybe I should hunt Jess down and discuss the bits and bobs. She might be able to help me sort them out. Of course, she could also tell me I was worrying too much over nothing and that I should leave it alone.

A dragonfly fluttered into the garden, and I watched, bemused as it landed on first one berry bush, and then a second.

My own sense of preservation was telling me the same thing. My conscience wanted to discover what had happened to Declan, why everyone was dreaming other people's dreams, and how it all connected together.

Besides, I loved solving puzzles, and this was a doozy.

I was so engrossed in my thoughts I didn't even hear any footsteps, but suddenly, Tara was next to me on the bench.

She must have come up the path behind me. "What are you doing here?" I couldn't help the tetchiness in my voice, and stood to face her, every muscle tensed.

The other woman got to her feet as well, standing mere inches from me. "I'm here to warn you off, you meddling cow. You're sticking your Yank nose in where it's not wanted. Stay away from Marcus, too. You're not wanted here."

I didn't want anything to do with Marcus other than friendship, but I bridled at her accusations. I knew de-escalation techniques from work, but she had me so riled up, I couldn't remember any of them. "I didn't realize Marcus was your lover now. I thought Liam had inherited that title. After Declan, that is. Is Nabil next? Do you plan on stringing them up in a garland?"

She growled and, if I hadn't been watching for it, her punch would have landed right on my Yank nose. But I was a nurse, and this was far from the first time I'd confronted an angry patient. I was paying attention to the signs and ducked, pulling her arm around the way they taught me.

Nursing sometimes required a lot of tricks to subdue patients. Tara was so tiny, and I could practically bench-press her. However, I satisfied myself with wrenching her arm behind her back. "Now, that wasn't very neighborly of you. I suggest you go away, Tara. This is my house and my land. Stay off."

"Not a feckin' hope, cow. We were doing just fine until you started messing about." She struggled and hissed at me, trying to get free.

"Declan was doing fine, was he? I didn't even know you people until he ended up dead in my pub. Did you do that? Was it a jealous rage? You do have quite the temper." I wondered if I could manhandle her off the property. I didn't trust her to leave of her own accord.

Besides, I'd had enough of her animosity and needed to eject her now. I stumbled forward, but she resisted every step, despite my grip on her arm behind her back. "Get. Out."

"Feck. Off. You. Massive. *Cow.*"

A few more stumbles, and she wriggled until she slipped out of my lock. She spun, her fingers clawing for my face. I jerked back, my nursing instincts setting in again.

I was about to kick her foot out from under her when a huge black mass flew at her head. Faelan had latched onto her skull, and by her screams, was scratching the heck out of her.

"Ow! Get him off! Off! Help!"

I wanted to laugh out loud, but I was the very model of grace. "If you leave, he'll let you go. It's as simple as that, Tara."

She darted along the side yard and out the front gate. Once she went through, Faelan leapt off her face and walked calmly toward me, his tail in the air. From his gait, he was full of smug satisfaction.

It took a few long moments of deep breaths before I could think again.

After her display of violence, I was more convinced than ever that Tara had killed Declan. I still had no real proof. All the evidence was purely coincidental.

But if she'd killed him, who'd beaten her up? I must be missing something essential, and it was driving me nuts.

The chill was getting bad again, so I lit a fire in the hearth. The earthy, tangy aroma of peat was still a lovely wonder to me.

With a fresh cup of Barry's tea in my hand, I paced in my parlour, trying to puzzle everything out, but every notion came back to Tara. With a growl of frustration, I pulled out a pad and pencil to create a grid of what had happened to who, where, and when.

When had the Moonlit Mystic Muckity-Muck group arrived in Ballybás? I wasn't entirely sure, but it must have been at least a week ago. My dreams started going wonky last Thursday. If the new-agers had done their ceremony and summoned this dream creature, then they must have arrived in town no later than Monday, September 21st.

If they did their first ritual that night, that would work out. It might have been a day or two earlier, but I hadn't gotten the impression from Jess that they'd been there longer. Besides, Eileen only let her B&B rooms out for a week at a time. She said that any more felt too permanent.

I took another sip of my tea, but it was growing cold. I grimaced and freshened it from the pot.

And then there was Audrey. Hadn't Jess mentioned that her sister had just shown up that week? She was at least nominally with the group, even if she didn't seem to partake in their celebrations.

She was so entangled in this mess. I was so glad I hadn't asked her to help with my accounting. I still needed to find someone, though.

Leaning against the table, I stared at all the notes. They started to swim before my eyes, dancing on the page like some demented cartoon.

I dug my fingers into my scalp. There were just so many things I didn't know. This might be impossible.

So, Tara and Declan used to date, but then they broke up. Had he broken up with her or vice versa? That could be essential information. Now, she seemed to be with Liam, but she'd acted all jealous when Marcus flirted with me. Maybe she just wanted all the men? Greedy much? But I'd seen crazier things.

I drained the dregs of my tea and poured another cup. This mess might even require a three-cup solution. Then, I wrote down more questions to be answered.

Did Nabil factor into this at all? He seemed the most level-headed of the group, by far. The type to just sit back and watch the antics of the others. Then again, the quiet types were sometimes the most dangerous of them all.

I couldn't forget about the mysterious stranger from the meeting. He certainly looked the part to have murdered Declan. But if mister tall, dark, and angry was some sort of hit man, why would he stay in town after the murder? Maybe he was hoping to get whatever money Declan owed from his girlfriend.

Or his ex-girlfriend. Suddenly, I was worried for both Audrey and Tara's safety.

Did Declan have any more ex-girlfriends? How many of them had hooked up in a row? Maybe I should chart them out. As I sipped my drink, I wrote all the names on my pad, with brackets for relationships, as far as I knew them.

Audrey, Tara, Marcus, Liam, random mafia guy; anyone could be the killer. Heck, even Nabil could be guilty, though he seemed pretty mild. Where was everyone on Friday morning when Declan was killed? I didn't even have any alibis to rule out suspects.

So, I pivoted to the dates. If they had their first ritual on Wednesday the 21st, the switched dreams began the next night, on the 22nd. Declan was killed on Friday the 23rd, which gave two whole days for tempers to rise to the point of murder.

Then, Faelan had that skirmish with the goat who had been a fairy creature, a púca. How did that fit into all of this? Was it related at all or just a coincidence?

Out of habit, I scanned the dark shadows for my cat, but none of the blackness had shining eyes.

After that, Marcus invited me and Jess out for a party at the stone circle. That was on Monday, the 26th, and we danced, sang, and drank. Then, we got drugged against our will, which I was still pissed off about.

Granted, I no longer had to worry about failing a drug test for work. But Armand had once slipped me something, and I'd failed a surprise drug test a few days later.

Now that I thought about it, that had happened shortly before I found out about him and Marie, who *used* to be my best friend. And Marie was friends with Teri, my ex-boss.

I hadn't connected the dots before, but that might have all been planned. A surge of rage tasted bitter in my mouth and it was several moments before I could wash it away with equally bitter tea.

I had truly loved and trusted Marie, once upon a time. Her betrayal with Armand had been so difficult to swallow. This realization was even worse.

Whether it was or not, once bitten, a thousand times shy.

Anyway, back to my timeline, and my third cup of tea. Fourth? Whatever.

Was Audrey already in town before their ceremony? Or had she arrived before that? I thought I remembered Jess saying she'd been there for a few days. So, if I operated under the assumption she'd come to town first, she had motive and opportunity. Did she have the means?

I wondered if she had long nails.

So, we went out drinking, and I found Declan's necklace. At least Tara said it was his. What if she'd been lying? I wasn't exactly thinking straight at that point and my memory refused to pull up any details about her body language. In fact, I'd wandered home high as a kite and had someone else's nightmares.

But what about the clues? I'd found that fabric from Audrey's belt next to Declan's necklace. What if Audrey discovered that Declan had been messing with someone else? I imagine she had quite the temper, too. She might have been the last person to see him alive.

Could Audrey really have killed her own boyfriend? She was worried about money to pay off his debts. It must have occurred to her that if he died, she'd be better off, money-wise. I had to consider it as a possibility, anyhow.

Killers were much more likely to be lovers or ex-lovers.

The next day, I'd returned to the stone circle and found the other items. A broken piece of mirror, some burnt herbs, a bit of hide, and a flint weapon. Which could all have been unrelated, for all I knew. They might have been there for weeks before the MMM muppets arrived.

Or they could have been the items for that ritual, the Tarbh Feis. Was it in Gran's diary or the library? Something about primitive tools and burnt herbs.

My head was spinning, and I couldn't think straight, but at least I was getting all the facts. When I stood to make myself a sandwich, the room spun. I sat right back down again.

What was going on? My brain felt like it was pulsing, sort of like it had at the stone circle. Only this time, I hadn't drunk any of Liam's homemade concoctions.

Had Barry's betrayed me? I stared into my swirling tea.

CHAPTER FOURTEEN

The rest of that day was a blur. I had no firm grasp on anything except the arms of my comfy chair and, occasionally, Faelan in my lap.

Despite that coziness, whenever I dipped into a nap, flashes of strange scenes haunted my dreams. Running from machine gun fire in a desert. Swamped in a busy kitchen. Lost in a grocery store. Each one pounded on my anxiety.

When I woke, my body ached. I pulled a full-body stretch and dragged myself out of the chair. The sun was no longer shining through the kitchen window. Instead, when I craned my neck to peer into the pub, it was streaming through those newly repaired stained-glass windows. A kaleidoscope of colors painted the pub interior. I didn't understand. How had the building spun around? Buildings didn't do that, right?

The sun wasn't where it was supposed to be. Why it was in the east? When I moved, my neck hurt. Rubbing it, I stretched back and forth, trying to relieve the crick. I must have slept the entire night in that chair.

Stumbling to the kitchen, I was about to make myself some coffee when I stared at the tap. I must have been drugged. Was it the water?

Then, I smelled my armpit. *No, that wasn't nice at all.* Instead of making some magical morning elixir, I trudged upstairs for a thorough shower and fresh clothing.

As I descended again, feeling marginally more human, I poured a glass of milk, hoping that was safe, and fell back into the cozy chair. My mind was still muzzy from whatever had happened last night. I stared at the pale liquid, marveling at the pristine white.

A rap on wood roused me from admiring the milk. "Miss Skye?"

Trying to clear the wool from my mind, I turned to find Finn gazing at me anxiously. When had they come in? A vague recollection of stumbling to the door and then falling asleep in the chair again gave me my answer. I cleared my throat and spoke in an almost normal tone, "What d'you need, Finn?"

"It's just that we've finished the painting, like. At least, the top part above the wainscotting. Would you like to take a look?"

I would dearly love to curl into my bed and finish riding out whatever I'd been tripping on, but I couldn't let the cousins see my state. How did I get dosed? Was it in something I drank last night? Some sort of contact contagion?

I glanced at the wall clock. How was it already past noon? A thousand possibilities ran rampant through my brain as I followed Finn into the pub, a small knot of doubt heavy in my stomach. Maybe I should call Adanna to give myself a drug test.

They had all the lights on, which were shining on the cream-colored walls. They'd painted the edging a dark brown, and it resembled half-timbered decoration. That gave the room a quaint, charming feel, and a smile crept across my face.

I had to admit, they'd done a pretty good job.

All the fixtures were taped, and the tarp protected the hardwood floor from random drips. The wainscotting itself had been removed and would be replaced once they applied striped wallpaper to the bottom half.

So, they'd probably be hammering away again for the rest of the day. My head definitely couldn't handle that right now. "It looks great, lads. Why don't you take the rest of the day off?"

Finn and Rory exchanged a concerned glance. "Off? But you're always saying as how you're worried about the job taking so long."

I waved a dismissal. "No, you boys deserve it. Go on. Have a pint on me." I handed them a €20 note.

Another glance, and they nodded as one. "Right you are, Miss Skye. We'll be back tomorrow."

Once they left, I sank back into my comfy chair. I didn't dare drink my cold coffee. What if my water supply were tainted? Could I get it tested? Maybe, but not right now. I didn't trust myself to walk outside in this state.

Someone knocked at the door. *Sheep nuggets, what now?* I pulled myself out of the chair and stumbled through the pub.

When I opened the door, Sean's grinning face greeted me, carrying two shopping bags. Then, Marcus entered the yard behind him, walking toward the door, also carrying shopping bags. I blinked, not understanding.

Sean gave a half-smile with a flicker of a glance toward the other man. "I hope I'm not intruding. I brought the fixtures I needed to repair those lights in your hallway. And a couple of treats for dessert." He held up a plastic container with what looked like cookies inside.

Numbly, I nodded and stepped inside to let him in, then turned to the blond man.

Marcus held up his bag. "I bring a peace offering. Would you care for some fish and chips?"

I glanced back at Sean, who was already down the hallway with his cookies. That's when I realized I hadn't eaten a thing yet.

My stomach rebelled at the very idea of food, much less something as rich and fried as fish and chips. That much grease and salt made great late night drunk food. Not so great on a stomach trying to figure out what drugs it was on.

Still, I didn't want to seem ungrateful. "Uh, come on in, but I'm not that hungry."

He gave a shrug and strode through the pub and into the parlour. That made me narrow my eyes. As far as I knew, Marcus had never been inside my place before. How would he know where to go? Had Gran had him over? I penciled his name onto my mental suspect list.

As he set the bag on the kitchen counter and pulled out the food, Marcus said, "Sean, here, was telling me about the work you're having done on the place. It looks good! When do you think you'll be opening the pub?"

"No idea. Maybe in two or three months, if all the inspections go well." The aroma of the fish slapped against me as I tried to keep my belly from roiling.

"In January? That's a rough time to be opening a pub, even in Ireland."

I tried to keep the impatience out of my reply. "The timing isn't planned on a marketing campaign. It's planned on a 'when can I get the work done' campaign."

Sean peered around the corner from the hallway, "She's perfectly competent to judge her own affairs, like."

A scowl flickered over Marcus's face, and he jerked a thumb toward the hall. "Are you his girl, then?"

Irritation turned my tone prickly, and I'd had about enough of him. "No, I'm not his 'girl.' I'm not anyone's 'girl.' I'm my own woman."

His eyes grew wide, but I was on a roll, and didn't feel like easing off.

"Where do you get these antiquated concepts? You're like those old men in the photos on the wall." I gestured toward the wall with my ancestors' fading portraits. "Do they teach such things in Irish schools? Some special class for manly men? Some red Kool-Aid that everyone has to drink?"

Marcus backed up, his hands up. "Whoa, there, Mizz Feminist. I meant no offense. Wait, what's that about Kool-Aid?"

Sean called out, "It's a reference to some cult from the seventies."

The other man cocked his head. My irritation had faded, but I was still miffed. "There was this cult guru who set up a compound in South America, and then commanded everyone to drink this poisoned Kool-Aid. Because he'd brainwashed them all into thinking he was a messiah, everyone obeyed, and they all died."

Marcus's eyes grew wide. "No, missus! I mean, we all had the typical Irish da for induction into the Irish school of misogyny. But we choose our own drugs."

I narrowed my gaze. "Drugs. Yeah, I meant to ask you about that. The other night at the stone circle, did Liam dose me with something?"

He furrowed his brow. "We were all pretty high, but I don't think he gave you anything special. You drank his concoction, right? We all did. That didn't make me any worse for wear."

"What did you take? Was it before you arrived?"

Sean came in, dusting his hands off. "What's this about drugs?"

Armand had gloated when I realized he'd drugged me. Memories of his smarmy face kept intruding on my mind, but I shoved them away. I needed to figure this out.

Turning to Sean, I said, "When Jess and I went up to the standing stones with this lot, I was dizzy and had hallucinations. Far more than just being drunk would make me. Besides, I only drank a few bottles of cider."

Marcus let out a snort. "And whatever Liam gave you in that bottle."

I took a deep breath. "I'm woozy today, too. But I haven't been anywhere near Liam and his bottles."

Sean placed a gentle hand on my shoulder, his expression worried. "Are you okay, Skye? Do you need to sit down?"

He glowered at Marcus. "What was in it? What did you give her?"

The Dublin man gave a shrug. "Who knows? Liam's always experimenting with new things. I doubt he'd put anything harder than alcohol, though. Sure, he loves his trips, like, but he wouldn't share with a stranger without consent. And I haven't even seen him today."

That made me feel a little less angry, but I still needed to know what was going on. "If he didn't dose me, who did? Both Jess and I were definitely on something. And today…"

Sean gave a rueful grin. "Come to think about it, I've had a couple odd experiences myself lately."

"Have you?" I glanced at Marcus, but he just shrugged. "What sort of experiences? Are you still having someone else's dreams?"

He scratched behind his ear as he thought. "Aye, we talked about that in the town meeting, but this is more than that.

Times when I was dizzy and needed to sit or I'd keel over. Or when I just knew I shouldn't drive. At one point, I swear Setanta was talking to me."

Faelan could talk, but he was a Cat Sídhe. I wondered briefly if Setanta was a Dog Sídhe. Was there such a thing? Or was this an audial hallucination?

Rubbing the back of his neck, Marcus said, "Uh, Liam might have more to do with that than you think."

We both turned to glare at him.

"Right. Well, there was this one time, up near Kells at this village called Crossakiel. Smaller than this place, maybe two hundred people."

"Go on."

"We'd done some rituals at Loughcrew, right? And then the whole place started acting strange. Surreal things, like people randomly running down the street, loud music everywhere. One woman was after drawing on the pavement with chalk, swirling designs in bright colors. Someone else couldn't stop laughing."

I pursed my lips. "And you think Liam had something to do with this?"

"Oh, he said not, but he loves experimenting, mostly on himself. That being said, he's talked us into it on occasion. He even got Tara so flying, she almost died one night."

His sour expression suggested he was pissed at Liam about that. Was he jealous of the two of them? That was an interesting data point.

There was a hint of steel in Sean's voice when he asked, "And is Liam capable of dosing us all? How would he do that?"

Marcus shrugged. "I'm not sure. He takes pride in his ingenuity. The more complex, the better, so. He always had this dream, an ultimate vision of nirvana."

I asked, "What sort of dream?"

"That we could all transcend this form into the next world. Not dying, like, but becoming something else. Something better, more spiritual." Marcus waved his hands above his head.

I was busy getting all the details down in my notebook. "I'll be fine. The dizziness has passed. I think we need to figure out what in the world Liam is doing and stop him." I glanced up at Marcus. "What do you know about hallucinogens?"

He gave a sly grin. "Not a whole lot. I've always preferred a pint of Guinness, myself."

"Fair." I stared at my notes, but I didn't see them. Other things kept bubbling up, reminders of Armand and his manipulation. Over and above dosing me on the sly, my ex-husband had spent a lot of my money on them. "Why would someone spend good money on drugs just to dose a whole village?"

Sean shook his head. "This Liam doesn't sound like a normal mate. More like a mad scientist, if you ask me."

"I'm really not liking your friend, Marcus." In fact, I wasn't liking Marcus much at this point. I wanted to ask him to leave, but it seemed so rude. Still, he did offer a few more details that might be relevant before the conversation tapered off again.

Sean came to my rescue. "Skye, I've got some questions for you about the décor you want in the hall. Do you have a moment?"

Marcus excused himself and, after he left, Sean lifted his eyebrows. "What do you think of all that? And are you sure you're feeling all right?"

What if it wasn't the drugs, or at least, not *just* the drugs? That dream-stealer was already affecting the town, but if there was more to it, the result could be some unholy terror across the entire town.

I didn't want to bring up the shadow creature with Sean, though. Did he believe in the Good Folk like Adanna did? What if he thought I was a moonbat by bringing up the subject? But he'd said he had a swapped dream. "Sean, have you ever heard of a... a dream-stealer?"

He wrinkled his nose. "No, that's a new one to me. Did you read about one?"

"No, but it seemed to be relevant to what's been happening. Unless these dreams are really just someone dosing everyone with drugs."

Sean gave a shrug. "It could be. Who knows?"

Now, I felt like a fool, so I switched to a safer subject. "Are you all done in the hallway?"

Not quite hiding a startled expression, he glanced down the hall. "More or less. You have new lights there, but a few in the utility room could use an update."

"That sounds great, thank you."

He stared at me for a moment. "I hope you don't mind me saying, you look pure knackered, Skye."

I gave him a scowl. "Oh, thanks for noticing how awful I look."

"No, I mean, you're just stressed. Why don't you come over and help me bake for the after-church crowd this week?"

"Bake? Me?" I let out a hearty laugh. "You do not want me anywhere near an oven, Sean. I am absolutely no good in the kitchen."

He gave me a half-smile and stepped closer, his breath warm on my face. "Let me know if you want to learn. It helps me relax, and I'm an excellent teacher."

My cheeks heated up. I shouldn't kick him out, as that would be hopelessly rude. But I didn't want him here watching me blush.

Also, I wanted to call Jess and Adanna and go over this theory about Liam and drugs.

After another heartbeat, Sean let out a deep breath. He gathered his tools and gave a jaunty wave as he exited through the pub.

After a moment to think about how Sean made me feel like a schoolgirl, but in a good way, I reminded myself firmly that I still wasn't ready for all that.

I grabbed my phone and texted Adanna.

I found out some interesting things. Do you have some time to come over for a cuppa? Oh, and bring some bottled water.

After sending Jess a similar text, my phone klaxon went off. Glancing at the number, it had a United States origin. I switched it off. A few minutes later, I had a voicemail.

With great trepidation, I listened to it. "Skye, *mi corazón*, it looks like you've been a busy beaver. Why won't you answer my calls? It's always so fun to make you angry. And so easy."

Goosebumps rose on my skin. Fear and anxiety warred with anger and frustration.

I clicked off and blocked the number. I didn't care if it wouldn't work. He'd been using different numbers each time he called. They weren't even Miami area codes, so he must be spoofing numbers.

Had it been three or four times in the last few weeks? I'd lost count. It wouldn't do any good to report him, as he hadn't done anything wrong except make me afraid. I could just imagine McCarthy's expression if I tried to file a restraining order on a phone call from Florida.

Besides, who would have jurisdiction? I was in Ireland, and he was calling from the States.

I hoped.

The notion that Armand was in Ireland brought those goosebumps right back.

CHAPTER FIFTEEN

Jess and Adanna arrived at the same time, chatting as they strolled through the pub and settled on the sofa. Adanna handed me a six-pack of bottled water. "Is your water off?"

"You could say that." I gave her a mysterious grin and put the kettle on. "I suspect there might be something wrong with my water. I got really dizzy last night."

A few minutes later, I poured the tea. Adanna said, "Have you had the water tested? Or yourself?"

I shook my head. "I'm still trying to get my senses back into order. I called the water department. They can't send anyone out just yet."

Adanna asked, "You said you'd found out something else, though?"

I took a sip of my tea, though it was still too hot. "I did. Evidently, one of that new age group has been in the habit of experimenting with drugs."

Jess let out a laugh. "Half of Ireland has been in the habit of experimenting with drugs. Both legal and otherwise."

Adanna rolled her eyes, but said, "She's not lying."

I waved that away. "No, I mean, actually doing experiments. Dosing people without their knowledge, making observations, that sort of thing. That's one reason I'm suspicious of my water supply."

Adanna sat forward. "And you think that's what's happening here? Some sort of drug trial, conducted on the whole village?"

Pressing my lips together, I shrugged. "It would explain a lot. But I don't think it's entirely that. There's something else to the dream shenanigans."

I took a deep breath before diving in, hoping my new friends wouldn't laugh out loud at me. "When I was up at the stone circle, something was watching me. Something shadowy and dangerous."

This time, Jess leaned forward, her gaze intent. "What did it look like?"

"Did you not hear the shadowy part? Just that. Darkness, glowing eyes, with a vaguely human shape." A shiver ran down my spine at the memory.

Adanna furrowed her brow. "How did you banish it?"

I gave a sharp laugh. "Banish it? There was no banishing. There was only running. Faelan helped me escape."

Then, I remembered that Jess didn't know about Faelan's Cat Sídhe status. She must have had her suspicions, because she didn't bat an eye.

Adanna tapped her chin. "So, we're talking about both human meddling and Good Folk meddling. That definitely qualifies as interesting."

"Marcus told us that Liam loved playing with LSD. I'm convinced that he somehow managed to dose us at the circle that night. And maybe a few times since."

I'd been watching Adanna's expression, and when I mentioned LSD, she blinked. Declan had tested positive for it, according to that toxicology report. The doctor narrowed her eyes. "'Marcus told *us?*' You and who else?"

"Sean was here, replacing my hall lights."

Jess had a silly grin on her face. "Of course, he was. Has he offered to bring you a cake yet?"

"What?"

Now, Adanna wore a grin, too. "Sean loves baking. It's his primary mode of flirting."

My cheeks grew warm, even though there was nothing going on between us. "He did offer to teach me how to bake."

Adanna raised her eyebrows. "And? Did you accept? Tell us!"

With a roll of my eyes, I said, "No, I did not. I'm a horrible cook. I'd probably end up setting him on fire. Anyhow," I raised my voice over their protests, "Anyhow, Sean said he'd also been having some dizzy spells. So, If Liam was dosing us, could he have dosed the whole village?"

Adanna shrugged. "It's certainly possible."

"Which brings me to asking, where *does* the village get their water supply?"

Jess waved inland. "There's a natural spring just up your hill here. That supplies most of our water. But if he added drugs to the spring, they'd be horribly diluted, wouldn't they?"

Adanna nodded absently. "Unless he added it closer in, like at the filtering station. Most folks wouldn't notice a difference, but Skye, the station is just on the other side of the empty farm on the corner. Your house would probably get the strongest dose."

Things were beginning to slip into place, and my antipathy toward Liam rose several notches.

What in the name of all that was holy was wrong with this guy? How dare he drug me? Sure, I took a chug of his alcohol, but LSD? Seriously? What if I'd had a bad reaction? We'd been miles away from a hospital.

I still didn't understand why he would do something like this. I clutched my cup so hard it slipped out of my grip and spilled on the rug.

Jess rushed to the kitchen to grab some paper towels while I retrieved Gran's china teacup from the floor. Luckily, it wasn't even chipped. After we mopped up the mess, we all sat back again.

Adanna still looked pensive. "And this shadowy figure, he's this dream-stealer, do you think?"

"I do. I did some research, but I can't quite figure out what he might be, if he's even a creature in the lore. The only thing I could find that might even be slightly related is the Tarbh Feis."

Jess nodded with a thoughtful expression. "The bull feast? Oh, for your group at the stones? Sure and that would be the sort of ritual they were up for. Which meant they were trying divination."

With a grim smile, Jess said, "It sounds like we need to give Liam a visit. He owes us several explanations."

In the ink black of the September evening, Adanna, Jess, and I marched down to the other end of the village, determined to find answers.

I was surprised to see a few pumpkins out already, carved with faces. Smaller carved faces peeked out here and there. I recalled Gran mentioned the Irish tended to carve turnips rather than pumpkins, and that they lasted longer. The turnips looked much more sinister with their flat slit eyes and tiny mouths.

My anxiety was shifting into hyperdrive. "What if he isn't there?"

Adanna let out a low chuckle. "Let me worry about that."

Once we arrived at Eileen's B&B, it loomed in the darkness. Every muscle in my body screamed that this was a horrible idea, but the stubborn side of my mind said that to stop now would be quitting. Besides, we were with Adanna, so we'd be safe from the Gardaí.

Adanna knocked on the door, which was decorated with a cardboard black cat. After a moment, Eileen answered, her eyes widening in surprise when she saw us. "Adanna? What are you doing here?"

I'd only met Eileen Donovan a few times. She ran the B&B and the local Irish language radio station. Her husband had died a few years ago, but that hadn't slowed her down a bit, according to Jess.

"We need to look inside Liam's room," Adanna said, her tone firm. "It's important."

Eileen hesitated, glancing between us. "What's this about?"

"Please, Eileen," Jess said, stepping forward. "We think Liam might be involved in something dangerous."

The older woman's eyes narrowed, but she stepped aside, allowing us in. Then, she reached for a board of keys behind her and handed us one. "This key will work."

Her front room was far fancier than mine, with polished oak floors that gleamed under the light of a crystal chandelier. Everything about her B&B spoke of experience, professionalism, and a touch of old-world charm.

Mine, by contrast, was still a work in progress. Sure, I'd painted the walls and sanded the floors, but the furniture was mismatched, and the décor screamed more "cozy fixer-upper" than "boutique getaway."

Then again, her B&B had six rooms, and mine only had three. A pang of doubt settled in my chest. Could I really pull this off? What if I'd bitten off more than I could chew? I shoved the thought aside, forcing a smile.

Three chintz-covered sofas faced a peat fireplace, burning with gentle heat. Two walls were covered with bookshelves, though one held board games as well. The clink of silverware came from the next room. Either interrupted Eileen's own dinner or she was serving her guests.

"He's not there just now, but he's due back soon. His is room two, first one on the left."

We climbed the narrow stairs to Liam's room, the floorboards creaking under our weight. When we reached the door, Adanna's hand clutching the key hovered over the lock.

"Ready?" she asked.

I nodded, my heart pounding in my chest. Jess gave a small, determined nod. Adanna unlocked and pushed the door open, then we stepped inside.

The room was a mess, clothes strewn everywhere, and the stink of sweat and stale alcohol hung in the air. First, I glanced over his suitcase, but other than dirty socks, I found nothing of note.

Jess ran her hands over the books on the shelf, but those would belong to the host, not the guest.

I studied the desk in the corner and found several snapshots in colorful frames. One of Liam and a white, fluffy dog. Another of him, Tara, and Declan, all laughing. They must have been great friends at one time.

Adanna had ducked into the small en suite bathroom, and from the clinking of bottles, was going through the medicine cabinet. "I think I found something!"

She came back in, holding a tiny brown bottle with a tissue. Bringing it over to the window to read the label, she squinted. "Ah, no, just prescription eye drops."

With a sigh of disappointment, I turned my attention to the small wooden table by the window. Tucked underneath, in the shadows, I found several whiskey bottles of various sizes.

One of them looked familiar and I went to pick it up, my fingers trembling.

Adanna said, "Stop! Use a tissue."

"Of course, sorry." I grabbed one from a lace-covered box on the windowsill.

The label said *Teeling 24-year-old whiskey*, with remnants of dust still clinging to the glass. "This looks like one of Gran's bottles," I said, turning it over in my hands. The dust felt greasy, like the other bottles in my pub. "The ones that went missing. That puts him at the scene of the murder, doesn't it?"

Jess frowned at the bottle. "Are you sure it's the same one?"

I peered more closely at it. There was a number indicating it was a small batch, but I couldn't tell if it was the right number.

Gran's voice tickled my mind. *That's one of mine. That eejit stole it, sure enough!*

Since I couldn't very well tell my friends that Gran had just verified it for me, I said, "I recognize the batch number."

With another tissue, Adanna took the bottle from me, carefully not touching the glass. She held it up to the light and shook it, peering at the tiny bit of liquid left. "We need to test the residue inside. If there's anything suspicious, it might be the break we need."

Just then, footsteps came down the hall. I spun around just as the door slammed open. Liam stood there, his face contorted in anger. "What the feck are you doing in my room?"

With a deep breath, I steeled myself for the confrontation. "We found this," I said, holding up the bottle. "Care to explain why you have it?"

Liam's eyes flickered to the bottle, then back to us. He lifted his chest and his chin. "That's *mine*. I bought it."

My voice shook with anger, and I took a step closer. Adrenaline fueled my words. "This bottle was stolen from my pub the night Declan was killed. We know you had something to do with it."

Liam sneered, taking a step toward us. "You have no proof. Get out, or I'll call the Gardaí."

"It's easy enough to check the batch number against Gran's records." Those were non-existent, but he didn't know that.

I glanced at Adanna and couldn't help a slight smirk. "Call the Gardaí, then." I doubted even Donal would arrest his own wife.

But she placed a hand on my arm, urging me back. "We're leaving, Liam. But this isn't over."

He tried to block us leaving but I stared him down and he stepped aside. I let out a breath of relief because I really wasn't up to a physical confrontation.

We hurried out of the room with the bottle, Liam's threats echoing behind us. As we descended the stairs, I realized Liam hadn't sounded nearly as laid back and chill as he normally did. Had that all been an act? What did he have to hide? Then again, we had been in his room without his permission.

A sneaking suspicion that Liam was the killer crept into my mind. I wrote his name below the others in my mind's list.

CHAPTER SIXTEEN

Back at Adanna's surgery, we gathered around her little conference table. The whiskey bottle sat in the center, as Adanna extracted a sample for testing. I paced back and forth, glancing up now and then.

Jess, perched on a stool, watched me with concern. "Skye, try to relax. We'll know soon enough."

I stopped pacing, taking a deep breath. "I just want this to be over. I want to know who killed Declan and why. I want to know who's been messing with our dreams. And how the two are related."

Adanna finished her preparations and held a vial up to the lamp. "I've got a decent sample, and I can do a preliminary test here, but these are wide-spectrum. For anything conclusive, I'll need to send it to a lab in Cork. It might take a few days to get the results."

I nodded with a mix of anticipation and fear. I'd worried that she didn't have testing kits for something specialized like this, but I'd held a modicum of hope. "Thanks."

We sat in silence for a few moments, the weight of the situation pressing down on us. Finally, Adanna spoke again. "Skye, I know you're anxious, but you need to be patient. We'll get to the bottom of this."

I sighed, running a hand through my hair. "I know. It's just, all of this feels so surreal. Like a nightmare I can't wake up from. And it's not even my *own* nightmare."

Jess reached out and squeezed my hand. "We're in this together, Skye. We'll figure it out."

Adanna's phone buzzed, and she glanced at the screen. "I need to take this," she said, stepping out of the room.

As she left, I looked at Jess. "Do you think we're right about Liam?"

Jess bit her lip, thinking. "I don't know. He seems suspicious, but there's still a lot we don't know."

The clues were just swimming in space. Nothing was clicking together. "I just hope we're not missing something important."

Later that evening, I lay on my sofa with Faelan curled up on my chest. The house was quiet, the only sound the soft ticking of the clock on the wall and an occasional crackle from the peat burning in the hearth.

My mind was racing with everything that had happened, and I found myself second-guessing our conclusions about Liam.

He *must* have taken the bottles of whiskey. But was it the same time Declan was killed? I wasn't even certain that the murder happened here.

What if we were wrong? What if someone else was responsible for Declan's death? What if McCarthy decided to arrest us for going into Liam's room after all?

I stroked Faelan's fur, trying to calm my racing thoughts for almost twenty minutes, but nothing settled in my mind. Then, my gaze fell upon Gran's diary sat on the coffee table. I pushed the cat off and sat up, reached for it, then flipped through the pages. Maybe there was something I'd missed, some clue that would point us in the right direction.

Flipping through several sections on the care and feeding of hearth fae, how to recognize if a fae was bothering one's cows, and how to charge water with magic, I came across a passage about divination rituals and the dangers they could bring. It didn't mention the Tarbh Feis but had some general warnings of how dangerous they could be. My mind flashed back to the shadow creatures and the sense of dread seeping into my bones.

My phone klaxon interrupted my study, and I reached for it, my heart pounding, checking to make sure it was an Irish number first. It was Adanna, so I answered.

"Skye," she said, her voice urgent. "I got the preliminary results, but they aren't conclusive. We need to wait for the lab results to be sure."

My breath caught in my throat. "What does your test say?"

"It tested positive for something, but the color isn't listed on the test kit," Adanna said. "Someone definitely drugged the whiskey, but I have no idea with what."

I let out a frustrated sigh. "I suppose you'll have to go back to Dublin yet again to get the proper test?"

She took a painfully long pause before responding. "Are my trips to Dublin inconveniencing you in some way, Skye?" Her tone was sharp.

Sheep nuggets! I'd definitely stepped in it with that comment, so I shifted to a safer topic. "No, no, I'm sorry. I didn't mean anything by that. But is this preliminary test enough proof to bring to your husband?"

"I'll talk to him when he gets back from his current call."

"Okay, thanks." I hung up, the phone still warm in my hand. A spark of determination lit in my chest, sharp and unrelenting. We were closing in, peeling back the layers of this mystery one stubborn piece at a time.

A mighty yawn reminded me that this had been a very long day, and an even longer night. I put away Gran's diary and trudged upstairs.

That night, as I tried to find sleep, the events of the last week spun through my head. Which is probably why another nightmare visited me.

The night was a void, cold and howling with wind. Each step plunged my feet deeper into the muck, the mud clinging and sucking at my boots. My hand stretched out blindly, brushing against a small mound of dried grass, brittle and stiff beneath my fingers.

I tried calling out, but my voice wouldn't work. I pulled one foot out with a disgusting sound and tested the ground in front of me, trying to find a solid spot, but there were none around me.

The hillock seemed pretty solid. I tried to lean on it, but that sank, too. The sinking feeling made panic rise in my chest, and my heart raced.

I shot upright with a yell, sweat dripping down my face and panting as if I'd just run a marathon.

A memory struck me of that night in May when we searched for Gerald. Adanna had flat-out refused to set foot in the bog, especially after dark. Now, still feeling the chill sinking into my bones and the mud clawing at my feet, I understood why.

This wasn't just fear. It was something deeper, something born of experience. A fragment of her past, something real and terrible, had taken root there.

No wonder Adanna refused to go into the bog.

The next morning dawned with pouring rain, although *dawned* probably wasn't the right word when I couldn't even see the sun.

I was about to make coffee with tap water, but remembered to use the bottled stuff I'd bought. While I was relaxing with my first coffee, the boys returned. Finn stuck his head in and let me know that they had some repairs to the molding before they hung paper on the lower half of the walls.

That told me all I needed to know. I had no doubt that the hammering would drive me outside, so I grabbed an umbrella and made tracks before the first headache started.

So much work to get that pub open again. If I'd known how much it was going to take, I might never have started the project. But it was what Gran would have wanted, and it was half-done already. Stopping now would be a huge waste. Besides, it was really my only plan.

My umbrella was big enough to keep my upper half dry, but by the time I arrived at the Blarney Scone, I was soaked from the waist down.

Once inside, I poked the umbrella back outside and shook the worst of the water off, before sticking it in the stand next to the door. No other customers were in the place, and it felt achingly empty.

I waved to Joshua, who was placing muffins in the glass display case. "Your usual, Skye?"

My stomach rumbled so loudly he must have heard it from the counter. Normally, I made do with a cinnamon scone slathered in blackberry jam, but with the rain drumming against the windows and the damp chill creeping into my bones, I craved something hot and hearty to chase the cold away. "I'm feeling like a change, so I'll grab a menu."

The laminated card was a little sticky at the edges, but I didn't mind. I slid into my usual spot by the plate-glass window, the best seat in the café for watching the world shuffle by. Outside, the rain was a steady curtain, softening the edges of the stone buildings and making the cobbled streets gleam like polished silver.

Not that many people were braving the weather. Máiréad bustled past clutching a plastic headscarf under her chin, her footsteps purposeful as she made her way to her shop. A cyclist wobbled by, his rain poncho flapping wildly behind him, while a pair of children splashed through puddles, their mother trailing behind with an exasperated look.

It wasn't long before Joshua appeared at my table, his easy grin as warm as the fireplace in the corner. He balanced a tray against one hip and tipped his head toward me. "What're you trying this bright and sunny morning?"

I smirked, glancing out at the misty gray downpour. *Bright and sunny, indeed.* "Bacon and scrambled eggs, please, with buttered toast. And a huge coffee!"

"Grand. It'll just be a few minutes."

The rain had eased but still fell in a steady rhythm. Ireland wasn't prone to heavy downpours, not like Miami, where from March through October, you could practically set your watch to the 2 p.m. storm.

In Miami, the rain came in fast and fierce, drenching the city in minutes before giving way to blazing sunshine. But the relief was short-lived. The heat returned with a vengeance, the air so thick with humidity it felt like wading through soup. Concrete and asphalt soaked it all in, turning the city into a sweltering sauna.

In Ireland, though, the rain lingered, soft and persistent, soaking into the earth and keeping everything green and alive. The air smelled of damp grass and peat, not hot pavement, and even on the grayest days, it felt like the land itself was breathing.

Someone bundled up against the weather hurried past outside, but I didn't recognize them.

Joshua returned with my coffee, and I flashed him a smile of gratitude. I cupped my hands around it and let out a sigh of contentment for both the warmth and the sweet, sweet caffeine.

The rain slackened more until it was barely a misty drizzle.

Finally, my warm beverage had cooled enough to drink. However, I barely had time to take a sip when the door swung open with a jingle, and in walked Liam and Tara, both looking like they'd rather be anywhere else but here.

I didn't have a good feeling about this.

Expecting another fight, I steeled myself as they stepped to my table.

Tara's cheeks were red. She spoke in a softer voice than I'd yet heard from her. "I wanted to…" she glanced at Liam, who nudged her. "I wanted to talk to you. About something important."

I didn't know how to deal with this quiet version of Tara. I glanced at Liam, who looked equally meek. What was going on with these two?

I tried to keep my tone even. "About what?"

She shook her head. "Not here, please. It's a private matter. Will you walk out back with us?"

Absolutely not. Not on your life. "How about out front?"

She let out a sign. "That'll do, like."

I caught Joshua's eye, and he raised his eyebrows. As I passed, he asked, "Will you be okay with them?"

I said in a low voice, "I should be, but if you'd peek out now and then, I'd appreciate it."

He gave a nod as I pulled on my jacket and went outside.

I stopped in plain sight of the café window, but Tara nodded to a side street. "Please. I don't want others to see."

That didn't sound at all suspicious. But I figured I was close enough that I could call for help if needed. We went to a side street but stayed a step away from the main road.

The rain had finally stopped, leaving the alley damp and rank. Cobblestones glistened with puddles, reflecting faint slivers of light from the café windows, while the air hung thick with the sour smell of wet earth and rotting garbage.

"Right," I said, folding my arms. "So, what's all this about?"

Tara's cheeks flushed bright red as she stared at her shoes, her usual fiery demeanor nowhere to be found. When she finally spoke, her voice was barely louder than the distant drip of water from the eaves. "I didn't want anyone else to hear my apology."

I blinked, certain I'd misheard. "An apology? From Tara the Warrior? Are you serious?"

I glanced at Liam, who leaned against the wall with an air of amused detachment. "Is she serious?"

Tara's head snapped up, and her enraged glare reignited with a vengeance. She stepped forward, shoving me hard enough that I stumbled back, my boots splashing in a puddle.

"You think this is funny?" she hissed, her voice sharp and venomous. "Is this another try to get him to ride you? You've been trying to push me aside ever since you got here. Is this your way of clearing the way for yourself to swoop in? To take Liam and Marcus too?"

Something snapped inside me. "Listen, if I'd wanted to get rid of you, I would have left your bleeding self on the cobblestones!"

"Ah, you couldn't do that. Your friends would know you for the coward you are. You just want all the men yourself, ye wagon!"

"What?" I shot back, genuinely baffled. "Tara, I just got divorced. The last thing I want is to deal with any more men. You can have them both, free of charge."

But she wasn't listening. Her anger boiled over, her voice rising. "You always have an excuse, don't you? Playing the victim, acting like you're innocent. But we all know the truth now, don't we?"

I furrowed my brow. "What truth? What are you talking about?"

"Ye bloody murderer!" Tara spat, pointing a trembling finger at me, her words echoing in the narrow alley.

I froze, the accusation hitting me like a slap. "Excuse me?"

"You heard her," Liam cut in, his voice low and cold. His smirk was gone, replaced by something darker. "You killed Declan. All this time, you've been pinning it on everyone else, playing detective to cover your tracks. Sure, you must have planted that bottle in my room."

My stomach flipped. "Are you out of your minds? I didn't kill anyone!"

"You're a liar," Tara snarled, her voice trembling with fury. "We see through your games now."

My heart pounded as my mind scrambled. They were turning on me. But why? To cover their own tracks? I opened my mouth to argue, but Tara didn't give me a chance.

She lunged at me, her fingers clawing toward my face. I stumbled back, slipping on the wet cobblestones as I threw my arms up to block her. Her nails raked the air inches from my cheek, and I barely kept my balance.

"Get off me!" I shouted, shoving her back, my voice echoing off the narrow alley walls. Why wasn't Joshua hearing me? He should be checking by now.

Liam stepped forward, looking like he might intervene, but I didn't want to find out. My pulse roared in my ears as I scrambled back to my feet. I headed toward the main road, but Tara clutched at my jacket and yanked me back.

I swung at her head. She ducked and kicked my shin, still gripping my jacket. The other girl wasn't tall, but she made up for it in ferocity. It was all I could do to hold her at arm's length. I glanced at Liam, but he just glowered at us, as if he was watching a show.

That was pretty much the truth, I supposed.

Tara's right hand got close enough to my neck that her nails stung. "Stop it! Get away from me, you rabid chipmunk!"

"Not until you pay for what you did to Declan!"

My arms were growing tired. "I haven't done a thing to him. I never even met him! You're a madwoman!"

Despite me being bigger and stronger, her nails were inching toward my eyes. I couldn't get the right leverage to twist her hands behind her back like I did before. I might just be out of luck with this one.

Out of nowhere, Faelan leapt at Tara, claws outstretched, and latched onto her arm, hissing and spitting.

Tara screamed and stumbled back, trying to yank Faelan off, but the cat stayed firmly latched on. He dug into her face, leaving angry red scratches.

Liam tried to pull him off, but Faelan jumped onto the man's thigh. Even through jeans, spots of blood seeped out. The cat climbed up his body and found the tender flesh of his face.

"Get this bloody cat off me!"

In the scuffle, Tara screamed something that caught my attention. "You don't understand! It wasn't supposed to go this far!"

What did that mean?

Tara managed to wrench Faelan off Liam's shoulders, and they stumbled away, leaving me breathless and more confused than ever. They disappeared down the wet, stinking alley, their shouts echoing off the walls.

Faelan sauntered back to me, looking pleased with himself. I scratched his head, trying to piece everything together.

What had gone 'too far?' And why did they think I was the killer? Did that mean they really weren't guilty?

If Liam and Tara were innocent, that left Marcus and Audrey, if I wasn't missing someone as a suspect. And Marcus had already shown some jealousy of Tara. Could he have gotten rid of the competition? If that was the case, then, why hadn't he moved toward being with her? Or had he done so, and got rejected?

I had a lot more questions than answers, but one thing was clear. Tara and Liam knew more than they were letting on. I wouldn't stop until I uncovered what happened to Declan.

Joshua popped his head out the café door, a worried look on his face. "Are you okay, Skye?"

I nodded, still shaken. "Yeah, I'm fine. Thanks for checking on me. It got intense."

He chuckled. "Aye, I could hear. You know, sometimes it's the quiet ones you have to watch out for."

I couldn't help but smile. "You've got that right."

Coming back into the café, I stared at my meal, which had now congealed into a cold mess. Joshua said, "Now, I'll make a new one, never fear. Hot and fresh!"

Before I could protest, he'd snatched up the old plate. "No arguing, now! I'll be back in a tick."

CHAPTER SEVENTEEN

The hot breakfast and coffee smoothed my hackles and calmed my adrenaline. It also improved my mood and warmed my blood. However, once I had a chance to percolate what Tara and Liam had done, it began to steam again. How dare Tara accuse me of killing Declan? She'd actually *attacked* me!

I'd had more than my fair share of combative patients, as well as men trying to cop a feel, or worse. I'd learned how to deal with these almost as a matter of course. But she'd been all rage and fury, like a summer Miami storm.

Well, I couldn't let her get away with that.

Once I paid for my meal and thanked Joshua, I grabbed my umbrella and marched toward Donal's Garda Station to file charges on her attack.

As I approached the door, though, my steps slowed. What proof did I have that she attacked me? My arms were longer than hers, and I'd held her at bay for the most part, despite her ferocity. She'd barely scratched my cheek.

Both Liam and Tara would have scratches where Faelan had exacted his punishment. Appearances were not in my favor, and it would be their word against mine. Two against one.

Despite what tentative truce Donal McCarthy and I had forged, I highly doubted he'd take my word against theirs in the face of that sort of evidence.

I stood in place as the rain began again, miserable and confused.

The Garda Station door flew open, and out stepped McCarthy himself. He glowered at me, closing the distance between us with a few strides. "Skye O'Shea. You're wanted for questioning. Please, come into the station."

My first instinct was to run, but that would have been the height of stupidity. Instead, I said, "What a coincidence. For once, I want to talk to you, too," and followed him into the building.

Tara and Liam were in the waiting room, their faces bearing Faelan's marks. Liam's jeans were ripped and had some bloodstains, as did Tara's shirt.

My delicious breakfast became a lump in my stomach.

"Miss O'Shea, please follow me."

Garda McCarthy led me past Garda Fitzgerald, typing on her computer. He swiped his card, and I followed him into the inner room. It was bare except for a table, two chairs, and what I guessed was recording equipment on the table.

He gestured for me to sit in one chair, and he took the other. "This interview will be recorded."

He pressed a button on the equipment, and it beeped. "The date is October 1st, and the time is 10am. We are in an interview room at the Ballybás Garda Station. I am Garda Officer Donal McCarthy. There are no other persons present. This is an interview with…Please, state your full name for the record."

"Skye Brigid O'Shea."

"And your address and date of birth."

I gave that information. I was sweating, and the urge to wipe my palms on my pants was strong.

He went on to advise me that I was free to obtain legal advice.

"Am I being arrested?"

"Not at this time."

Only a few of the butterflies in my stomach settled down. I declined the offer of a solicitor. I couldn't shake the feeling that asking for one would make me look guilty, or worse, like I had something to hide.

"Miss O'Shea, I'm questioning you in relation to the events that occurred approximately a half hour ago in the alley behind the Blarney Scone Café. Can you please share your version of the events?"

Trying to stick to actual facts, I gave a blow-by-blow of what happened. At least, until I got to Faelan's involvement. How in the world was I going to explain a faerie cat defending me? Dogs, sure. Dogs will defend their owners. But a cat? Most cats couldn't care less.

That didn't matter. Pay attention to the matter at hand, and stick to the facts, Skye. Stick to the facts. Let him sort out the reasoning.

"Your cat attacked her? Is that what you said?"

"It is. He jumped on her arm and bit her. Then, he scratched her face. When Liam tried to pull him off, Faelan attacked his leg and climbed up him to scratch his face."

McCarthy leaned back, crossed his arms, and glared at me for a few long moments. "I am not in the mood for fairy tales, Miss O'Shea."

I kept my tone as even as I could. "I'm not telling one, Garda McCarthy."

"Are you certain you wish that statement on the official record?"

"I am."

He let out a breath. "So be it. What happened next?"

After I finished my retelling, I said, "I was on my way to the Garda Station to report the incident to you when you came out."

He pursed his lips. "Is that so." It wasn't a question.

"It is. I understand you don't believe me about my cat, but please examine the scratches. They were not made by a human."

There. I'd gotten *that* on the record. No matter how much McCarthy thought I was lying, I had that juicy bit of evidence on my side. And if there was a DNA test, even better.

"Very well. Thank you for your cooperation. I will now end the recording." He pressed something on the equipment, and it beeped again.

I very much wanted to be elsewhere. "May I leave now?"

His tone was icy but not overtly hostile. That was an improvement over my first encounters with him. "You may, but we'd appreciate it if you remained in town until the investigation is concluded. I will walk you out."

I strode past Tara and Liam. She gave me such a glare that, if looks could kill, I'd be on the floor, as dead as disco.

Once I escaped the station, I headed straight home. Those butterflies had started fluttering in my stomach again. I wanted nothing more than to be alone in a safe, quiet place.

Before I could reach my haven, I ran into yet another of the Mad Moonies. Nabil came out of O'Leary's pub just as I walked by. He wore an expression of concern as he approached. "Skye? I heard there was a row."

I clenched my teeth. "If by row you mean Tara attacking me, then yes! Now, if you'll excuse me, there's a hot cup of coffee waiting for me at home."

He placed a gentle hand on my arm. "Please, she's not a bad person. Declan, well, he wasn't kind to her. She's got a lot of healing to do before she's human again."

Which made her sound like one of the Fair Folk or something. But having been a victim of abuse myself, my judgment of her softened.

Wait a minute. *Was* Tara human? She certainly looked like one of the fairies, if storybooks were to be believed. Five foot nothing, full of rage and strength, with no self-control. A shiver ran down my spine.

My expression must have given my thoughts away, because Nabil was speaking again, "No, nothing weird, I swear. She just has a fierce temper, especially about those she cares for."

I let out a snort. "I haven't hurt anyone she cares for, so she can just leave me alone, okay?"

He pursed his lips. "I'll let her know. Deal?"

"Deal."

I turned toward my house, but he touched my arm again. "I heard you were going to ask Audrey to work on your accounts?"

This small-town gossip thing was getting out of hand. I shrugged away from him. "How did you hear about that?"

Nabil rubbed the back of his neck. "Well, she told me. I'm an accountant, too, so we chat. Trade talk, like."

I let out a rueful laugh. "Gossiping about accounting. That sounds so exciting."

He chuckled and said, "Well, gossiping about nursing would probably bore me to tears, so fair play to you. Listen, the reason I bring it up is that Audrey isn't great at personal taxes. That's not her specialty, but it is mine."

Was this another attempt to get cash from me? After my experience with Audrey, I was suspicious. I hadn't really considered Nabil as a suspect, but maybe I should have.

Raising my eyebrows, I asked, "Are you offering to do my taxes?"

"If you're game, I am."

"You're a chartered accountant?"

He gave a disarming grin. "I even have the club card to prove it." As if to prove it, he handed me a business card. I took it with a nod.

And not one word about wanting cash up front. Nabil definitely seemed the most stable of the lot.

I reached the sanctuary of my home right at noon. Once inside, I blinked a few times to get used to the lights Finn and Rory had rigged up, making the pub unusually bright.

The cousins glanced up and waved, and I waved back. At least they weren't actively hammering. Instead, they were applying paste to strips of wallpaper for the lower half of the walls. The acrid paste stank and tickled my nose.

I'd debated the décor choice. Striped wallpaper felt horribly old-fashioned to me, but Jess assured me it was common in Irish pubs and would set the right atmosphere.

I probably should have eaten something for lunch, but my nerves were shot from McCarthy's questioning, and my stomach was still churning.

Instead, I grabbed one of Gran's crossword puzzle books and a pencil, then sank into the comfy chair. A distraction would be lovely.

This one had cryptic crosswords, and was more difficult than the ones I was used to. Each clue had layers of knowledge, puns, and clever tricks like jumbled words or synonyms. Sure, regular crosswords had most of those, but each and every clue in this one had all of them.

Perhaps a half-hour later, I put the puzzle book down. So many of the clues had references to the UK or Ireland, such as politicians or shows I didn't know. Maybe they were beyond my level, at least for now.

My phone buzzed, and I remembered to check the number first. It was a US number, so I just clicked deny and blocked the number. I'd had enough of Armand and his mind games.

Without warning, Faelan appeared out of nowhere and scratched my leg. "Ow! Hey, what was that for?"

He let out a low growl.

"What? Were you hurt in the fight this morning? Thanks for that, by the way."

He shook his head.

"Then, what? What do you need?"

Sigh. Time for bribery again. I went to the cupboard and pulled out a bag of cat treats I'd bought.

When I shook the bag, Faelan rubbed against my leg, his black fur shedding on my jeans. I pulled out a treat and held it in my palm, bending down to offer the tribute.

Faelan sniffed it daintily, then gobbled it. Once he finished the treat, cleaned his whiskers, and looked up, he said, "Your break is over."

"Oh, it's talking time again, is it? I wish you'd share the rules about when you can talk and when you can't."

He let out a light hiss. "That is not for you to know. You have work to do now."

I blinked at him. "What are you talking about?"

Faelan growled, as if explaining something incredibly obvious. "Tonight is the full moon."

"So? Do you turn into a pumpkin at midnight or something?"

With a slight gurgling meow, he said, "At midnight, you must fight the Scáth na tromluí."

My stomach tightened with a mix of dread and determination. "The what of the what?"

"The Shadow of Nightmares."

A chill ran down my spine. "Oh, that sounds fun. Why me?"

"Because your grandmother was the protector of this village. That duty has now fallen to you."

I scowled at the Cat Sídhe. "And what if I don't want it?"

"That is not permitted."

Great big fermented sheep nuggets on a platter. Was this the real reason Gran had bequeathed me her pub and B&B? So I could become a shield against random Fair Folk?

Then again, this felt almost like a natural progression from being a nurse. In a way, I was caring for the whole village, right? If I couldn't be a nurse anymore, at least I can save people's lives in some way. This place had been Gran's home, and was becoming mine.

Fighting a fae creature wasn't exactly on my to-do list, but I was learning better than to argue with Faelan about such things. "And you're just telling me this now?"

He shot me a disdainful look. "I told you when it was permitted."

"Are you ever going to tell me all the rules? Or who even makes the rules?"

He let out a faint his and his hackles rose. "Perhaps. Some day. But not today. Today we must prepare for battle."

"Fine. How do I prepare?"

Faelan stretched and licked his paw casually before answering, "You'll need an iron chain."

I rummaged through my mental inventory of the house and outbuildings. I'd cleared out a lot of the trash, and there wasn't a lot left. "Sorry, I must have left my spare one back in Dublin. We're fresh out."

He flicked his tail. "Of course. Then, you'll need rowan wood wands."

Were there any rowan bushes in the garden? I shook my head. "Nope, don't have any of those either."

Faelan narrowed his eyes, clearly annoyed. "Your third option is a bundle of yew branches."

I thought for a moment and nodded. "Yes, there's a yew tree in the back garden, near the creek."

"You will also require a bell, and some water charged with magic. I shall instruct you on how to perform that spell."

The house sat on five acres, with a creek running along one edge.

Digging out a rusty pair of gardening sheers from the garden shed, I marched to the bank and stared up at the ancient yew tree.

I remember reading about how yew trees grew in an unusual way. Drooping branches can root and form new trunks when they reach the ground. This one was old enough that the center of the trunk had rotted away, forming a chamber almost big enough for a child to crawl inside.

As Faelan instructed, I gave a brief prayer of thanks to the spirit of the tree. At first, the secateurs refused to cut into the wood. I grunted and pushed on either side with all my strength until the blades finally snapped through.

As I held my prize, the branch felt old and powerful in my hands, a connection to the ancient earth. A tingle ran through my body before I placed it on the ground.

Then, I chose a second one to cut. Once I had a bundle of nine branches, we returned to the house.

"You will need salt." I grabbed the tub of salt from the cupboard.

"Now, the bell," Faelan instructed.

I searched through the pub, eventually finding a rusty iron desk bell. I wiped it off and brought it back to Faelan, who nodded approvingly. "That will do. Now, for the water."

I grabbed a sports bottle and went to the sink, but Faelan growled.

"What? Is there something wrong with the water?" Then, I remembered my suspicions about Liam and drugging the water supply. But I hadn't felt dizzy for the last day or so. Surely, it had diluted out by now?

"Go to the creek."

"Ugh. I was just out there. Why didn't you tell me before? I could have done both at once."

With resentment fueling my steps, I marched back out to the creek, filled the stupid sports bottle, and stomped back inside again. "It's filled, okay? Now what?"

Per Faelan's instructions, I sat on the ground in my garden. The rain had slowed, but my jeans were quickly soaked by the grass. I tried to ignore that.

I closed my eyes, held my hands over the water, and focused on infusing it with my energy. Faelan told me words to chant three times. I didn't understand the Irish and reminded myself I needed to take lessons. Then, I chastised myself for swerving off-topic.

Once I finished, the water seemed to shimmer slightly, and Faelan purred in approval. "Now, you must wash yourself."

I wanted to protest that I wasn't dirty, but many religions valued ritual cleanliness, so I took a shower, dressed in fresh clothes, and descended again. At least I wasn't wearing damp jeans now.

"Now what?"

"Now, we wait." Faelan began grooming his back, totally nonchalantly.

I glanced at the clock, but it was still only nine. While I wasn't hungry, I made myself eat a sandwich. I tried to work on the crossword, but my nerves were too jumpy.

Would I be able to fight this thing? I had never really fought a fae creature before. I might have seen or heard them, but battled one? Not yet. But Faelan and Gran seemed to think I could, so I used that as fake confidence armor.

As the clock neared ten, I gathered my supplies. A tied bundle of yew branches, a bowl, the bell, and the charmed sports bottle, placing them all in a grocery bag. Since Faelan mentioned building a fire, I also grabbed a lighter. Gran had the long-handled type that clicked to light a fire.

Faelan and I got into the car, and he directed me to the standing stones parking lot. We climbed the hill, using my phone as a flashlight up the narrow, muddy path.

The dark shapes of the surrounding trees clad the stones in secret seclusion. The air was thick with the aftermath of the day's rain, and everything smelled damp and heavy. Every shadow seemed ready to strike out at me, and my arms were permanently covered with goosebumps.

After gathering some fallen branches from the surrounding trees, I created a fire pit in the center, though the wood was soaked.

A whisper in the back of my mind told me I shouldn't light a fire in the center of the stones, but Faelan insisted.

It took at least a dozen clicks of the lighter, but I finally got some kindling lit and stoked the fire until it burned on its own. Still, the flame sputtered and sparked until Faelan sat next to it, said something in Irish, and then it blazed strong, as if the wood had been dry as a bone.

Then, Faelan directed me to place yew branches around the stones in a huge circle. The air seemed to tingle with anticipation. Either that, or my own nerves were jangling. Both? It could be both. Both was good.

"Now, prime the water," Faelan instructed.

"I thought I did that back at the house?"

"You charged it. Now, you must prime it."

I muttered, *this is fairy magic, not a stupid car engine,* as I held a bowl over the flames, feeling the heat and a tingling rush through my blood intertwining.

Realizing this must be my own magic, it almost made me falter. But Faelan told me ancient Irish words to whisper, calling upon the power of fire to protect us. Once again, I repeated the chant three times.

Once we finished that step, I gathered some deadwood from the surrounding woods. It might have been wet, but wet wood was better than no wood. Besides, maybe Faelan could make it dry with magic again. Then, I glanced at my phone. Another half hour to midnight.

"Let me guess. More waiting?"

His tail jerked once. "We wait."

CHAPTER EIGHTEEN

As midnight approached, I stoked the bonfire to keep it strong. After making peat fires in my hearth, it felt odd to have a regular wood one. The smell was sharper and actual flames gyrated in the darkness.

Faelan leapt on the recumbent stone, settling in the very middle like he was sitting on a throne. "Now, you will repeat my words."

I wanted to tell him no. In truth, I wanted to run screaming down the hill and huddle in the safety of my car. Better yet, my cozy parlour, in front of my hearth, surrounded by Gran's love. But earning Gran's place meant taking care of her town, so here I was.

If I couldn't care for people as a nurse, I could care for them this way.

With my arms in the air, I called upon the power of flame to protect us. I felt foolish and if someone saw me, I might just die of embarrassment.

As I finished the third repeat, flames crackled and climbed high in a surge, casting eerie shadows across the stone circle.

Next, I dinged the desk bell, calling upon the power of air to help us. The sound echoed through the night, sharp and clear. The murmur of wind became a sudden gale, whipping my hair. Then, it settled with a whisper of energy.

One by one, I fed the yew branches to the fire, calling upon the power of earth. The flames leapt higher with each branch, casting a warm, golden light. Amorphous shapes danced on the standing stones around us.

I poured the salt in a circle around the stones. The last bit was a bit thin, as I was running out.

"What about the rain? Will it wash the salt away? Can we cover it or something?"

Faelan paused a moment, thinking. Then, he nodded. "You might bury the line, to preserve it."

I shot him a glare for not having mentioned this in the first place, but hastily grabbed a thin stone and worked my way around the line, burying the salt and patting the dirt firmly on top.

Once that was done, I sprinkled each stone with the charged water, working clockwise, calling upon the power of water. The droplets sizzled as they hit the stones, creating tiny puffs of steam. The spot where they fell throbbed with a dull light, then faded.

As the last branch burned and the final chant left my lips, a chilling howl echoed through the darkness. I recognized the sound from the other night. The shadow creature had arrived.

Its malevolent presence was a cold, creeping dread that seeped into my bones, threatening to overwhelm me. The flames surged higher, forcing me to stumble away from their intense heat, but I didn't dare step past the circle of stones.

The shadow creature prowled around the edge of the circle, its dark form pulsating with rage. I caught glimpses of ink-black fur, burning red eyes, and the hint of curved horns in the darkness. A shiver gripped my spine and shook it until my teeth ached.

It was testing the boundaries, seeking a weakness. I'd have to act quickly to banish it before it found a way in.

"Faelan, what do I do?"

The cat's tail twitched, but he remained silent.

"Oh, fermented sheep nuggets! Now is *not* the time to go silent! What do I do? It's going to get in!"

That maddening feline still said nothing. But he'd told me what to do while we were waiting. I had my instructions, I just had to do them. Fire, earth, water, air. Chanting and magical powers. I had all the tools I needed, but no experience in using them.

Just as I was gathering my courage to start, another sound surrounded us, a high-pitched bleat that rattled my bones. "What fresh madness is that?"

Now, the cat decided to speak, anger clear in his hisses. "The púca is back." Every hair on his back had spiked up and he growled into the darkness.

"Púca? Great. Is he related to the dream-stealer, then?"

"They are connected, yes. I will convince the púca that tonight is a bad night for him. You fight the dream-stealer."

The Scáth na tromluí poked and prodded the magical barrier, each touch stinging my senses. Another roar shook the stones. Panic grew in my blood, and my heart threatened to burst out of my chest.

Skye, use the fire, Gran's voice urged. *Fire purifies and protects.*

Relief swept through me. "Oh, thank all the gods you're here!"

You must take up the task I have left behind. If you don't banish it, the entire village will fall into madness.

"You're choosing now to tell me this?"

You are capable, my granddaughter. Your ancestors are helping.

I hoped they were more capable than I was.

Now, how to use the fire safely? Faelan had explained how, but I doubted my ability. I stepped closer to the flames, their heat making sweat form on my face. The scent of burning wood and damp earth mixed with the sickly stink of the creature.

With each step, I whispered a prayer, calling upon the flame's strength to protect us. To my surprise, the flames responded, growing brighter and more intense. They formed swirling designs similar to the Celtic knotwork on Gran's diary.

As I chanted the strange Irish words, the flame reached higher. The nightmare screamed, and I spoke louder. It screeched into the night, and again the flames shot up. My skin crawled with a million ants as the energy crackled between us.

Back and forth, flame and cry, cry and flame. We battled for a seeming eternity, and my voice grew hoarse with chanting.

Finally, its screams turned to whimpers, and a wave of triumph and exhaustion swept through me.

Just as that faded, a horrific cat's yowl filled the darkness, followed by an unearthly scream. Silence followed.

As the malevolent power began to fade, Tara erupted from the shadows, an iron axe gripped tightly in her hands. Her eyes burned with frenzied fury as she charged straight at me.

She stumbled as she crossed the salt circle, but regained herself quickly. I barely registered the movement before she swung the axe. I twisted to the side, but the blade scraped across my hand, sending a jolt of pain through me. A sharp screech escaped my lips.

Desperation surged as I seized her arms, keeping the axe from slashing across my face. But Tara was relentless. She kicked out, hooking my leg, and we both crashed to the muddy ground.

We fought in a tangle of limbs, each of us struggling for control. I seized her wrist, but she wrenched it free with a feral twist. She lashed out with her claws, raking at my face. I jerked back, blocking her strike with my arm, the mud-slick ground making every movement a battle for dominance.

"You're just like Saoirse!" she hissed, her face inches from mine. "Always thinking you're better than everyone else!"

I shoved her off and scrambled to my feet, panting. "What in seven hells are you talking about?"

"She was supposed to be my *mentor*," Tara spat, standing and swinging the axe again. "She betrayed me, and now you're following in her footsteps!"

Snatching up a branch from the embers, I parried her attack, using every ounce of focus I had. The smoldering end swept close to her face. "I have no idea what you're talking about, but if Gran betrayed you, I'll bet you it wasn't without reason."

Liam appeared out of the darkness, looking torn.

Tara screeched at him, "stay out of this, Liam!" She swung wildly at me. "This is between us."

I stepped backward, putting the pyre between us. Tara feinted first to one side, then the other, brandishing the axe at each move. Finally, we settled in the middle, watching each other through the flames. I eyed her weapon, but she didn't look like she was going to throw it.

"Your sainted grandmother was involved in things you can't even imagine. She used me, just like she used everyone else. Playing politics with emotions! And now you're doing the same."

"Me? What did I do?"

"You stole Declan!"

I let out a snort. "I never even met the man! You're delusional."

Tara didn't seem to register my words, her eyes wild and unyielding. "But I fixed that, didn't I?" she shouted, her voice crackling with fury. "He won't ever reject me again!"

A sickening realization hit me like a blow to the chest. *Fermented sheep nuggets.* She *had* killed Declan.

Her grin twisted into something feral as she darted to the side, feinting with calculated precision. I held my ground, refusing to be baited. Her voice lashed out like a whip. "Your grandmother rejected us all because we wouldn't worship her like she wanted! She thought she was better than us!"

The venom in her words cut deep, sparking doubt. Could there be truth in what she was saying? Had Gran tried to manipulate them? The question burrowed into my mind, and with it came another chilling thought. Was Gran's death not as innocent as I thought?

Exhaustion should have been coursing through me after the stress of the day. The ritual, the battle with the nightmare creature, the suffocating tension…but adrenaline surged in my veins, overriding everything. I couldn't stop now. Not until this was over, no matter what dark truths waited for me.

With a surge of resolve, I lunged at her, the bonfire's heat licking at my face. Tara twisted at the last second, slipping to the left, but her movement was too sharp. She stumbled into Liam, who had crept behind her unnoticed. The collision sent them both sprawling into the mud.

Launching myself at her, I grabbed her axe-wielding arm and yanked it back. The blade inched dangerously close, but I twisted her wrist with every ounce of strength I had. We rolled, the earth beneath us wet and unforgiving. Mud clung to my hands as I clawed at her grip, her resistance fierce and unrelenting.

"Let go!" I snarled, digging my fingers into her wrist until the axe thumped to the ground. Tara's scream ripped through the night, raw and piercing, echoing off the trees like a wounded animal. Without pausing, I kicked the weapon out of reach and scrambled to drag her upright, my hands locked around her arm like iron bands.

Liam stumbled to his feet, his face pale and stricken. His voice quivered as he stepped forward. "Don't hurt her!" he pleaded, his wide eyes darting between us.

I tightened my grip on Tara, my chest heaving, my mind racing. Hurt her? She'd just confessed to murder, and the battle wasn't over yet.

I nodded, ready for whatever came next. "I won't if I don't have to. We need to finish this."

The creature howled in the darkness. The scream almost sounded familiar, an echo of the one Tara had let out earlier.

I had been so close to banishing the creature before Tara's attack. That ill-timed interruption had given it a chance to recover strength.

Liam stared out at the woods. "Jesus, Mary, and Joseph! What was that?"

I rounded on him, my temper flaring again. "That was the creature *you* lot summoned! You and your Mystic Midnight

Moonbats. Whatever idiotic ritual you performed last week, you botched it up big time."

His eyes darted back and forth, confusion clear on his face. "What? That can't be!"

"You were trying to see into the future, right? To find out who should lead your pathetic little group? Well, this nightmare thing came instead. It's been stealing our dreams and mixing them up!"

Liam shook his head, backing up with his hands out. "No, the dreams were from me! I did that."

I narrowed my gaze at him. If he was going mad, too, I wouldn't be able to hold both of them. Heck, I could barely hold Tara. She was struggling with such insane strength.

"What do you mean, you did that?"

He had the grace to stare at his feet and mumble something.

"Speak up, Liam."

"I said, I dosed the well. The transfer point's near your home, so you probably got the heaviest dose. Sorry."

A cold shiver ran down my spine. My heart pounded in my chest, my mind scrambling for words, but all I could manage was, "Why in the name of all that's holy would you do that?"

He shrugged, as if the weight of his betrayal didn't exist. "It's the only way for everyone to be free. Spiritually, I mean. I didn't realize people would swap dreams, though."

"But your drugs didn't cause the dream swaps. The creature I've been trying to banish did that!"

Then, the realization hit me like a punch to the gut. He'd drugged the entire village. And me, the one person meant to protect them. My vision blurred as anger and disbelief twisted into something darker. The weight of his confession crushed the air from my lungs. What had I just heard? How could I let this happen?

I wanted to scream, to rage at him, but all I could do was stand there, the rain mixing with the hot tears I hadn't even realized were falling.

Gran's voice spoke in my mind. *Definitely an eejit. This is one reason I left.*

Lightning flashed, forcing me to shut my eyes. A boom of thunder shook the ground and the scáth na tromluí roared. Again, there was a familiar tone in his voice.

Then, Tara shouted something at Liam. I turned to look at her. That was what was familiar.

The Shadow of Nightmares has Tara's voice. Just a bit, but it was there. They must be connected somehow, beyond the fact that her group had called it forth.

A few drops of rain fell, and then a deluge hit us.

The rain beat down in sheets, the world reduced to a blur of blackness and relentless water. Tara's muscles, her breath coming in ragged gasps as her head swiveled back and forth. Her voice barely rose above the storm. "Is it coming for us? We're going to die!"

I clenched my jaw, shoving my own panic down, forcing myself to focus. I couldn't let her see the storm brewing inside me, the tightening of my chest, the cold fingers of fear creeping up my spine.

Tara was trembling in my grip, her wrist cold beneath my hand. I tightened my hold, trying to steady both of us. She let out a small squeak of discomfort, but I didn't release her.

"Calm down!" I snapped, the words coming out sharper than I intended. "You aren't going to die. What you *are* going to do is help me banish that thing once and for all."

I sounded so darn sure of myself, my voice unwavering even as the panic clawed at my insides. But deep down, I was a mess. My mind screamed with questions. Was Tara really connected to that creature? I had no idea how that had happened, or if me banishing it would hurt her. My heart hammered in my chest, and my breath caught, even though I forced myself to stay steady for her sake.

Every drop of rain that hit my face felt like a shock, my entire body taut with tension. Tara, with her wide, terrified eyes locked on the darkened sky, was someone I needed to care for, too, even if I hated her. I couldn't leave another human to that creature's mercy.

I wanted to believe my words. I had to. I knew I was lying, even if only to myself.

Another roar surrounded us, dispersed by the pouring rain. The previously raging blaze sputtered, fighting against the downpour. If flames were protecting us, what would happen when they died? And where had Faelan run off to? He needed to supercharge the fire again. I let out a small prayer of thanks that I'd buried that darned salt circle.

Liam gulped. "What do we do?"

After all Tara had done, I didn't want to do it, but I needed their help. I gave the woman a long stare before responding. "Look, we'll need to work together. You both promise to help? We settle anything else after this is done, okay?"

Tara gave a sullen nod, and I let go of her arm. The first thing I did was grab her axe. She shot me a resentful glare and rubbed her wrist. I wondered if she *knew* she was connected to the Shadow of Nightmares. *Was this all on purpose? Or was she innocent?*

Maybe that was why she'd been so cruel all along.

I took a deep breath and tried to find Faelan, but could barely see anything in the rainy gloom, much less a black cat. "I'd already started to banish it when you interrupted me. I was using iron, fire, water, and yew branches."

Lightning illuminated the stone circle, and the shadow creature's dark form flickered in and out of view, just past the closest stone. *Too close.*

My brain screamed at me. Why wasn't I running? I had perfectly good legs. I ought to be running as fast as I could.

I bet Gran wouldn't have run.

"First, the iron," I shouted over the rain, pulling out the rusty desk bell. "Iron repels fae creatures."

Tara snorted. "Every eejit knows that."

The rain was relentless, but the flames still flickered, fueled by the charged yew branches. Sizzling smoke spit and popped. "Fire purifies and protects," I shouted, echoing Gran's words. "Tara, feed in the rest of the branches."

She hesitated, but a glance at the encroaching shadow creature spurred her into action. She fed the wood to the blaze, and the flames leapt higher, casting an eerie, protective ruddiness, sizzling loud in the pouring rain.

I rummaged through my bag, pulling out the last bit of charged water. "I can throw this in its face, like holy water on a vampire, if we get that close." It felt ridiculous talking about throwing water when I had to wipe the rain out of my eyes every few seconds.

Finally, I placed the little iron desk bell on the recumbent stone again. The pelting rain made it ping constantly, almost musically.

A horrible screeching scrape filled the area, like the sound of chalk on a board. The scáth na tromluí might be pulling a claw across a stone. We all winced.

With the elements in place, it was time to draw in the magic. I stood at the center of the circle, the energy of the earth beneath my feet, the flame's warmth, the air's whisper, and the water's life-giving force pounding relentlessly on my head.

Use the elements, Gran's voice whispered in my mind. *Use the words Faelan taught you.*

I was going to, Gran!

I raised my arms, chanting first in Irish. *"Tine, aer, uisce, agus talamh, cabhraigh linn!* Fire, air, water, and earth, help us!"

The wind picked up, swirling like a tornado. Then, the rain intensified, but instead of being oppressive, it felt cleansing, purifying. The flames roared higher, defying the deluge, and the ground beneath us hummed with power.

The shadow creature howled in time with the next peal of thunder. It lashed out, a tendril of darkness striking the edge of our circle. It stopped short of crossing the line of salt, buried beneath the dirt. My muscles burned with the touch, but iron, fire, and salt held firm, repelling its attack.

"We're almost there," I said, my voice steady despite the fear screaming inside me. "We need to banish it."

I shook the desk bell, the sound piercing through the storm. *"Scáth na tromluí, díbrím thú!* Shadow of Nightmares, I banish you!"

The creature recoiled, its form flickering violently. It let out another agonizing roar, and a surge of power surrounded us. Burning energy flowed through my blood and out my fingers, making every hair on my body stand on end.

Draw upon the strength of your ancestors. They are with you.

I shut my eyes tight, reaching deep within myself, and remembered those fading portraits on the parlour wall. Their faces swam in my mind's eye. Each one smiled at me, unlike their photographs. A crowd of strangers linked to my soul like a daisy chain, fortifying my strength.

Tingling power soared through me, strength from these strangers flowing into my bones, merging with the power of the elements.

I opened my eyes, filled with a newfound determination. "Liam, Tara, join hands with me."

As they did, our combined energy intensified. Together, we chanted the banishment spell, our voices shaky but steadily rising above the storm.

"*Scáth na tromluí, imigh an áit seo!* Shadow of Nightmares, leave this place!"

The creature writhed and shrieked, its form unraveling in the face of our united power. The wind howled, the pyre blazed, and the rain poured, all converging in a final, explosive burst of gorgeous sparks, better than any fireworks display.

Light poured down from the sky, like a spotlight chasing away the shadows. The blinding flash of light coalesced into a thousand sparkling stores.

The horrific screech made me want to rip my ears off.

Then, in a shower of fading embers, the shadow creature dissipated, its presence vanishing into the light.

The storm calmed, and the rain eased to a gentle drizzle. The stink of scorched fur and rotting leaves tickled my nose.

We stood in the stone circle, panting and soaked, but victorious. The oppressive weight of the shadow creature's presence had disappeared, replaced by a sense of peace and relief.

Tara let out a screech and collapsed to her knees, tears mingling with the rain on her face. "Thank you," she whispered, a mix of disbelief and exhaustion in her voice. Then, she keeled over, curled into a fetal position.

Liam looked at me, his expression filled with awe and respect. "Skye, that was incredible."

Sheer exhaustion seeped into every muscle of my body. I could barely whisper. "We did it together."

The village was safe, and I saved them. That sounded strange, even within my mind, but that was what Gran had charged me to do. A certain satisfaction at completing the task warmed me. I may no longer be able to save people as a nurse, but I could help the people who had accepted me into their home. My home, now.

As the adrenaline wore off, my knees wobbled, and I collapsed. Tara lay curled up a few feet away, sobbing. Liam knelt beside her, looking torn and guilty.

I studied her through the haze of exhaustion, recognizing the signs almost immediately. Her pale, clammy skin, rapid, shallow breathing, and unfocused, glassy eyes.

I looked at Liam, my voice weak but firm. "She's in shock. We need to get her back to the village. To Adanna's surgery."

"Shock? Is she hurt?"

"She's not bleeding, but this isn't about wounds." I pushed myself up against the recumbent stone, steadying my trembling legs. "It's her body reacting to everything. Fear, exhaustion, maybe dehydration. If we don't keep her warm and calm, it'll get worse."

I stumbled toward Tara's prone form, reaching out to gently touch her shoulder. "Tara, it's Skye," I said softly. "You're safe now, but we need to help your body recover." Her sobbing slowed, though her breaths still came in shallow gasps.

I wished I had thought to bring a blanket, but I hadn't considered this eventuality.

We tried to lift her, but even as little as she was, we had no strength left. I slipped and fell backward, my bum squelching in the mud. Frustrated but refusing to give up, I crawled back to Tara, shielding her from the wind with my body.

"Tara, breathe with me," I urged, taking slow, exaggerated breaths to guide her. "In and out. That's it."

Her eyes fluttered, the faintest hint of focus returning. We had to keep her stable until we could get her somewhere safe.

By now, the rain had finally stopped, and I heard a noise down the path. Had the shadow creature returned? Fear sped down my spine, but I asked. "Who's there?"

Someone turned on a phone, and the light from the screen illuminated Jess's face. "Skye?"

CHAPTER NINETEEN

The rain came back as a miserable drizzle as Jess clambered to the hilltop and crouched beside me. Her phone light under her face gave her an eerie visage. The stink of burning dream-stealer flesh and fur mixed with the rain and sodden fire, which had finally sizzled out.

Liam sat cross-legged with his head in his hands, next to Tara. The nurse part of me ached to go check her vitals, to make sure she was okay. The petty human part of me wanted her to suffer for attacking me and killing Declan. But if that had been because of the Shadow of Nightmare's control, I should try to be kinder.

She moaned occasionally, so I knew she was still alive. That helped to salve my conscience.

Jess asked, "Is it gone?"

"Is what gone?"

"The dream-stealer. Faelan told me you'd need help once it was gone."

"Wait, he *told* you?"

Jess gave me a sheepish grin. "Well, sure. Did you not know he's a Cat Sídhe? He talks to me all the time."

I stared into the darkness, trying to find a hint of the cat. Two glowing eyes blinked in the gloom. "He only chooses to talk to me when he deigns it to be important."

She giggled. "I can't get him to shut up, sometimes."

"Great. He's more your cat than mine, then?"

With a fierce shake of her head, she said, "Oh, no, he's his own cat. You're his human, though. You can't get out of that."

I leaned against the ancient stone, cold seeping through my sodden clothes. The misty rain drizzled around us, and the eerie quiet of the standing stone circle warned me not to let my guard down yet.

If Jess could talk to Faelan, maybe she was more magical than I'd thought. That yellow glow had to mean something. I remembered the incident in her store where Tara's dress had ripped after she acted all nasty.

I was about to ask her when Tara let out a loud groan, and Liam helped her sit up.

I rubbed my temples, looking at the two of them. "I need to know what happened to Declan. So, who's going to start? Tara? Liam?"

Tara crossed her arms, glaring at the ground. Liam shifted uncomfortably, avoiding eye contact.

"I'm not stupid," I continued. "I know there's more to Declan's death than what's been said. You two were involved.

So, spill." Before they could think about it, I retrieved Tara's axe. I'd much rather have that in my own hand.

Faelan chose this moment to reappear, right against Liam's legs. He let out a yelp and hopped back, but then let out a nervous laugh. I suppose, despite Faelan's attack on him, he was less frightened of a cat than the creature we'd just banished. Logical, at least.

The cat continued to rub against his legs, and I wondered if this would have the same effect as sitting on Adanna's lap, which made her more talkative.

Liam leaned over to pet Faelan, cautiously. "It wasn't supposed to go that way," he muttered, almost to himself.

"What wasn't supposed to go which way?" Thunder rumbled across the sky. Was the storm coming back? We needed to hurry this along.

Liam glanced at Tara, who gave him a sharp look. He swallowed hard. "Tara and Declan had a row. In your pub."

"Why in my pub?" I asked, narrowing my eyes.

Faelan sauntered over to Tara to rub against her foot. She glared at the cat, and for a moment, I thought she'd kick him. That would earn her a punch in the nose. Luckily, she left him alone. "It used to be Saoirse's place," Tara said, finally looking up. "Declan went there for some whiskey, maybe for the ritual. We'd just had an argument, so I followed him in. Liam followed me."

Jess asked, "How did he get in? The door was locked, wasn't it?"

Tara said, "Sure and he'd made a copy of the key from when she led our group. She'd given me a copy. Saoirse used to give me private lessons."

I narrowed my eyes, remembering Gran's diary note about the feisty warrior girl. "Lessons in what?"

Tara gave a feral grin. "In being a strong woman and taking no faff from anyone."

"Well, you took that one to heart. So, Declan had the key, and he went in to steal some whiskey. What happened next?" I pressed.

Tara's jaw tightened. "He wouldn't shut up about being our leader now, about how Saoirse would've wanted him to take over. I lost my temper."

Jess, sitting beside me, raised an eyebrow. "You've seen Tara in an argument. It's not pretty."

I snorted, the memory of our last fight flashing vividly in my mind. The shouting, the wild swings, the bruises I still carried. "Not pretty? She fights like she's got something to prove, and she doesn't hold back. I've got the scars to prove it." My fingers brushed the faint mark on my forearm, a souvenir from our first encounter.

My voice dropped, a simmering mix of annoyance and begrudging respect. "So, what next? Do I need to brace for round three, or are we finally calling a truce?"

Shaking her head, she said, "I'm over that, sure. It's like someone drained the rage from me."

Or banished a rage-filled fae creature from her mind. She must not have any clue they were connected. Thunder rolled again, and I redirected us back to the murder. "Then what happened next with Declan?"

Tara stared at her feet. "He started talking about how I needed to admit he was in charge, that he was stronger and had the right to be the leader. Then, he tried to prove how strong he was."

I swallowed. "How did he try to prove that?"

The younger woman shot me a glare filled with fire. "How do you *think* he tried? He grabbed me and tried…well, he tried. But I made sure he wouldn't try that again with anyone else. Ever again."

Liam placed a hand on her arm. "You don't know he would have done that."

Tara spun on him. "Oh, yes, I did! I knew exactly what he wanted to do to me. In living, graphic detail! Hadn't I been having his dreams night after night, living through my own…" Her voice faded and she shut her eyes. "When he attacked me, I had no doubt."

Stealing my resolve, I asked, "How did you kill him?"

She stared at the ground and gave a shrug, her voice now cold and flat. "He was already high with Liam's drugs. I'd broken his grip and hid behind a table. It was pretty easy to jump out from the darkness, to pretend to be some fae creature attacking him."

Tara swallowed and looked out into the darkness. Her expression was terrified and sympathy welled up in my breast. For all her anger, she'd been through a heck of a lot.

"So, what happened?"

"When he stumbled back, he hit his head on the bar."

She stared into nothing and said, "But it felt like the shadow creature stayed with me after that." Then, she shook her head. "But that's gone now. Saoirse promised me it would go away, and it did."

What did Gran have to do with it? I'd have to ask her when I had the chance.

Liam chimed in, his voice shaky. "I walked in right after it happened. Tara was freaking out. I didn't know what to do, so I thought if we made it look like a robbery, it might confuse the Gardaí."

I groaned. "Stealing whiskey bottles? *That* was your big plan?"

Liam shrugged helplessly. "It seemed like a good idea at the time."

The misty rain finally faded to nothing. The scent of pine and mud mingled with the scorched fur stink.

Jess whispered, "He's not exactly the sharpest knife in the drawer."

"Obviously," I muttered. "So, you didn't go to the Gardaí, and instead, you decided to cover it up? What about the scratches on his face?"

Tara and Liam exchanged a glance. She said, "We used his fingers to scratch himself. To confuse any investigation."

I let out a snort. "At least that was more effective as a red herring than the stupid bottles. It meant they had to test for DNA. Was it you I bumped into when I left?"

He gave a sullen nod. "I almost screamed when I realized how close you came to finding us. I tried to convince *her* to turn herself in," Liam pointed to Tara, "but she wouldn't listen." His tone had turned to a pleading whine.

Tara scowled. "I wasn't going to prison. I panicked, okay?"

"And the drugs?" I asked, eyes narrowing. "Why did I get a dose at the bonfire? And the day after?"

Tara rolled her eyes. "Liam's always been into finding nirvana through chemical means."

Liam scowled at her. "It's a legit thing!"

"After Declan died, he started drinking and doing drugs to cope with the guilt. I got sick of it and dumped his stash in the pond."

Random details were fitting into place with satisfying clicks. A thrill ran down my spine as I added each clue. "The pond that feeds into my well? That's why I was hallucinating?"

Tara nodded. "Yeah. I didn't exactly think that one through."

Jess shook her head. "A dumb idea, but considering the circumstances, not surprising."

My anger flared. "And then you accused me of killing Declan? You were just going to let me take the blame for the murder?"

Tara looked away. "It wasn't supposed to go this far."

I stared at them, with a mix of anger and pity.

Jess, evidently sensing the need to lighten the mood, nudged me. "Well, at least we know the truth now. I'll give a call to the Garda Station, and they can come pick these two up."

Glancing back to where Faelan's eyes had been, I spied them. They still glowed, and a faint growl came from that direction.

I sighed, looking up at the sky. A few stars twinkled in the ink-black night, so the clouds must be breaking up. "Yeah, we know the truth. And Gran would be rolling in her grave."

CHAPTER TWENTY

I had no dreams that night.

In the morning, I woke fresh and rested for the first time in over a week. When I glanced at my phone, it was already past ten, which meant I had slept a lot longer than I normally did. Evidently, my body needed it.

The hot shower felt like heaven after the battle in the pouring September rain. Okay, technically, it had been past midnight, so the pouring October rain. That was a song, wasn't it?

After dressing, I padded downstairs. Jess was lying on the sofa, reading a book. "Ah, Sleeping Beauty is awake!"

I halted on the bottom step. "Did you stay here all night?"

She nodded. "I wanted to make sure the scáth na tromluí didn't return."

My cheeks grew warm. I wasn't used to other people caring for me, much less inconveniencing themselves to help me. "Th-thank you."

"No worries. Also, Faelan wouldn't let me leave."

I spied the big black cat on my comfy chair, staring at me, his tail twitching. "Well, he can be an insistent jerk sometimes."

"Indeed, he can."

I finally took the last step into the parlour and turned into the kitchen. "Would you like a cuppa? Or coffee?"

She held up a mug. "I made myself one already. The kettle should still be hot."

It was, and I poured myself a hot drink, then returned to the parlour. I glared at Faelan for a moment. "May I have my chair back?"

He stared at me.

"Seriously, Faelan. Get up."

When he remained still, I pressed my lips together and went to the cupboard. Pulling out the laser pointer, I held it up for Jess to see. She stifled a giggle.

Then, I pointed it at the floor and turned it on. It was slightly diffused on the carpet, but I could still make out the bright red dot.

With deliberation, I moved the dot closer to the chair that Faelan was hogging. When it crossed his line of vision, he stared at it, his tail whipping back and forth.

I wiggled the dot a few times, then slowly moved it away from the chair, toward the bookcase.

Without warning, Faelan pounced on the red dot. I scooted into the chair, shut off the pointer, and we both burst into laughter.

The Cat Sídhe growled, his tail whipping even harder. "What is this tomfoolery?"

Trying to keep my guffaws under control, I held up the pointer. "Just a toy, Faelan. Would you like to play some more?"

"I would not. This is beneath my dignity."

With a mostly straight face, I said, "Then, I shall respect your dignity."

"Your polite words are acceptable." And he marched out of the room, his tail held high.

With a last chuckle, I held the hot mug in my hands, relishing the warmth as it seeped into my skin. *Maybe I should light the hearth.*

Jess must have read my mind, as she rose to do exactly that. Once she got the peat burning, she settled back down.

For some reason, Audrey's performance at the meeting sprang to mind. "Your sister, Audrey. When did she come to town?"

"Oh, at least two weeks ago. She didn't come by my place at first, though. She said she had some things to take care of."

Interesting. I wondered if she'd ever gotten the money to pay off Declan's debts. "Where did she disappear to, anyhow?"

Jess rolled her eyes, and her yellow glow flickered. "She got spooked. Some guy was asking questions about her, and *poof!* She disappeared. Back to Dublin, presumably, to find some other loser to play the sucker for. Gods, for a smart woman, she is so dumb."

So, she'd left the scene of the crime. "A guy? What sort of guy?"

She shrugged but wrinkled her nose. "One of those sour Dublin types. He only asked a few questions before I told him to feck off."

"You don't know who he was?" I suspected Jess was talking about the mafia-type who had been hanging around the town meeting. He hadn't looked like he was here for the sights.

A fleeting expression of impatience crossed her face before she rubbed the back of her neck. "Not really."

Faelan chose that moment to leap onto Jess's lap. She stroked him for a moment before saying, "I didn't want to say, but I did recognize him. He used to help Liam with his, uh, experiments."

"The drug experiments? Was he a dealer?"

"More like the financing side of it."

I supposed that explained his presence. This guy had been supplying the money for Liam and his drug experiments as well as Declan's gambling habit. He'd been searching for Audrey to, what, collect what he lost? "Would he hurt her, do you think?"

She shook her head. "I'm not sure, but he did try to shake her down. She ran to me just before I came to your place that morning."

Even if she was the killer, I worried for her. "Your sister's safe, isn't she?"

Jess gave a solemn nod and stroked Faelan's back a few times. His purrs filled the room for a couple of moments. "She's not really in Dublin. That was a rumor I'm spreading. She went to a cousin's in Donegal for a while."

"I'm glad she never ended up doing my books."

"Oh, she's okay as an accountant! But her choices in men leave a lot to be desired."

Maybe I should let Nabil do my books, after all. Or maybe I should just wait a few months. They wouldn't be due until next October, right?

In the meantime, I felt like I needed to find out more about Gran, especially how she had acted in the Mad Moonie Mob. And what she had told Tara about the Shadow of Nightmares.

"I wish I knew what happened to Gran in the group. Do you know anything about all that?"

"Well, according to Audrey, Saoirse was the leader of Mystic Meadow Moon for about a decade. However, one of the men, Aidan, decided he was going to be co-leader."

"Just decided?"

She gave a nod. "Exactly. As you might expect, Saoirse didn't agree, and there was a power play."

"Tara said Gran played politics with emotions."

Jess shrugged. "Do you know much about pagan group dynamics?"

"Not in the slightest."

"Well, usually there is one leader, but if there's two leaders, they are often folks who are together."

"As in…?"

"As in. Saoirse had no desire to be with Aidan, so she kicked him out. Some of the others took offense, and everyone took one side or the other."

I took a sip of my tea. "And which side was Declan on? Or was he with the group then?"

"Saoirse's side. He'd had a thing for her, evidently."

I sat up, horrified. "A thing? She must have been at least forty years older than him!"

Jess waved her hand. "Not a sexual thing, more like a mentor thing. But she'd left by then. Which really pissed Aidan off, because they're cousins."

"Wait, Aidan and Declan were cousins?"

"Sure, and Aidan and Marcus, from what I recall. Distant, though."

"Right. Everyone in Ireland is cousins."

Faelan let out a growl, jumped down from Jess's lap, and disappeared down the hall. Was it something we'd said?

"Ha! Fair play. Well, the group had returned here to do a ritual in her memory, but Tara and Liam had other plans."

"That divination thing?"

Jess took a long drink from her mug, draining it. Then, she got up to refill it. "Exactly. The Tarbh Feis. They wanted to know who should be leader."

"That's about what I figured. And all this was because of a botched ritual to divine something they could have just decided for themselves?"

"That's it."

I rubbed my temples. "Fermented sheep nuggets. This is a mess."

Jess gave a shrug and topped off her tea. "A mess that started when Saoirse left them in the lurch, to be fair."

"She wouldn't have stood for that sort of shenanigans, I'm sure."

I stared into my mug. Evidently, I didn't know Gran as well as I thought. I had only been corresponding with her via letter for years. What else didn't I know?

"I still don't understand why Tara followed Declan to the pub. What did she think he was going to do? Gran's been dead for almost a year, now."

"She passed on Samhain."

That sent a chill down my spine. The lawyer had told me the date of her death, but I'd never made that connection before.

Jess shrugged. "Tara must have figured he was moving on to the next generation, so to speak."

"He was here for *me?* I never even met him!"

"So you keep saying."

I shot to my feet and started pacing. "It wasn't me! I swear it. I would have remembered, don't you think?"

I scoured my memory, trying to think. "Wait. I did remember bumping into a guy in a leather jacket coming out of the pub. That was probably Declan, but that wasn't exactly a meeting."

"Liam swears he saw Declan with someone who looked like Saoirse. It had to be you, like."

I halted. "*Liam* said that? The same Liam who thinks hallucinogens are a sacred rite?"

After a moment of silence, we both laughed. Jess said, "He *is* an unreliable witness. But Skye, what if he *did* see Declan with Saoirse?"

Gran spoke with me now and then. Could she also manifest as a ghost? "Did Liam say she was shimmering and white?"

"No, but again, unreliable witness."

Jess obviously believed in the Good Neighbors. Why not ghosts, too? I wasn't sure I wanted to know, so I changed the subject. "So, is Tara in custody now? And Liam? Last night was sort of fuzzy."

"They are."

"What about Marcus and Nabil?"

She shook her head. "From what Garda McCarthy could find out, they knew nothing about all this."

I mulled that over a bit. Marcus had been a pushy jerk, but at least he wasn't a criminal pushy jerk. His aggressiveness reminded me of something else. "Wait, what about Tara's attack? Who did that?"

Jess let out a snort. "We aren't sure, but my guess would be Audrey."

"Your sister? Why?"

"That money I wouldn't lend her, for her new deadbeat boyfriend. Like I said, she's never made smart choices with her men."

I wrinkled my nose. "That sounds pretty weak. Are you sure that's what happened?"

Faelan, who had jumped up on the kitchen counter where he darn well knew he shouldn't be, twitched his tail.

Turning to the cat, I asked, "Do you know something?"

With a tiny growl, he said, "The angry woman hurt herself."

That threw me for a loop. "What? Why would she do such a thing?"

Faelan licked his paw, then looked up. "To confuse you. You were close to the truth."

I'd been considering Tara as the top suspect up to that point. So, to be fair, her trick had worked perfectly.

"And why did she say 'Saoirse promised me it would go away' about the Shadow of Nightmares? What's the connection there?"

His tail flicked again. "Your grandmother had fought the creature in the past. The angry woman was your grandmother's protégé, so it attached itself to her as a way to get at you."

I rubbed my temples to stave off the incoming headache.

Faelan leapt off his perch land left the room. I stared after him. "Where's he going?"

Jess just shook her head. "Cats do as they please."

"Isn't that the truth."

I'd only enough time to take my mug back to the kitchen and place it in the sink before he returned. He carried Declan's shell necklace in his mouth, trailing under him like a pale pink snake.

"Where did you find that?"

He dropped it at my feet. "I didn't find it, foolish human. I took it from the púca."

"I forgot about that thing! Did you kill it?"

He let out a low growl. "I did not. You cannot kill the púca. I did make it leave for now. It will be back, and you will need to be better prepared next time."

"You were the one who prepared me! Maybe give me some more time to learn it next time?"

"It will be as it must be."

I don't like the sound of that one bit. Cold fingers of fear ran down my spine.

"Now, it is time to use the necklace."

I knelt to pick it up. "Use it? How?"

"Must I teach you everything? At the Wishing Tree."

As the sun burned through the October clouds, a modicum of warmth touched my face. It hadn't taken long for Jess, Faelan, and me to climb back into the garden of the abandoned farm.

Following Faelan's instructions, I chanted some Irish words and draped the shell necklace around a branch, closing the clasp so it wouldn't fall off.

I really needed to learn some Irish. Casting a magic spell using words I didn't know made my skin crawl. Knowing the words for fire and water weren't nearly enough.

What should I wish for? A dozen more wishes? A dozen more wishing trees? That seemed like a silly thing. For the pub to be finished? That would happen eventually. Why waste a perfectly good fairy wish on that? I could wish for McCarthy to back off, but his confession earlier suggested that was on the road to resolution.

No, I knew what to wish for. Something I had no control over. I wished that Armand would stop calling. That he'd forget about me and never bother me again.

Just as I stepped back, the sun dimmed. I looked up as storm clouds gathered above us. The wind chilled, and I pulled my jacket closer. Samhain was growing closer.

The first drops of rain hit. We rushed back to the house to escape the impending rain, but a gale smacked us in the face. Stinging chunks of hail pelted us as we ran.

Finally, just as we reached the pub door, the sun re-emerged, as if it had never left.

I asked Faelan, "Does that mean that the wish worked?"

But, of course, Faelan was nowhere to be found.

EPILOGUE

Two days later, Finn had a good grip on my shoulders, leading me into the pub. "Now, keep yer eyes closed, Miss Skye. I'll let you know when it's okay to open them."

I stumbled, but Rory had my arm and kept me from falling. "You're grand, you're grand."

"Okay, you can open them now!"

I gazed around at their work. Every light in the pub was shining brightly on the walls. A rich cream color on the top half of the walls set the bottom half nicely. Below that, a thin chair rail of dark wood separated it from the thick stripes of darker cream, maroon, and thin lines of forest green.

The boys had even hung some of Gran's old photographs, with her and some mildly famous people who had visited her pub over the decades, along with the obligatory metal Guinness ad signs.

Just as I clapped Finn and Rory on the shoulders, two of the Guinness signs fell with a clatter. At first, there was a moment of dead silence. Then, all three of us burst into laughter.

"Never you worry, Miss Skye. We'll get that fixed up in a tick."

"I trust you will. Would you care to join me in a whiskey?"

Glancing at the empty spots where the three missing bottles had been, I pulled down one of the more expensive bottles. I wiped off the dust and poured three glasses. Finn held his up to the light, swirled it a few times, then knocked it back. "Aye, that's the stuff."

Rory, however, sipped his drink, made a face, then took another sip.

"Don't you like the whiskey, Rory? I thought every Irish man loved the stuff like mother's milk."

He wrinkled his nose. "Sorry to say, I don't. Da always tried to get me to drink it, said it was just a matter of getting used to the taste." He gave a shrug. "I never did."

As I poured Finn another, I wondered if Gran had loved her whiskey. I mean, she owned a pub, right? She must have enjoyed drinking.

Which brought my mind back to her activities in the Mystic Meadow Moon group. I wished I knew more about what had happened with them.

Had Gran been unfair to them? Had she played politics with emotions?

Had my grandmother been a bad person?

Finn held up the empty bottle. "You'll need to buy another before you open. This one's a favorite of the locals."

Someone knocked on the door. I opened it wide to let in Jess and Adanna. They both hugged me and I gave them a quick tour of the renovated space.

Adanna shook her head. "This looks amazing, Skye. You've really brightened the place up, while keeping the charm. Your gran would be proud."

My phone klaxon went off. Expecting to see a United States number, another of Armand's spoofing attempts, I realized it wasn't from overseas. An Irish phone number.

Thinking it could be Gran's Dublin lawyers, I answered, "Hello?"

"Miss Skye O'Shea?" He had an American accent, but it wasn't Armand.

Just because it wasn't my ex-husband didn't mean it was someone safe. "Who's asking?"

"We have a delivery for you. Can I get your address to verify the location?"

I clicked the phone off and gave in to the shakes. Armand was getting clever.

Everyone's getting excited for Samhain. Can this savvy ex-pat spot a harbinger of doom before destruction descends?

Start reading Pranks, Poitín, and Púcas to embark on a thrilling journey into the heart of Celtic legend today!

THANK YOU!

Thank you so much for enjoying **Whispers, Whiskey, and Wishes.** If you've enjoyed the story, please consider leaving a review to help others discover Skye's adventures!

If you'd like to get updates, sneak previews, sales, and **FREE STUFF**, please sign up for my newsletter.

You can also see all the books available
through Green Dragon Publishing at:
www.GreenDragonArtist.com

DEDICATION

For those whose past holds skeletons that you're too frightened to face.

ACKNOWLEDGEMENTS

I have such a wonderful group of friends, both authors and readers, who have helped me with this book. Beta readers like Ian Erik Morris, Natasha Reyes, Mattea Orr, M. A. Hoyler, and so many others.

Following a successful first book with an equally good sequel is a huge challenge. But I've had lots of support, and I appreciate everyone who has helped me.

PRONUNCIATION GUIDE AND GLOSSARY

Aengos Óg – [AYNguss OHG] One of the Tuatha dé Danann.
Ballybás – [bah-lee-BAWS] Town of the dead.
Bean sídhe/Banshee – [bahn SHEE] A fairy who wails for the dead of a particular family.
Bodhrán – [BOW-rin] An Irish hand drum.
Brigid – [BRI-jid] An Irish goddess.
Cabhraigh linn – [CA-vree LINN] Help us.
Caer Ibormeith – [CARE ee-BORE-mee] One of the Tuatha dé Danann.
Cat sídhe – [kat SHEE] A fairy cat.
Cipín – [chip-EEN] A wooden instrument for playing the bodhrán.
Clurichaun – [CLUR-i-kawn] A fairy creature.
Dearg-Due – [DAH-rugh DOO-ah] A vengeful Irish spirit who steals blood.
Dia daoibh – [JEE-ah DEEV] Hello (to more than one person) (literally, God be with you).
Dullahan – [DOO-la-hawn] A fairy creature.
Dumbek – [DOOM-bek] A tall drum designed to be held between the knees.
Ethal Anbuail – [EE-hal an-BWAL] One of the Tuatha dé Danann.
Go raibh maith agat – [Go ruhv MAH ug-AHT] Thank you.
Hola, mi corazón – [HO-lah, mee CORE-a-zone] (Spanish) Hello, my heart.
Imigh as seo – [ih-MEE ass show] Go away, out of here.
Leannan Sídhe – [LAN-ann SHEE] A fairy creature.

Leprechaun – [LEP-ri-kawn] A fairy creature.
Máiréad – [MY-rid] A woman's name.
Mo chroí – [muh CROY] My heart.
Muirgen – [MIR-gen] Born of the sea/A woman's name.
Púca – [POO-kah] A fairy creature.
Qué pasa – [kay PAH-sah] (Spanish) What's happening?
Samhain – [SOW-inn] November/Hallowe'en.
Saoirse – [SEER-shah] Freedom.
Scáth na tromluí – [SCAH nah TROM-loo] The shadow of the nightmare (not a creature in actual Irish folklore).
Sétanta – [sheh-TAWN-the] an ancient Irish hero.
Tá tú curtha ar deoraíocht – [taw too CUR-ha ar DEE-o-ree-acht] You have been exiled.
Tarbh feis – [TARV fesh] Bull Feast.
Tine, aer, uisce, agus talamh – [TEE-neh, air, ISH-keh, AH-gus TAH-lahv] Fire, air, water, and earth.
Tir na nÓg – [TEER nah NAWG] Land of the young.
Tuatha dé Danann – [TOO-a-ha day DAWN-ann] The people of Danú.

ABOUT THE AUTHOR

Christy Nicholas writes under several pen names, including Rowan Dillon, C.N. Jackson, and Emeline Rhys. She's an author, artist, and accountant. After she failed to become an airline pilot, she quit her ceaseless pursuit of careers that began with the letter 'A' and decided to concentrate on her writing. Since she has Project Completion Compulsion, she is one of the few authors with no unfinished novels.

Christy has her hands in many crafts, including digital art, beaded jewelry, writing, and photography. In real life, she's a CPA, but having grown up with art all around her (her mother, grandmother, and great-grandmother are/were all artists), it sort of infected her, as it were. She wants to expose the incredible beauty in this world, hidden beneath the everyday grime of familiarity and habit, and share it with others. She uses characters out of time and places infused with magic and myth, writing magical realism stories in both historical fantasy and time travel flavors.

Social Media Links:
Blog: www.GreenDragonArtist.net
Website: www.GreenDragonArtist.com
Facebook: www.facebook.com/greendragonauthor
Instagram: www.instagram.com/greendragonartist9
TikTok: www.tiktok.com/@greendragonauthor